Dear Reader,

Truth and consequences is this month's theme for Harlequin Duets. In volume #19 Julie Kistler tickles the funny bone with her arrogant Jones boys, heroes used to getting whatever they want in *Calling Mr. Right.* However, when they buy and transform a radio station, Griffin Jones finds himself assuming a false identity to help Nell McCabe keep herself from getting fired—by himself! Complications ensue and emotions run amuck. Then Connie Flynn weaves a tale of comic adventures and misadventures in *The Wedding Dress Mess* as the hero tries to protect his mother from the consequences of her folly.

In volume #20 Charlotte Maclay returns with *Not Exactly Pregnant.* Is she or isn't she? turns out to be the frequently asked question in a town that is overrun by pregnancies. But what happens when a very good girl and the ultimate bad boy are about to become parents? Then we welcome Liz Jarrett to Duets with her first novel, *Darn Near Perfect.* When workaholic Michael's boss decides he needs to learn how to be more altruistic, to learn that it truly is better to give than to receive, Michael gets a lot more than he expected when he hooks up with a group of matchmaking senior citizens.

I hope you enjoy this month's Duets.

Malle Vallik

Malle Vallik
Senior Editor

Why had she acted so foolishly with Jack?

At the time it had seemed so *right*. But now Lindy knew that getting intimate with Jack had been all wrong. One crazy night together didn't make a future. Sighing, she searched through her closet for something that would cover him up while his clothes dried, something so she wouldn't keep remembering how handsome, how powerfully male he'd looked naked.

The best she could find was an old chenille bathrobe. He'd look ridiculous in it, which would be just fine with Lindy.

Moments later she learned how wrong she'd been. Jack Colby in a chenille bathrobe was still the sexiest man she'd ever seen.

Damn! Until the ridiculous rumor about her being pregnant had surfaced, she'd put Jack out of her mind. Now what she wanted more than anything was to repeat her foolish mistake…right this very second.

For more, turn to page 9

Michael Parker was all wrong for her,

Casey kept telling herself.

She had to remember he was a man rooted to the fast track. And last night had been one big fluke—a fluke that wouldn't happen again. She had way too much at stake to risk it all on a case of lust—regardless of how strong that lust was. If she didn't get a grip on herself soon, she'd end up pulling petals off flowers saying, "He loves me, he loves me not."

"You are such a sap," she muttered to herself as she glanced out her open office door into the main room. There she saw Michael talking to two of the seniors. Darn his hide, he looked incredibly...tempting. Drat. Lust she could fight. But he'd better not turn out to be a nice guy after all.

That would be way too much for her to take.

For more, turn to page 197

CHARLOTTE MACLAY

Not Exactly Pregnant

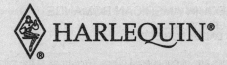

HARLEQUIN®

TORONTO • NEW YORK • LONDON
AMSTERDAM • PARIS • SYDNEY • HAMBURG
STOCKHOLM • ATHENS • TOKYO • MILAN • MADRID
PRAGUE • WARSAW • BUDAPEST • AUCKLAND

Dear Reader,

I believe that smiles, laughter and happy endings are
necessary to feed the soul. That's why I love writing for
Harlequin Duets. Indeed, humor generally sneaks into all
of my books whether I intend it to or not.

I also enjoy travel as a way to find new inspiration. When
my husband and I visited Kentucky we were delighted by
the small towns and sumptuous horsebreeding farms.
While we were there we didn't exactly meet Jack and
Lindy, the hero and heroine of this story, but it was easy to
imagine them as we drove through the countryside or
stopped for a quick lunch at some small café.

I hope you'll enjoy getting acquainted with all of the
people in my fictional town of Goodfellow, KY. I certainly
had fun creating them.

It's always a pleasure to hear from readers. Write to me at
P.O. Box 505, Torrance, CA 90508

Charlotte Maclay

Books by Charlotte Maclay

HARLEQUIN LOVE & LAUGHTER
29—ACCIDENTAL ROOMMATES
61—COURTING CUPID

HARLEQUIN AMERICAN ROMANCE
788—DEPUTY DADDY
806—A DADDY FOR BECKY

Don't miss any of our special offers. Write to us at the following
address for information on our newest releases.

Harlequin Reader Service
U.S.: 3010 Walden Ave., P.O. Box 1325, Buffalo, NY 14269
Canadian: P.O. Box 609, Fort Erie, Ont. L2A 5X3

Special thanks to Lupe Riders
for my daily dose of smiles and laughter.
Luv y'all!

1

"LINDY, IS IT TRUE? Are you pregnant?"

Blurry-eyed, Linda Montgomery stared at the phone in her hand, which moments ago had startled her out of a dead sleep. Then she glanced at her alarm clock—6:02 a.m. "Marcie, do you have any idea what time it is?"

"I'm your very best friend in the whole entire world and you didn't even bother to tell me you're pregnant. Dang it, Lindy, I'm hurt. Very hurt."

With a groan, Lindy collapsed back onto her pillow, picturing Marcie's wide dark eyes and pixie-cut hair. Her friend, dear as she might be, had a flair for the dramatic...dramatically *wrong* in this case. "Read my lips, Marcie. I am not pregnant."

"Of course you are. Everybody says so."

"Like who?"

"Everybody at Paddy's, that's who."

The singles' bar across the county line was a hotbed of rumor and gossip, as well as the local meat market. Lindy hadn't been there in weeks, not since her birthday. Nor did she intend to go back anytime soon. "Why would they say a ridiculous thing like that?"

"Why would it be so ridiculous? It's not like you're too old."

"Thanks, Marcie. It's really nice of you to say that to your oldest friend."

"Well, most of our friends have already started families. You could easily have diddled a little—"

"I repeat, I'm not pregnant. I'm not even seeing anyone."

"Well, you could be and you're keeping that a secret, too."

"I'm not." At this point, Lindy had pretty well given up on men. The choices in Goodfellow, Kentucky, were so limited there seemed little chance she'd ever find a husband…or get pregnant, for that matter, except by artificial insemination. And her goal of owning her own pet grooming store right now was far more important than either having a husband or children. There'd be plenty of time after she established her own independence to fall in love. The one good thing she'd inherited from her moonshine-making father was an entrepreneurial spirit. Of course, his still had been the death of him when it blew up. She didn't expect a grooming shop to be fatal.

"But everyone says—"

"Marcie, I'm not interested in discussing my nonexistent love life at six o'clock in the morning."

One tiny little slip to celebrate her twenty-fifth birthday—and bring an end to her virginity—did not qualify as a love life, in her view.

Her golden retriever padded into the bedroom and jumped up onto her bed, nuzzling her neck and licking her face.

"Quit that, honey," she muttered, shoving the big dog to the other side of the bed.

"Oh, I get it. You've got someone there now and you don't want him to know. I can keep a secret. Just say yes or no—"

"There's no one here, Marcie."

"I heard you talking to him. I'm not deaf, you know. You're in bed right this very minute with some guy and you won't even tell your very best friend."

Lindy rolled her eyes. "I'm in bed with Tootsie, not a man."

Marcie paused for a heartbeat. "That's kinky, Lindy."

"Marcie!" She came up out of bed in a rush, startling Tootsie, who shot off the bed in the opposite direction, all gangly legs and clicking toenails on the hardwood floor. "I'm hanging up now. I'm not going to talk to you about my love life, and I am *not* pregnant. Goodbye!" She slammed the phone down.

Who on earth would start a rumor that she was pregnant? Lindy wasn't exactly known as fast and loose. Heavens, her mother would have a fit—even a bigger fit than the one she'd thrown when Lindy refused to go to beauty college like her mother had wanted her to. Instead, she'd apprenticed with D'Arcy McDrew at Fluff 'n Cut Grooming. Now she operated the shop on a lease with an option to buy. In one year, she'd have enough money invested so that the business would be hers—and the bank's.

Then she'd have all the respect she'd yearned for and failed to receive as a moonshiner's daughter.

But in a town this size, Lindy never even had a chance to be bad. When she jaywalked, the news got back to her mother at the unlicensed beauty shop she ran on her back porch, before Lindy made it to the other side of the street.

Hadn't Mama heard by dawn the next morning about her leaving Paddy's Bar with Jack Colby, the town's most notorious bad boy? And hadn't her mother gotten cross-legged about Lindy seeing a man she didn't think fittin' to roll with the pigs? After all, he came from bad blood, his father killed by a fellow convict in state prison, his older brother a frequent inmate of the same institution.

In horsebreeding country, bloodlines meant everything. Jack's line was tainted.

Linda shivered slightly, trying to repress the delicious memories of that night she'd spent with him and wasn't entirely successful in the effort.

She'd known Jack forever, but always from a distance, and had made it a point to stay away from his crowd. But one time in high school she'd seen him come to the defense of a runty kid the other guys were bullying. From that moment on, she'd had a soft spot in her heart for the sinfully good-looking bad boy who'd fought his way through school. Not that she'd ever expected or wanted anything to come of her crush.

And nothing had, until that night five weeks ago at Paddy's.

But a one-night stand? Lordy, she hadn't intended that. She'd been so embarrassed, she hadn't even returned his phone call the next day.

And of all the men in town, he'd be the one most capable of poisoning her prospects for a successful business of her own. Folks in these parts simply wouldn't patronize her shop if they thought she had anything to do with one of the Colby boys—criminals all, they'd say.

"Come on, Tootsie. Let's get ourselves some breakfast. The good folks of Goodfellow can count on their fingers all they'd like and still come up with zero. No way am I pregnant." Though, despite the precautions they'd taken, she'd sweated out the month until her flow started after she'd been with Jack.

From the corner of the kitchen came the muffled cry, "Heads up! Heads up!"

"I'm coming, Petey," she told the parrot, removing the cover from his cage.

He ruffled his feathers. "Heads up! Heads up!"

"You're supposed to say good morning," she reminded him. "Good morning. Good morning."

"Heads up! Heads up!"

Grimacing, she wondered why she'd ever agreed to give remedial speech lessons to the stupid bird. But poor Mrs. O'Toole had bought the creature for company after her husband passed on. All she could get out of the parrot was "Heads up! Heads up!" Which made Petey not exactly a stimulating conversationalist.

Goosing Lindy with her cold nose, Tootsie let it be known she was still waiting for breakfast. "I know you're hungry, sweetheart. I'm coming."

Petey sang his one-note tune again.

She'd just scooped a panful of dog food out of the fifty-pound bag in the broom closet when the phone rang again.

"Hang on," she called across the room, pouring the pellets into Tootsie's yellow Snoopy dish. The dog nearly upended her in her eagerness to get to the food. "Sheesch! You'd think I'd been starving you for weeks." She gave the retriever an affectionate slap on her rump, which she ignored.

The persistent phone was more difficult to ignore. Telemarketers certainly had nothing on Lindy's friends for poor timing.

She snatched up the phone with a *"yes."*

"My, my, we are a little testy this morning, aren't we, dear?"

"Mama, it's barely past six." Balancing the phone on her shoulder, Lindy reached for the coffee in the cupboard.

"Yes, dear, but I have to get to work early and I'd like to know what to tell my customers."

"About what?" She spooned two measures into the two-cup coffeemaker.

"You may think you don't have to worry about your reputation and don't mind getting caught, but I hold a position of respect in this town."

"Of course, Mama." The widow of a man who had personally consumed more of his own white lightning than he'd sold? Some reputation. Despite that, her mother had a way of holding her head high that Lindy couldn't help but admire. Of course, moonshining was a long tradition in Kentucky if not actually an admirable one. Certainly better than robbing the pari-mutuel window at the racetrack or stealing the mayor's car, part of the Colby family's sins. Not that Jack had been guilty of anything more than a quick temper and too many fights.

Running the water, Lindy filled the pot and poured it into the top of the coffeemaker, then set the pot on the warmer. The curling phone cord stretched to its limit across the room.

"And whenever you decide to tell me the news,

I'll be as supportive as I can be, given the circumstances.''

Lindy frowned. A little hitch formed in her mental flow. "What news?"

"Now, now, don't you fret for a minute, dear. A little birdie told me but I won't say a word. Not a word. Not until you're ready."

"Mama! What are you talking about?"

"Well, dear, I know folks are always surprised to learn I'm old enough to have a grown daughter. I do try to take care of myself, you know. Beauticians have to do that. Now they'll be shocked, absolutely shocked, to hear I'm going to be a grandmother, too."

A groan escaped Lindy's throat. "Whatever you've heard, Mama, it's not true."

"Fiddlesticks, girl! You don't have to keep your news a secret from me. Why, this is the time when you need your mother the most to help you get through these next few months and answer all of your questions for you. Being pregnant is such a difficult experience, you'll need a mature woman to guide you."

Lindy gritted her teeth. "I'm not pregnant, Mama."

"I am put out that you haven't even so much as brought your gentleman friend to supper but I'm sure he'll do the right thing."

"I don't have a gentleman friend."

''Now, I ain't saying what you've done is wrong, gettin' caught short 'n all before the wedding. I try very hard to be modern about these things. But I do wish you'd been just a bit more careful. When it gets right down to the get-go, a girl's reputation is all she's got. An' I'm surely hoping the young man's a respectable sort. Not like that Colby boy.''

Lindy never got headaches. She had one now. The pounding started right at the base of her skull and was working its way up to the top.

As hard as she tried, Lindy couldn't jar loose her mother's notion that she was pregnant. Whoever had started that rumor had sure done a bang-up job. The news was spreading as fast as fleas on an old hound dog.

The town of Goodfellow was like that. As warm-hearted and caring as the folks might be, the community thrived on gossip and rumor. Even so, Lindy couldn't imagine living anywhere else. Her roots went back for seven generations in this bluegrass county; her relatives had worn both uniforms during the War Between the States. She wasn't about to pull up stakes and leave her roots behind.

Finally Lindy begged off the conversation with her mother. She had to get to work, and while she was at it she'd have to find a way to squelch the rumor.

Still, she had nothing to worry about. Rumors of

this sort burned themselves out in no time when there was no evidence to support them.

She hoped.

LINDY BARELY ESCAPED Pumpkin's snapping teeth.

"Come on, Pumpkin," she crooned, contemplating a muzzle in the back room that was exactly Pumpkin's size. "You know you love being groomed. All that nice brushing, a pretty pink bow—"

The Pekingese snapped again.

"Now, now, sweetums," soothed Mrs. Allensworthy, the miniature monster's owner. She wore a floppy-brimmed hat to disguise that her hair had thinned to only a few wisps of white. "Mummy wants you to go with this nice lady so babykins can be all pretty. I'll give you a tiny-weeny treat when you're all done. Promise, promise." She smacked her lips.

Lindy reached across the counter for the dog.

Pumpkin bared her razorlike teeth and growled.

The front door to the shop opened, the bell tinkled, and a man appeared.

Lindy gaped at him. A dizzying sensation swept over her as though all the air had been drawn from her lungs and her heart did a joyous leap before she could stop it.

Jack Colby, wearing his signature black jeans and matching black T-shirt, looked for all the world to be the bad boy the town of Goodfellow had labeled him. His physique was lean and hard—a man not to be messed with. His gaze assessing, he flashed her a smile that slashed his cheeks with vertical creases, and did something warm and melting to Lindy's insides. A smile that was an invitation to trouble.

His reputation as a born heartbreaker was well deserved. Lindy would be wise to remember that. And to protect her reputation.

As she was about to speak, to say something rather than stand there like a mute, Tootsie sauntered out from the back room to check on the new arrival. Pumpkin objected to the presence of the much larger dog. In a panic, she yelped and scrambled out of Mrs. Allensworthy's arms, leaped off the counter and flew toward the doorway to escape.

Except Jack blocked her path.

Like any red-blooded Pekingese who felt overwhelmed and trapped, she used her only remaining defense. She squatted. Shivered.

And peed on Jack's booted foot.

A hush descended on the shop. Painfully, Lindy dragged her gaze from the damage the Pekingese had done, up the long legs encased in form-fitting jeans, scanned his broad chest, and the breadth of his shoulders until she met his dark-eyed gaze. He winked, the corners of his sensual lips sliding into another of his patented smiles.

"Sorry," she whispered, swallowing a relieved giggle and trying to ignore the chill bumps that sped down her spine.

Her gaze shifted to Mrs. Allensworthy, whose jaw had dropped noticeably, looking like the hinge had come loose.

In a slow perusal, Jack glanced from the dog to Lindy and then to Mrs. Allensworthy and her floppy hat. "Ma'am," he said in a sonorous voice that had the power to command a squad of tough Marines— or make little old ladies cower. "I reckon that poor excuse for a dog has got some kind of a bladder problem. I think you'd best take her on over to Doc Townsend's right away before something bad happens to her."

Despite his hard-edged tone, surely he was teasing. Or so Lindy hoped.

Getting her jaw back on track, Mrs. Allensworthy sputtered, "Well, I never—" Intimidated by Jack's presence and his reputation, she scooped up her pet.

"Now wait a minute," Lindy objected, coming to her senses. "You can't throw my customer out of the shop. Mrs. Allensworthy—"

"Is leaving." Bowing slightly, he opened the door for her.

She scurried outside, her hat brim flapping like wings, no doubt relieved to escape with her life.

"You had no right to do that." Lindy started around to his side of the counter, to go after Mrs.

Allensworthy, then thought better of it. Having the counter between her and Jack Colby offered at least some protection from her own wild impulses. "She's been a regular customer for years. She comes in almost every week. You can't barge in here and disrupt my business."

Reaching into his back pocket, he pulled out his wallet. "What's the going rate?"

Heat flooded her cheeks as memories of their one-night stand came back to her. She lifted her chin. "I don't know what you're talking about."

"By chasing ol' Mrs. Allensworthy off, how much money did you lose?"

"Oh, that." Humiliation bore a little deeper into her chest. "I don't want your money."

"Maybe not. But Mrs. Allensworthy was in the way." Opening his wallet, he slapped a twenty dollar bill on the counter. "We need to talk."

"Now? I've got a business to run." D'Arcy had given Lindy a chance to eventually own the business when she and her husband moved to California to be nearer their grandchildren. Lindy had jumped at the opportunity. But she didn't need Jack's charity to make a go of her shop.

"Lindy, this is serious." His gaze swept over her, effectively undressing her, reminding her in intimate detail of the night they'd spent together. A moment of panic warred with the sensual onslaught of memories.

The shop door opened again, and an Irish setter bounded into the shop. Colleen and Tootsie nuzzled each other like two old girlfriends telling secrets, playfully nibbling on each other's ears.

Marge Salter, the country club women's golf champion, a six-handicapper, and a former amateur tennis champion for all of Kentucky bounded in after her dog. "A shampoo and trim, if you please," she said lightly, as full of herself as a big dog with a brass collar. "And you, my dear, have been keeping secrets from us all," she said to Lindy, wagging her finger. "Naughty, naughty."

"Hi, Ms. Salter." Sparing Jack a quick glance, Lindy grabbed Colleen by the collar. The eager bitch had Tootsie pinned beneath her in a display of pack dominance. "No secrets here. What you see is what you get."

Ms. Salter shifted her attention to Jack, looking him up and down. "You brought your dog in to be groomed, too?"

"No, ma'am. Out at my place, we just squirt ours with a hose."

She lifted her permanently etched brows, those that had been created by a plastic surgeon who'd tucked, folded and rolled her face until it was a mask pulled taut over her skull bones. "Well, then, maybe there's another reason why you dropped by to see Lindy so early?" she asked suggestively.

"If there was, it wouldn't be any of your business, would it, Ms. Salter?"

Before he could drive this customer away, too, Lindy quickly said, "What time would you like to pick up Colleen?"

Ms. Salter dragged her gaze back to Lindy. "Oh, about four, I suppose. I have a board meeting this morning and a golf date this afternoon."

"Perfect." Lindy was due to attend a friend's bridal shower luncheon and would be back in plenty of time. "Colleen will be ready at four."

With a knowing look at Jack, Marge said, "I'd say if a certain someone is responsible for your pregnancy, you'd be better off not admitting it."

Jack's expression darkened.

Lindy bristled. "I'm not pregnant, Ms. Salter. That's a totally false rumor you've heard."

"Really?" She cocked those artificial brows again. "I know your mother will be relieved to hear that. Though naturally she must be eager for you to find a *suitable* husband. Someone respectable." With a haughty lift of her chin, she turned and left the shop.

Lindy ignored the verbal slap in her face but she couldn't help wincing at Ms. Salter's insult of Jack. He didn't deserve that.

Jack speared her with his dark eyes. "The rumor's false?"

"Absolutely." Giving Colleen a yank, she

dragged the setter off Tootsie and pulled her toward the back room. "Good to see you again," she called over her shoulder. "As you can see, I've got work to do."

Jack Colby wouldn't leave it at that. She'd known he wouldn't. But she wasn't thrilled with the way he marched right into her back room.

"I want to know the truth," he said.

She shoved Colleen into a cage and snapped the latch shut. "What truth is that?"

"Are you pregnant with my child?"

Breathing should come naturally. Usually it did. But for a moment Lindy couldn't seem to recall how it was done. "*Your* child?"

"That's what I asked you."

"And that's why you're here?" How in hell had he heard the rumor before she did? "Come on, Jack. Do I look like I'm pregnant?"

His dark brows drew together as he examined her, and she really wished she hadn't put on an extra five pounds since her high school days.

"No, you don't," he said.

"There, you see? Nothing to worry about."

"So who's the guy?"

"What guy?"

"The one who got you pregnant. Is he going to marry you?"

"Don't you people listen? I am *not* pregnant now and I never have been."

She headed toward the front of the shop, but he snared her by the arm. "Wait."

"Sic him, Tootsie," she ordered, knowing full well her dog was too much of a wimp to attack anyone.

"If it's just a rumor, it's damn well all over town. I don't like people talking about you like that."

Despite the ridiculous rumor, pleasure curled through her midsection that Jack would want to defend her reputation. "In a few days, when it's obvious the whole cockamamie story is unfounded, the rumor will die down and they'll find something else to talk about."

"Lindy, look at me."

She couldn't. He was simply too dang potent and she kept remembering what they'd done together. All of it.

Catching her by the shoulder, he turned her and lifted her chin. "Something's up. You're not being straight with me. Why do I get the feeling you're lying to me?"

She wasn't lying. Heaven knew, with him touching her, she could hardly speak much less breathe.

His eyes narrowed, wonderfully dark, expressive eyes. Bedroom eyes. "I'm not going to leave until I know for sure you're not pregnant."

With a twist of her head, she pulled away. "What are you planning to do? Give me a pelvic exam?" She clamped her mouth shut. For a woman given to making dumb comments, she'd outdone herself this time. The way Jack was looking at her, his eyes narrowed, the band of dark brown becoming almost black, it wasn't exactly a pelvic exam he was thinking about. His thoughts were close enough to the same idea, however, that Lindy's nipples puckered all on their own and her skin flushed clear down to her toes. Jack Colby was the hottest, most seductive man she had ever met, in or out of bed.

From the moment she'd seen him beating up a school bully, she'd been drawn to him. No one else had taken his side. He'd stood alone to protect a younger child and suffered a cut lip and a black eye for his efforts plus a suspension from school. Just one of a dozen fights he'd been in, but this one had been totally righteous.

Lindy had never thought of him as a bad boy after she'd seen that much courage in him. Not that it had helped his image a great deal in the community. With a convicted felon for a father and a stepfather known to use his fists freely, Jack had never had much of a chance to make something of himself in Goodfellow. Which made her wonder why he had come home after his hitch in the Marines.

The bell on the shop door tinkled again.

"There are tests you can take," he said, showing no interest in the latest customer to arrive.

Lindy had to. In fact, she wanted to pay attention

to her customer to the exclusion of Jack. "I'm sure you'll excuse me," she said, pulling away from him. "I've got a lot to do today. Five dogs to groom—well, four now that you ran off Mrs. Allensworthy—and then there's a wedding shower I have to—"

"No."

Stubborn, butt-headed man.

"Yoohoo, is anybody here?"

"Coming."

Roberta Fawlty waited for her on the far side of the counter. "Oh, dear, I hope you weren't suffering with a bout of morning sickness. It can be just awful in the early months, can't it? Why, I remember with Jacob—"

"No morning sickness, Mrs. Fawlty. I'm fine."

"I'm so glad to hear that. Do remind me, dear. Who is it you're dating?"

"No one." One night with Jack did not constitute a date. Or a relationship. "I'll have Miss Bee ready by four. You can pick her up then." Lindy took the leash from Roberta, gave a tug and the honey-blond spaniel followed her docilely into the back room.

Before she could get Miss Bee settled in one of the wire cages, the bell tinkled again. She passed the leash to Jack. "If you're going to stick around, you can make yourself useful. My assistant is late."

To Jack's credit, he didn't balk at her order. He didn't look thrilled however when Miss Bee began sniffing at his damp shoe, and he led her toward an empty cage.

Lindy welcomed the remaining two scheduled dogs plus Mrs. Anratty's unexpected cat, who'd escaped outdoors long enough to roll around in a combination of broken duck eggs and cow pies. A delightful experience, no doubt, for the usually confined house pet. Less pleasant for those around her.

Wrinkling her nose, Lindy dropped the furry bundle into a cage well away from the dogs.

"Are you still here?" she asked, blithely carrying on with her tasks as Jack's gaze followed her around the back room. Not that she was all that comfortable with him so close at hand. Picturing him, as she had from time to time in the past five weeks, naked beside her in that fancy motel room was decidedly troubling, an image she tried to block. Whatever had gotten into her that night?

Besides Jack, she thought wryly.

"Business appears to be booming." His T-shirt fit snugly, revealing well-defined muscles across his chest and arms strengthened by hard work. Or perhaps he'd honed his physique in the Marines. He still wore his saddle-brown hair close cropped, despite the fact he'd been a civilian for several months.

"It's a living." A tuft of hair the same attractive shade peeked out at his throat above his T-shirt, a particularly intriguing sight because she knew how it swirled across his chest and arrowed below his waist.

Her mouth went dry at the memory.

He moved into her space, standing so close she could see variations in the dark brown of his eyes, flecks that could be black or a deep green. He caught her chin between his forefinger and thumb, lifting gently.

"Why didn't you return my phone call?" he asked.

2

JACK COLBY WATCHED a flush steal up Lindy's slender neck and stain her cheeks. He wasn't used to being treated like a near stranger by a woman he'd slept with—or even one he'd dated casually. Women liked him and he reciprocated the feeling. Which meant, among other things, he wasn't ready to settle down yet. Certainly not until he got his horsebreeding business going, and maybe not even then.

But if push came to shove, he'd do the right thing—unlike his own father who'd felt no compunction about getting a woman pregnant then moving on—right into prison, as it turned out.

"You did get my message, didn't you?" he asked when she failed to respond to his first question.

"Jack, we both got carried away that night. I didn't see much point—"

"I don't do one-night stands."

"Neither do I. Usually."

"And I was the exception? That doesn't say much about my technique."

"Your technique was just fine. We just shouldn't have."

"But we did. And now you may be carrying my baby."

She shook her head, the long blond hair that she'd formed into a single loose braid shifting behind her shoulders. "I've already had my, ah, flow since we…" She swallowed visibly, and her tongue swept out to dampen her lips. "…were together."

He felt the gesture right behind his fly. "We made love."

"That doesn't mean we have a lifelong commitment."

"It could if you're carrying my baby."

She pulled away from him, tossing her head like a high-strung filly. "I'm really getting tired of that broken record everybody's been playing this morning. I'm not pregnant. Even if I were, which I'm not, the problem wouldn't be yours."

Her honesty was like a sharp stick right in his gut. "You wouldn't want to admit the kid was mine," he said tautly.

"Jack, we're both from the wrong side of the tracks. I'm trying to better myself—"

"And I wouldn't be much of an asset."

She sighed, an act that raised her full breasts in a thoroughly enticing way. "That's not exactly what I meant."

"Sure it is. As Ms. Salter graciously pointed out, I come from poor white trash. Bad blood. Not much future in being associated with a guy like me." As Jack's stepfather had told him a thousand times. And the school principal. And practically everybody else in town including his mother. Not that he gave a damn.

"I *meant* that we're both trying to better ourselves. Neither of us is ready for a permanent relationship...or having babies. Besides, we used protection. I may have been foolish that night, but I'm not stupid. And neither are you."

"No protection is a hundred percent sure."

Ignoring his comment and turning away, she slipped on a rubber apron to cover her blouse and jeans, lifting her braid free of the yoke. Except for a stubborn set of her jaw, she looked innocent and slightly vulnerable. A trace of makeup smoothed her already perfect complexion and enhanced the green of her eyes.

He'd wanted her that night at Paddy's Bar. He'd been thinking about her ever since, barely able to concentrate on training his Thoroughbred, his ticket to success, the future of Colby Farms. Hell, he wanted Lindy now.

"I suggest if you don't want to get soaked, you'd better step back." She released the Irish setter from her cage. Apparently sensing what was coming, the other dog, a golden retriever ambled to the front of the shop. "Giving a dog a bath is wet work."

"I've never been afraid of a little water." Which had been doubly true that night when they'd showered together. Or rather the next morning. And he wasn't a hundred percent certain he'd used a condom that time. Hell, he'd been so hot even after the night they'd spent together, he'd been lucky to remember his own name.

With amazing ease she lifted the dog into a deep, porcelain sink that was scarred by wear. She wasn't a large woman but she was strong, her legs capable of pulling a man to her and holding him there with great endurance.

He'd wondered why he hadn't noticed her around town before. Then again, he'd just come back from the Marines a few months ago. He'd been too busy trying to get his own life together to think much about dating anyone.

Until that night at the bar when he'd danced with Lindy. He'd surprised himself by inviting her onto the small dance floor at Paddy's Bar. As a rule he stayed well away from "nice" girls, and Lindy had "nice girl" written all over her face. But her laughter, her genuine smile had drawn him across the room. At the time he had thought she'd been surprised herself when she'd stood and accepted his hand. But then she'd stepped into his arms, her body fitting perfectly with his, and he had the oddest feeling he'd finally come home.

Now he wondered if they both had reasons to regret that night they'd spent together—Lindy far more than he.

The dog panted, drawing his attention. He

seemed to be enjoying having his thick coat lathered with shampoo. Jack had been equally pleased with a similar process when he and Lindy had showered together.

"I don't get how you heard that silly rumor before I did." She aimed a hose to rinse the lather off the dog.

"I've been going back to Paddy's almost every night hoping to see you again."

"You have?" Eyes wide, she whirled. The hose sprayed water in all directions, but mostly toward Jack.

He stepped back but he wasn't quick enough.

"Why in heaven's name would you do that?" She seemed unconcerned Jack was drenched from the waist down.

"You didn't return my call. I wanted to see you again." Water puddled around his feet.

"Because you thought I'd be easy to get into bed again?"

"Because I enjoyed being with you." Even when he knew it'd be better for Lindy if he kept his distance.

She dropped her gaze, fixing her eyes on the wet setter.

Water dripped from his pants, turning from warm to chill. "I don't know why you're so surprised. We had a good time."

"Jack, as far as I can recall, you've never lacked for girlfriends. Why me?"

He wasn't sure how to answer that. Lindy wasn't as beautiful as many of the women he'd known, and certainly more innocent than most. But he'd been attracted to her energy, her willingness to tackle life head on. Her slight southern drawl made him think of mint julips and magnolia trees. And home. "Maybe I like that you're different from the other women I've known."

She raised her brows. "You mean I'm uglier? Or just plain mule-headed?"

He chuckled. "Probably the mule-headed part."

She fought back a smile. "Thanks, I think."

"Look, this rumor is all around town. Why don't we just make sure—"

"I am sure. If you must know, I had a routine physical exam a week ago. I'm sure the doctor would have mentioned a little detail like me being pregnant." She wrapped a large towel around the setter.

"Why don't you just take one of those home pregnancy tests? Then you'd know for sure."

"God, you must have been a balky child! And you haven't changed one bit, have you?" She lifted the dog from the sink, set her on the floor and pulled the towel away.

"Not much."

The setter shook herself, starting at her tail and working her way to her floppy ears. A spraying arc of water soaked Jack's shirt. As relationships with women went, this one was hard on his wardrobe.

"I assume you did that on purpose," he said dryly.

A wicked glint of amusement sparked in her jade-green eyes. "I told you this was wet work. You wouldn't believe me."

"And that means I have to believe everything you tell me?"

"Jack, we met at Paddy's. We both had a lot to drink. I went with you to a motel and we had great sex. End of story. Now go home."

"Indulge me. Take the test."

"I will not demean myself further by doing any such thing."

"Fine. You can call your doctor and let him confirm that you're not pregnant." He gestured toward the phone. "I'll listen in."

"Lord, do you put every woman you sleep with through this?"

Lindy shoved Colleen into the drying pen and turned on the blower. This man was not going to go away until he got the answer he wanted. He was so self-assured, he didn't even look silly standing there dripping wet. He looked sexy as hell, and so tempting she wanted to jump his bones.

But she'd done that once. A repeat performance was not a good idea.

"You're the only woman I've slept with that's become the talk of the town because she's suddenly pregnant," he said softly. "We both need to be certain."

Not ready to admit defeat, she stalked across the room to the phone and punched in the doctor's number. She had to make this man go away before she did something really stupid. Like fall in love with him.

The receptionist answered. While Lindy waited for the doctor to come on the line, she glared at Jack. He had the most penetrating eyes, sexy, heavy-lidded, bedroom eyes. And the way he looked at her she felt as if she was the only woman in the world. But she knew his reputation from high school days—the good girls had kept their distance and the bad girls... Well, they'd fawned all over him.

She swallowed a sigh. Guess she now qualified for the bad-girl category.

"Hello! Hello! Who is this?" the doctor asked when he finally picked up the phone.

She forced herself to drag her gaze away from Jack. "It's Lindy Montgomery, Dr. Jennings."

"Ah, the lovely lady of the haircuts. How are you, Kathleen, my dear?"

"No, doctor. This is Lindy." She raised her voice to accommodate his increasing deafness. "It's not my mother."

"Of course you're not my mother. She died years ago. Still miss the old dear, though."

Jack came close. Too close. With his head next to hers, Lindy caught his scent, masculine and very elemental. For the past five weeks, she hadn't washed the blouse she'd worn that night. In her imagination, at least, the fabric still held a faint trace of his presence.

Gritting her teeth, she concentrated on the need to get Jack to leave. Soon. "Dr. Jennings, there's something I'd like you to confirm for me."

"Of course, my dear. Anything I can do for the health of my patients."

"Was there any indication during my physical that I might be pregnant?"

There was a long pause on the other end of the line. "Kathleen, why at your age would you think you're pregnant?"

"Not Kathleen, doctor!" she shouted. "I'm Linda, her daughter."

"I can't tell you anything about Linda. That's confidential information, doctor-patient privilege, you know. You'll have to ask your daughter yourself. If she wants you to know—"

"But Dr. Jennings, I *am* the patient. I'm Lindy. You can tell me the results—"

"I can't simply discuss my patients willy-nilly with anyone who calls, now can I? Not even their mothers."

"Dr. Jennings!" she wailed. "You were there when I was born. You know who I am."

Grinning wryly, Jack stepped back. He did have the most attractive smile but now his timing irritated the hell out of her. A little lopsided, those two creases appeared in his cheeks when his lips canted—

"And I have no desire to feed any rumors that might be flying about," the doctor said.

Lindy didn't know which man she wanted to throttle first—Jennings, who was a suture or two short of a full count, or Jack. She imagined Jack would reach the top of the list if he said one more word about taking that damn home pregnancy test.

As she hung up, Jack said, "I should have thought to pick up a test before I came this morning."

Boing! Give that man at the top of the list a red carnation!

She manhandled Colleen out of the drying cage and hefted her onto a grooming table. Why hadn't she fallen for some other guy years ago, a man with a spotless reputation—a butcher or baker, a candlestick maker. A dull man. Not the town bad boy. Life would be eminently less complicated if that had been the case.

"I want you to go away," she said. "I want you to never come—"

"Hi, Lindy, I'm really sorry I'm late." Her assistant, an eighteen-year-old with the heart of an elephant and the sense of a rabbit, bless her, came bounding into the room through the back door.

"Late is not good, Roseanne," Lindy said.

"I know but I—" The girl's eyes filled with tears and her freckled face turned as red as her hair. "I'm so sorry,'' she wailed, making a dash for the tiny rest room at the back of the shop.

Jack's forehead puckered. ''What was that all about?''

''Who knows.'' She handed him a stiff grooming brush. ''Here, make yourself useful while I find out.''

Roseanne wasn't exactly forthcoming about what was bothering her.

''Are you sick?'' Lindy asked.

''No.'' Using toilet paper, she blew her nose and wiped her red-rimmed eyes.

''Did someone hurt your feelings?''

Her chin trembled. ''Not really.''

''Roseanne, we have four dogs to bathe and groom before noon and Mrs. Anratty's cat. I don't have time to play twenty questions.''

''I can't tell you,'' she wailed. ''It's too terrible.''

The town of Goodfellow ought to open a playhouse. Between Marcie and Roseanne, there were plenty of drama queens around.

''Fine. When you're feeling better, come on out and let's get to work.''

Jack relinquished the brush and Lindy got down to business. Roseanne soon joined her, occasionally sniffing and blowing her nose.

Eventually Jack wandered off. Lindy hoped he'd taken her advice to heart and gone home—back to the squalid farm that had belonged to his mother and stepfather. But she didn't have time to worry about his absence. And it only irritated her a little that he'd left without saying goodbye.

Or maybe it galled her a lot. They had, after all, slept together. He'd made such a big deal about that silly rumor and then poof! He'd vanished.

Which was probably just as well. Her nerves couldn't have handled much more of Jack hanging around. He was simply too sexy for her own good.

As soon as she and Roseanne finished grooming the dogs—and the abysmally smelly cat—she returned to her cozy little house, a hundred paces back of the shop, a two-on-a-lot deal that was part of her option to buy.

As she showered and brushed her hair to get ready for her friend's bridal shower, Lindy had trouble keeping Jack out of her thoughts. Falling for him would place her whole future at risk. If nothing else, D'Arcy McDrew had always been the Queen Prude of Goodfellow. If she got wind out in California of Lindy messing with Jack Colby, Lindy could kiss her lease goodbye. And her future.

But sometimes reality wasn't enough to stop a girl from dreaming. Bad boys, after all, did have their appeal.

AN EARLY SPRING breeze drifted in through the open windows carrying with it the fresh scent of new grass from the horse pastures that lay on the outskirts of town. This was the season that wealthy horsebreeders waited anxiously for the birth of new foals, hoping for the founding of new bloodlines. Their fortunes rested on their breeding programs being successful, and being a success was the only thing that counted in Goodfellow.

Lindy and her friends were not a part of that circle. Not that she wanted to be. Respectable was good enough for Lindy.

Inside Marcie's house, the shower guests crowded into the small living room and spilled out onto the back porch. The floor around the bride-to-be was stacked with opened presents, torn wrapping paper and the standard paper-plate bouquet made of ribbons. Everyone was talking at once of boyfriends, weddings and school chums who had moved away.

Sitting on the chair next to Lindy, Addie MacKenzie balanced a paper dessert plate with a slice of cake on it and a cup of punch. She leaned forward.

"I didn't want to say anything earlier," she whispered. "But I'm just so happy we'll be having our babies about the same time."

"You're pregnant?" Lindy asked. Like many of Lindy's classmates, Addie had married her longtime boyfriend right out of high school. He drove a truck for the local feed store, and she checked groceries at Graham's in town.

She glowed with her good news. "We haven't told anyone yet. Well, only close friends. We've been trying so long, Chuck was afraid it might be his fault. You know how these macho men get if they can't do the deed. Just yesterday I took the test. We got a great big pink plus. Isn't that grand?''

"Terrific. Does that mean you're going to have a girl?"

"Oh, no, silly." Her giggle was like tiny champagne bubbles popping. "We won't know the sex for ages yet. Chuck is hoping for a boy, of course. Maybe you'll have a boy, too. 'Course, it's a real shame you of all people got caught short, without a husband 'n all, but I'm sure—"

"I'm happy for you, Addie. I really am. But I'm not pregnant."

Addie's eyes widened. Because of her fair hair and complexion she'd had permanent eyeliner applied. It made her look as though her eyelids were particularly heavy and hard to open. "But I'd heard—"

"There's not an ounce of truth to that rumor." And Lindy was getting darn tired of denying it.

"Oh, that's too bad. I mean, I guess it's good—under the circumstances 'n all—but I'd been hoping our babies would grow up together just like we did."

Smiling weakly, Lindy shrugged. "Sorry." She could only wonder if everyone at the shower had heard the same stupid story.

Marcie flounced over to the couch and situated herself on the floor in front of Lindy and Addie. "Isn't Addie's news the most terrific thing. You two will be raising your babies at the same time. I'm so envious. And here I don't even have a boyfriend in sight, unless you count Jasper Tolliver, which I don't. Not after what he did last night.''

''Marcie, Addie is pregnant. Tootsie is pregnant. Thousands of women across the country are pregnant. I'm not.''

''You have to be,'' Marcie protested. ''Mrs. Murdock heard it from Bette-Jane Fetzer, who heard it from Allison Worth. And she'd gotten it straight from Jean Neff who'd heard it from Joan—''

''Marcie! I don't care if they heard the news directly from a burning bush! I am *not* pregnant!''

Lindy should not have raised her voice in an unladylike manner. Her mother had always warned her about that. She'd been right.

A hush descended on the room. Not a soul moved. No one spoke. They all gaped at Lindy while her cheeks flushed as hot as that same legendary bush.

Propelled by embarrassment, Lindy tried for an air of mock cheerfulness and leaped to her feet. ''Why don't we all help Marcie and her mom with the cleanup?''

''You don't have to do that, dear,'' Mrs. Goodlet called from across the room. ''Marcie and I will take care of everything after you're gone. I just want everyone to enjoy themselves while they're here.''

Lindy was not enjoying herself. Somebody had

apparently tattooed a giant *P* on her forehead, which was better than a scarlet *A* on her chest, she supposed. But only marginally.

Flitting from one cluster of friends to another, she tried to make conversation about any subject except that of pregnancy. Or babies. She didn't have much success. Amazing how many times those two subjects come up when you get a group of women together. And the horror stories about actually giving birth didn't bear considering, nor did the displays of blue birthing veins that scrolled up the legs of half the women present.

Gritting her teeth, Lindy silently vowed she'd have her tubes tied before she ever got to a wedding night.

Not that she hadn't enjoyed her evening with Jack. Lust could be a good thing. And attraction. A little chemistry—well maybe a lot. But it had only been a passing moment. She had her goals set, a path she intended to travel. Establish a successful business, hold on to her respectability.

Jack wasn't a part of that.

By now, he probably realized he didn't have to worry. Knowing she wasn't pregnant, he'd drop out of her life as quickly as he'd dropped in.

Checking her watch, she noted she had just enough time to get back to the shop before her customers began arriving to pick up their pets. Roseanne wasn't real good yet about the details of paperwork and collecting the amount due.

Lindy did not expect to return to the shop to find her young assistant in frantic pursuit of a pack of freshly groomed dogs who were chasing an orange-and-yellow tabby around the parking lot.

Nor did she expect to find Jack Colby in the middle of the melee.

3

THE CAT SCAMPERED onto Lindy's porch and jumped to the railing. Balancing easily, she bristled and hissed at her pursuers.

From inside the house, Petey frantically squawked, "Heads up! Heads up!"

Yapping and barking, tails wagging, the dogs viewed the cat's feline display as an invitation to fun and games.

Jack darted after the animals. He was quicker on his feet and more athletic than Lindy expected, though she should have remembered he'd always been a jock.

Since she'd seen him last, he'd changed clothes and was now wearing jeans so old they were nearly faded white. Unfortunately, he'd apparently taken a swan dive into the flower bed. Mud streaked both his shirt and pants.

He cornered Colleen between Lindy's porch and the front steps to her house, and grabbed her collar, going down on his knees in the process.

Roseanne went after Miss Bee, who'd scampered

up onto the porch to harass the cat from that direction.

Wearing a dress and high heels, Lindy couldn't be of much help pursuing the dogs, but she waded into the mess anyway. She whistled twice before Tootsie came to heel and she ordered the dog to sit. The two black poodles in her charge flung themselves into the air like circus performers, yapping hysterically, all in a futile effort to get at the cat.

"Roseanne, take Miss Bee inside and get some leashes," she ordered.

Panting, Colleen's tongue lolled to one side. Lindy got the impression Jack would like to do the same but was too macho to admit defeat.

"Hell of a way to run a business," he muttered.

"I thought I'd promote it as an innovative exercise program."

"For the dogs...or their keepers?"

In spite of herself, she smiled. "I'm still working out the details."

A reluctant flash of amusement sparked in his eyes. "So far I'd say there were a few flaws in the plan—unless you're planning to sell it to the Marines." Without releasing his grip on the dog's collar, Jack levered himself to his feet. The knees of his jeans were now covered in dripping mud and stained green from the grass.

Roseanne returned with the requested leashes. "I'm so sorry, Lindy. I was getting the cat ready for pickup and the phone rang. I got distracted, it was Billy and, well, gee…'' Her eyes filled with tears. "I'm sorry."

The poor kid either had the worst case of PMS in the world, or something serious was troubling her.

"It's okay, Roseanne." She took the leashes from the young woman and tossed one to Jack, then eyed the poodles. Their paws were caked with mud. Colleen and Miss Bee were probably in the same fix. "We'll have to bathe them all again but at least they won't need to be trimmed." Not eager to cause Roseanne additional tears, Lindy put the most positive spin on the fiasco that she could.

"It's practically time for the owners to come," Roseanne said with dread.

"Then we'll have to hurry, won't we?" She snared one poodle, snapped the leash in place, and went after his brother. He eluded her. She tripped over the six-inch high ornamental wire fence that marked the boundary between the lawn and flower bed, and landed hard on her knees. "Damn," she grumbled as she felt her pantyhose rip.

Jack, who'd handed over Colleen's leash to Roseanne, went after the second poodle. He caught him before he reached the end of the porch.

"You're getting good at this," Lindy commented.

"It's an acquired talent. Practice is the key."

He'd said something that night they'd been together about practice being the key to good sex.

"And experimentation," she added softly, remembering how determined he'd been to discover what pleased her the most, to learn each and every one of her erogenous zones, pleasuring her in ways she hadn't imagined possible. Not that anything he'd done had *displeased* her. On the contrary. And he seemed to relish her far less experienced efforts to satisfy him.

Heat flooded her cheeks as she remembered the details of their erotic acts—his and hers.

"Yes, there is that," he agreed, and she knew he had read her thoughts.

Tugging on the leashes, she pulled the yapping poodles toward Roseanne, who dragged three unwilling dogs toward the back door of the shop.

Meanwhile, Tootsie's obedience to Lindy's "sit" and "stay" commands was being sorely tested. Her tail twitched, the fur along her back rippled.

"Guess the cat is next," Jack said. "I'll get her."

Sitting on the porch railing, the cat feigned indifference, licking her coat and cleaning her paws. Lindy didn't buy the act.

"I'd better do it," she said. "She's used to me."

Too late. Like an attacking Marine, Jack had already entered Amelia's comfort zone through which she allowed few humans to pass except her owner and occasionally Lindy. As though she'd been launched on a Mars probe, the cat leaped off the railing and made a dash for the droopy cypress trees at the edge of the property. Tootsie's patience snapped, hours of training forgotten as she joined in the fray once again. One look over her shoulder to confirm Jack and Tootsie were still after her, and Amelia raced up the trunk of the largest tree.

Tootsie barked.

Jack cursed.

So did Lindy.

They all tipped their heads back. Assorted twigs rained down and the very top of the tree wobbled.

"Looks like you'll have to call the fire department," Jack said.

"They don't rescue cats from trees anymore. It's not in their budget."

"Then how do we get her down?"

"Leave a dish of food out for her. When she gets hungry she'll come down."

"How long is she likely to hold out?"

Lindy sighed. "Depends on how scared she is. It could be days."

"Your customer is due back any minute now."

"True."

He cocked his head, studying the tree and the cat perched almost out of sight among the topmost branches. He grimaced. "I'll get her."

"No, you don't have to—"

He started shimmying up the trunk, and when he got to the branches he swung his leg over the first one and used the rest as a ladder to climb up. The problem was the tree was tall. The branches at the top couldn't possibly hold his weight. The whole tree was beginning to shake like it was being buffeted by a violent windstorm.

"Jack, you don't have to do this."

"I thought in business, the customer was king." He glanced down at her, a challenging gleam in his eye as if this were only one more obstacle he'd been asked to face and conquer.

The tree swayed precariously.

Darn him for being so macho, for trying to come to her rescue—along with the cat. Why was he trying to impress her? As if she hadn't been impressed enough during her adolescent years.

"You're going to break your neck," she warned.

"Possibly," he agreed amiably. He scrambled up a little higher. The tree bent under his weight.

"Jack!" she screamed.

"I've got her—"

The cat howled.

The limb Jack was standing on cracked. Debris scattered to the ground. Branches bowed one after the other, allowing Lindy to follow the path of Jack's descent. She considered closing her eyes. She really hated the sight of blood. But since he was rescuing the cat that had been in her charge, she owed him enough loyalty to watch him crash to the ground. Then she'd call 911.

He reached the ground with a thud, rolled over and staggered to his feet.

"The fire department has the right idea," he groused, thrusting the cat into Lindy's arms. A scratch mark crossed his cheek, and his knuckles were red and scraped.

"Thanks." She cuddled the frantic cat as best she could, trying to calm her. "At least Amelia doesn't stink as much as she did this morning."

"Small blessing." He honored her with one of his lopsided grins.

An elemental awareness rose in Lindy, something hot and needy, filled with forbidden memories. She wanted to taste him again, his sharp, distinctive flavor. Wanted to sink her fingers into the thickness of his hair, feel the texture. Wanted to lose herself in him, lose her reserve with him as she had on that one glorious night.

Not exactly a good idea if she wanted to stay in the good graces of the folks in Goodfellow who could afford her grooming services.

Her mouth gone dry with a combination of wanting and disappointment, she forced herself to say, "Looks like I have lots of work to do before my customers show up."

"I'll help you."

"I'd rather you didn't."

"I'm volunteering for purely selfish reasons. I don't own a whole lot of civilian clothes and right about now, I look like I've been wallowing in a pigsty. Maybe I could convince you to wash my pants and shirt."

She could understand his concern. He did look a mess; it was her fault, or at least her employee's fault. It wasn't too much for him to ask her to repair the damage as best she could.

"I'll have to take care of the animals first," she said.

He gave her a lopsided grin which sent her heart spinning.

It took more than an hour to get the dogs bathed, blow-dried and brushed out. Jack was as good as his word, shampooing Colleen while Lindy and Roseanne performed the finishing touches on the two poodles. In nature's way, the cat took care of her own grooming needs.

After the dogs had been dutifully delivered to their respective owners, and Roseanne had left for the day, Lindy walked Jack to her house on the back of the property. Tootsie trotted along between them, guarding her from the stranger. Or perhaps as intrigued by him as Lindy was.

The air was still. What little traffic the town of Goodfellow had was quiet, and starlings flitted through the twilight sky in search of one last edible morsel before they slept.

Suddenly conscious of being alone with Jack and the dangers that lay along that path, she let him into the house. Tootsie left her side to plop down on her favorite place, a hooked rug in front of the yawning fireplace. Like most pregnant females, Lindy supposed, Tootsie had taken to doing a lot of dozing lately.

From the other room, Petey squawked, "Heads up! Heads up!"

Scowling, Jack half crouched. "Are we about to get some incoming fire?"

"That's a parrot. I think he's got post-traumatic stress syndrome."

"He's a vet?"

"His owner isn't sure." She shrugged. "You'll have to strip so I can wash your pants. I'll see what I can find for you to put on."

"I'm not modest. My shorts will be enough."

She shot him a censuring look. "No, they won't." *Not for me!*

He grinned. "While you're at it, you'd better strip, too."

"Thanks, but no." This time she intended to remain fully clothed.

"Your dress has seen better days."

Looking at the mud streaks and water stains on the dreadfully expensive dress, she had to agree. Usually frugal, she'd splurged for once. Bad mistake.

"Teal-blue. It's a good color for you. It deepens your eyes."

She hadn't turned on the lights in her small living room, and the shadows cast him in shades of gray. His rich baritone voice came out of those shadows, tempting her, inviting her to repeat a foolish mistake, his masculine tone and easy drawl caressing her like dark molasses.

"Make yourself at home. I'll be right back." She fled. There could hardly be another word for it, except cowardice under fire.

In her room, she shed her clothes and pulled on an old sweatshirt and baggy pants. She wanted to hide from him. Or maybe from herself. Certainly from the feelings he set off in her. And her memories.

Why had she acted so foolishly with Jack? It hadn't been the liquor alone that she had consumed that night. Or the feeling of celebration. At the time it had seemed so *right*. But now she knew that getting intimate with Jack had been all wrong. There was no future there, not if she—the daughter of a moonshiner—ever hoped to earn the respect of the townspeople and see her business thrive.

Sighing, she searched through her closet for something that would cover him while she washed his clothes, something so she wouldn't keep remembering how handsome, how powerfully male he'd looked naked.

The best she could find was an old chenille bathrobe. He'd look ridiculous in it, which was just fine with Lindy. Perhaps the memories of the erotic night they'd shared would disappear in the humor of the situation.

Moments later she learned how wrong she'd been to hope for such a reprieve.

Jack Colby in a pink chenille bathrobe was still the sexiest man she'd ever seen.

The robe gaped open, revealing the hair-roughened, muscular legs of a man who'd been hardened and shaped by the Marines. The crisp hair on his chest was equally apparent. Lord, what she wouldn't give to run her fingers through those curls one more time and feel his skin warm and rippling beneath her touch.

She snatched the pants and shirt from his hands and escaped to the back porch. Dumping the clothes in the washing machine, she turned on the water and sprinkled in some detergent.

Damn! Until the ridiculous rumor about her being pregnant had surfaced, Lindy had put the *incident* with Jack behind her. Now he was in her house again, half-naked, and what she wanted more than anything else was to repeat her foolish mistake.

WAITING FOR LINDY to return Jack examined her home. Her dog watched him alertly, as though one misstep would be Jack's last.

Periodically, the parrot announced its presence with an unpleasantly ear-splitting squawk.

More cottage than house, the place was in better shape than the shack where Jack had grown up and far cozier. A jacket had been tossed carelessly over the back of a chintz-covered couch, her tennis shoes had been left by the front door, and unopened mail lay strewn on a small maple dining table.

Scattered on every available surface was an assortment of dofunnies, mostly small ceramic animals. A pink elephant with purple polka dots shared space with a whimsical cat licking its paws. The clock over the fireplace—a wide-eyed owl—was surrounded by dogs of every imaginable breed.

In the bathroom where he'd taken off his muddy clothes, he'd noted her stockings hanging from the shower bar. Pots of makeup scattered about gave off a womanly scent, one he remembered and inhaled with pleasure. Like spring honeysuckle.

Tootsie's ears swiveled as Lindy returned to the living room. "It'll take about an hour to get your things washed and dried."

"I'm in no hurry." Though it was clear she'd be happy to see the back of him. For his own reasons, he was determined to stay, at least until he knew the truth. No man—or woman—would ever say Jack was as worthless as his father, not when it came to acknowledging his responsibilities. Though he might not be doing Lindy any favors. Having her name linked with his wouldn't earn her any bragging rights in a town like Goodfellow.

"Quite a collection of animals," he commented, nodding toward the row of dogs on the mantel.

She flushed slightly. "People keep giving me little keepsakes."

"Because they know you love animals."

"I suppose. One of my weaknesses."

Jack didn't think she was weak at all, but rather a determined, hardworking woman.

"While we're waiting, you can take care of other

important matters.'' He pulled a slender box from the robe pocket.

Lindy's eyes widened as he produced the home pregnancy test, a benign little box which he'd claimed not to have that morning. ''Where did you get that?''

''The Goodfellow Pharmacy.''

''Right here in town?'' she gasped.

''It seemed like the logical place to buy one.''

''Oh, swell.'' In frustration, she pushed strands of flyaway hair back from her face. This man was far too determined, like a dog that wouldn't quit gnawing on an old bone. ''Half the people in town saw you in my grooming shop this morning. Then you pick up a pregnancy test at the friendly corner drugstore with that awful rumor going around town? God, if people connect you with me—''

''More importantly, I need to know if you and I are connected in a far more binding way.''

''We're not.'' She gritted her teeth. She could be stubborn, too. As well as foolish.

''So you say.''

''Okay, let's for a moment say I am pregnant— which I'm not. Why would you be so sure it's your baby? I am, after all, well beyond the age of consent.''

He studied her in a silent perusal that skated along her nerve endings. ''Did you really think I wouldn't notice you were a virgin?''

The slow heat of guilt crept up her neck.

"What was I? A birthday present to yourself?"

"No, it wasn't like that. Not really." But maybe a little bit. A woman of twenty-five ought to know what all the fuss was about.

He held out the box to her. "Take the test. If the results are negative, I'll leave you in peace."

Tootsie stretched and yawned hugely.

Lindy snatched the box from Jack's hand. "I'll take your dang test, but only because I want this whole ordeal over with and you out of here. Maybe when the results are known, I can get a headline in the newspaper. Rumor Of Pregnancy False."

She stomped into the bathroom, slammed the door and locked it. This was the most ridiculous thing she'd ever done. She'd already had her flow once since that night. They'd used protection. Mostly. How could Jack possibly think she was pregnant with his child?

Was he feeling some misguided guilt because he'd been her first lover?

If she hadn't succumbed to temptation, she wouldn't be in this fix.

Irritated as much with herself as with Jack—and whoever had started the rumor in town—she read the instructions on the box. When the test turned out negative, she'd have to post the results on the bulletin board down at Graham's Grocery. Assuming she couldn't get the newspaper to cover such an astounding story. Then maybe everyone would shut up about the whole thing.

She followed the prescribed steps and waited the appropriate amount of time before checking the results.

"Oh, my God..." she groaned, staring at the markings on the cylinder.

She snatched up the box and reread the directions. Twice. Word by word.

Vertigo nearly doubled her over.

Tootsie scratched on the bathroom door.

"Not now, sweetheart."

She couldn't possibly be pregnant. But there it was. Slowly the shattering implication of the pink plus sign sank in. In her mind's eye, it became a huge neon sign blinking over the town of Goodfellow announcing the news of a not-so-blessed upcoming event.

She was going to have Jack Colby's baby.

4

THE TEST WAS positive.

Jack knew that the instant he saw her. She had the look of a shell-shocked soldier. Pale. Glassy-eyed. The plastic wand trembling in her hand.

For Jack, her pregnancy was like a punch in the gut with the butt end of a rifle. Not that he didn't like Lindy. He did. She was beautiful and fun to be with. Sexy as hell. He simply hadn't intended to get *any* woman pregnant, had never planned to pass on the stigma of being a Colby, of having bad blood, to a child. A youngster's shoulders weren't broad enough to carry that burden. He knew that for a fact.

At the very least, he'd wanted a chance to prove he wasn't his father's son before he started his own family.

But the deed was done. He'd do the right thing.

His own legs a little unsteady, he stepped forward.

She held up her hand to ward him off. "Don't."

"We've got to talk about this, Lindy."

"I can't." She shook her head. "I won't."

"God, I'm sorry. You know I never meant for this to happen."

She gave a hysterical little cry. "And that's supposed to make me feel better? That you never intended to get me pregnant?"

Lacking an answer that would placate her, he shrugged helplessly. "We'll figure out something. I want you to know right up front, I'm willing to marry you."

"Oh, that makes everything fine and dandy, doesn't it. Except *I'm* the one everybody will be talking about. *I'm* the one who'll get all fat and sloppy. Like all menfolk, you'll go on about your business while I..." Her voice broke. "I'll lose my dream."

"Tell me your dreams, Lindy."

"The Fluff 'n Cut. A roof over my head and enough money in the bank so me and mine won't ever go hungry or not have a decent dress to wear to school. I know it's not a big dream compared to some, but it's mine, dammit! And I'll lose..." A strangled sob caught her again.

"I have dreams, too," he said softly with a touch of reproach.

She pressed her lips together, her chin trembled and tears welled in her eyes, making them glisten like emerald pools.

"I'm sorry, Jack. I know you do." With a trembling hand, she rubbed at her forehead. "Neither of us wanted this."

Jack couldn't handle it. She might not want him for a husband—or the father of her child—but he couldn't simply stand by while she fell apart. So he stepped forward, ignoring her earlier rebuff, and wrapped his arms around her. She tensed for a moment like a high-strung Thoroughbred, then eased, accepting his touch. Her head rested on his shoulder as she drew a shuddering breath, and he caught the sweet scent of her honeysuckle shampoo. Down deep, his body reacted with a force that amazed him.

By sheer determination, he stifled the natural urge that rose up in him. The urge that had been so insistent the night he'd seen Lindy at Paddy's Bar. Despite her "nice girl" appearance, he'd still been surprised she was a virgin. And *proud* she'd chosen him for her first lover. When he had realized the truth, he'd vowed to go slow, to make the experience special for her. A memory she wouldn't regret. Getting her pregnant, passing on the Colbys' "bad blood" hadn't been a part of the plan.

Now was not the time to act on those same insistent urges again.

"It's going to be okay, sweet sugar," he whispered, rubbing his cheek across the top of her head as he pulled her more snugly against his chest. "Somehow it's going to be okay."

She shivered as though she'd been caught in an unexpected summer storm. "I...I think you'd better go."

"I'll leave, if that's what you want. But tonight won't be the end of this."

"I have to have time to think. This is all so…"

"Awful?"

"Sudden." She looked up at him, devastation in her eyes. "I was so sure I wasn't…that I couldn't be—"

"But you are."

With a nod, she accepted the truth of the test results with the same stoic finality as a convicted spy facing a firing squad. "Please go," she whispered.

"For appearance's sake, I think it'd be best if I put my clothes back on. Going out in your bathrobe might cause a few raised eyebrows. The good folks of Goodfellow are a bit stodgy when it comes to things like men in pink chenille bathrobes."

His comment almost got a smile out of her but not quite. "The wash cycle is done but they're not dry—"

"It's okay. I've worn worse than wet jeans." He released her, and she stepped back.

From her spot in front of the fireplace, Tootsie stretched and yawned, shifting into a more comfortable position.

"I know you're not any happier about this than I am, Jack. I'm just so sorry…"

He let his gaze sweep over her. After a day's work, strands of blond hair had escaped her braid to frame her face and tease along the column of her neck. Her breasts rose high and proud beneath her sweatshirt. The swell of her hips invited a man's caress.

"It wouldn't be a burden to marry you, Lindy," he said carefully. "No burden at all."

Color stained her cheeks as she nodded toward the kitchen. "The washer's on the back porch."

"Got it." Feeling like he'd made a mess of things, that he'd failed to find the words that would reassure Lindy, he took a step into the small dining room.

"Heads up! Heads up!"

Startled, Jack swore. "What's this bird's name?"

"Petey."

"He's never heard of 'Polly want a cracker'?"

"Apparently not."

"Heads up! Heads up!" the bird screeched.

"At ease, Petey. At ease."

The parrot purred, his head dropping to his chest. "At ease," he muttered.

Jack snapped around to look at Lindy.

She looked back at him with surprise. "Did I hear what I think I heard?"

He cocked his head toward the bird. "Ten-hut!" he commanded Marine-style.

The parrot righted himself on his perch and fluffed his feathers. "Heads up! Heads up!"

"I'll be damned."

Lindy burst out laughing, the sound so wonderfully warm it wrapped around Jack like a wool blanket on a cold night. His chest tightened. This amazing, caring, resilient woman was pregnant with *his* baby.

"Is Petey a Marine, do you think?" she asked, her voice laced with humor.

He tried not to think about her pregnancy, about the child that could be his son or daughter. "Could be. Or an army brat."

"I never even considered…" She came to stand beside him, their arms brushing. "What else do you suppose he knows?"

He could barely think at all with her standing so close to him, her sweet perfume teasing him. "Uh, let's try…semper fi!"

"Semper fi!" the bird echoed followed by a sound resembling a trumpet flourish.

"Oh, good Lord," Lindy cried, laughing so hard tears ran down her cheeks. "Mrs. O'Toole is going to have a hissy fit. She got herself a *Marine* for company after her husband died."

"Could be worse," Jack said straight-faced. "Better than a jet-jockey who only knows how to waggle his stick."

She looked at him wide-eyed. "I can't believe you said that. Mrs. O'Toole is seventy years old."

Swallowing a grin, he shrugged. "Just a little military humor."

She leaned into him, and he wrapped his arm around her.

"You'd better go before I do something really stupid," she warned.

"Like what?"

"Hmm, don't ask."

Chuckling, he said, "I'll call you tomorrow, sugar." He placed a kiss on the top of her head.

Reluctantly, he released her and headed through the kitchen to the service porch. He wanted to stay. He wanted to hold her all night, to bury himself in her sweet warmth. He couldn't do that, not now. Maybe never. He'd been a loner most of his life. Things like that don't change much. But some days it hurt more than usual.

Pulling his damp jeans out of the washing machine, he tugged them on, grimacing. His wet T-shirt clung like a second, sticky layer of skin.

"I'll just head out the back way," he called to her, half-afraid of what he might do if he went back inside, afraid he wouldn't have the sense to leave.

He opened the back door and stepped out onto the porch. The night air chilled him; the winking stars in the sky mocked him to make a wish as he went down the two steps to the backyard.

"Jack! You shouldn't go out that—"

Something clipped him right at the knees. Hard. He sprawled forward, eating dirt and grass.

"What the hell!" he sputtered.

Suddenly the backyard was lit up by a floodlight. "Oh, Jack, I tried to warn you."

He rolled over and found himself looking up into

the eyes of a… Good God! A goat! A goat that was considering him for her next meal.

"Lindy!" he bellowed, scrambling to his feet.

"Isabel won't hurt you."

The hell she wouldn't! There was a feverish look in her rectangular eyes. A *hungry* look. "Call her off, okay?" The goat butted him again, and her lips nipped at his hip pocket.

Jack dodged out of the way but the goat came right after him.

"Get outta here."

Lindy came down the steps and hooked her arm around the goat's neck.

Curious about all the activity, Tootsie pushed out through the screen door, her tail wagging.

The goat bleated.

"I'm sorry," Lindy said, still corralling the goat. "Sometimes she thinks she's a billy goat. I should have fed her when I got home but I forgot."

"Guess you had other things on your mind." He brushed a clump of grass off his knee. "I didn't know you owned a goat."

"I don't. Not exactly. Terrance Mulvaney and his wife are touring Europe and they didn't want to leave Isabel alone because she's pregnant. From what I've seen, she's eating more than enough for…" Her voice trailed off.

Ignoring the killer goat, he closed the distance to Lindy and cupped her cheek. "A lot of that pregnancy business going around lately, isn't there?"

His voice was soft and husky even to his own ears in the stillness of the spring night. His gaze held hers, unfamiliar emotions bubbling in him. Wanting, even needing to feel a matching response from her.

Closing her hand over his momentarily, her fingers as gentle as a breeze, she said, "Good night, Jack."

He hated to leave her. Hated that he didn't have a right to stay, that she hadn't returned his phone call after that first and only night they'd been together. Hated that he'd never wanted a woman to carry any part of the burdens he'd shouldered for as long as he could remember.

"Good night," he whispered. Turning, he found the gate and let himself out of the yard. If Lindy never admitted to a soul that her baby was his, he'd understand.

Damn, that would hurt.

But hey, *No pain, no gain*. He'd live with it.

GRATEFUL FOR SOMETHING warm and alive to hold on to, Lindy hugged Isabel while she watched Jack walk down the driveway toward the grooming shop and out to the street. She heard the engine of his pickup start, then fade away as he drove down Second Street. Only then did she release the goat.

She squeezed her eyes shut. With a shake of her head, she tried to dislodge the fears that gripped her.

"Chow time, Izzy." She got out the bag of feed

from a small shed in the yard, pouring a generous portion for Isabel, but her thoughts were on her own pregnancy, not the goat's.

Pregnant.

Instinctively, she rested her hand on her tummy.

It didn't seem possible. One night with Jack— one glorious night, she amended—and she'd been caught. Talk about unfair! She'd never in her life been able to get away with anything. Someone always discovered her least little failing.

Like the time she'd inadvertently shoplifted an ice-cream bar at Graham's Grocery. She'd fully intended to pay for it, had the precious dollar bill in her pocket. But she'd been laughing with Marcie and some of their other friends. And she'd walked out the door without paying.

Old Mr. "Grouchy" Graham had grabbed her by the ear, dragging her back inside. "No better than po' white trash," he accused. "Moonshiner's daughter."

Despite her tears and her offer to pay double the price for the ice cream, he'd called the police. Chief Pickles had read her the riot act. Terrified, she'd thought he was going to put her in jail, though he'd finally let her go with only a warning and had never made the threatened call to her mother.

It was years before Lindy had the nerve to set foot in Graham's Grocery again and then only after "Grouchy" Graham died of apoplexy during a dispute with the IRS about deducting his tabby cat as a business expense because she was such a good mouser around the store.

Poor white trash. Both the Montgomerys and Colbys qualified for that label. Lindy had thought she could rise above her station through hard work and impeccable behavior. Having a baby out of wedlock wasn't exactly a step in that direction.

Marrying Jack Colby would be even more devastating to her hopes and dreams.

Except she'd dreamed of Jack since their night together. Erotic dreams filled with wanting.

"Dang it all!" she muttered, scratching Isabel's wiry coat and stroking her distended belly. Unlike the goat, an unintended pregnancy would turn her world topsy-turvy. What in heaven's name was she going to do?

No matter which way she turned, D'Arcy was likely to cancel her lease—assuming by the time the news spread to California Lindy had any business left at all.

SHE STILL HADN'T found an answer to her dilemma when dawn lightened the sky the next morning. Nor had she had a wink of sleep.

Staggering up from her sleepless bed, she swept her tangled mass of hair back from her face and headed for the kitchen. Slower to get up, Tootsie stretched, raising her rump into the air, her pregnant tummy beginning to drag some.

"At least you aren't likely to get breeding veins," she promised her dog.

"Heads up! Heads up!"

She groaned. "At ease, Petey."

"Heads up! Heads up!" He strutted on his perch.

She glowered at the parrot whose cage she had forgotten to cover last night. "Why can't you be a normal bird? You know, you could purr like a cat or something. Bark like a dog. Lots of parrots do that. You don't have to be a Marine." But Marines were nice. Honorable. Hadn't Jack offered to marry her the moment he discovered she was pregnant? Not every man would do that.

But just because she'd had half a crush on him for years and thought he was the sexiest man she'd ever known, she couldn't accept his proposal. That wouldn't be fair to either of them. And it certainly wouldn't enhance her reputation.

Petey squawked his same old tune.

She tried "semper fi!" and "ten-hut!," but Petey was back in his old rut.

It finally occurred to Lindy that she shouldn't be wasting her time talking to a fine-feathered enlistee in the Marines but to the real McCoy. She had to talk to Jack.

Not that she knew what to say. But Petey, bless his heart, would furnish a perfect excuse to drive out to Jack's house.

Glancing at the clock over the stove, she decided it wasn't too early to show up at his horse farm.

He'd be out with the animals. Unlike most of the big-time Kentucky breeders in the county, Jack wouldn't have a trainer plus dozens of groomers and exercisers to handle the workload. Sunday wasn't a workday for her so she'd have plenty of time to—

Well, *talk* to Jack.

Energized at last, she fed the animals, showered quickly and dressed, giving as little thought as possible to what a woman should wear when she was planning an early-morning call on the gentleman who had accidentally gotten her pregnant. Casual would do. Jeans, a comfy T-shirt and tennis shoes. And maybe just a tiny drop of cologne behind her ears. Simple earbobs...

"Oh, quit it, Lindy!" she muttered.

On the way out the door, she grabbed a gooey Danish she had stashed in the bread box. Purse slung over her shoulder, she carried Petey's cage out to her Blazer. Tootsie leaped into the rear seat without an invitation, always eager for a ride in the truck.

All the while, Lindy's heart was doing a fluttery thing and her stomach was filled with butterflies the same way it had been that night when Jack asked her to dance at Paddy's Bar. And when he'd taken her down the road a piece to one of the fanciest motels on the outskirts of Lexington.

She didn't have many occasions to drive south of Goodfellow, through the hollows and wooded areas, past subsistence tobacco farms, an area that was considered the wrong side of the tracks even if there wasn't actually a railroad running through town. No white rail fences or wide expanses of bluegrass grazing pastures. And folks who lived here didn't use the services of a groomer. They were too poor.

So when she turned off at the Colby place she wasn't surprised that the house was rundown and in need of a good coat of paint. A huge walnut tree shaded the clapboard structure; an ill-kept bed of irises and a raggedy honeysuckle bush near the front porch were in dire need of attention. So was what used to be a lawn.

What surprised her was the white rail fence bordering a beautiful horse pasture of dusty-blue grass and a practice track circling the well-tended property.

She smiled to herself as she pulled the truck to stop beside a newly constructed horse barn. Jack Colby had been working hard since his return from the Marines. What he'd accomplished in a few short months was amazing and spoke convincingly of his own dreams.

Which probably didn't include a wife and baby right now any more than her plans involved a hasty marriage.

As she got out of the truck, she spotted Jack leading a strikingly handsome Thoroughbred out of the barn with a jockey mounted in the saddle. Even though Lindy had never spent much time around horses, she could tell the stallion had the potential to be a winner. Sleekly muscled. Long, powerful legs. A broad chest.

Rather like his owner, she thought as her admiring gaze shifted to Jack. He definitely had all the same magnificent attributes.

She shivered slightly, remembering how it had been to be in his arms.

Calling Tootsie to heel, she walked toward where Jack stood at the rail fence watching as the horse and rider began to lope around the track. He turned before she reached him.

The heated look that filled his eyes made her go all hot inside; the smile that creased his cheeks made her breath catch. Chill bumps raced down her spine. Dressed in black from head to toe, Jack Colby was the most potently masculine man she'd ever known.

He thumbed his worn cowboy hat farther up on his forehead. "Hey."

She swallowed hard. "Hey, yourself."

"You come to take a look at My Family Jewels?"

Sputtering, she felt heat flood her face. For the life of her, she couldn't prevent her gaze from dropping to the zipper fly on his jeans, noting the way the black denim pulled tautly across his pelvis. "I did no such thing. I wasn't even thinking about—"

"My Family Jewels is my horse." He gestured toward the Thoroughbred circling the track.

She blinked. "You named your horse—"

"Not me." He gave an innocent shrug while keeping a straight face. "The prior owner. I understand he owns a chain of jewelry stores throughout the midwest. The name's registered and everything. Of course, I'm extra careful to make sure nobody damages My Family Jewels."

Unable to repress a giddy smile, she said, "I'm sure you are."

He studied her a moment before letting his own smile appear. "I was going to call you this afternoon."

"I know. I...I couldn't get Petey to say anything except 'heads up!' again. I thought maybe you could..." She shrugged, knowing Petey was a lame excuse to be here, that something rather closely related to Jack's personal family jewels might well come closer to the truth.

He glanced toward her truck, the logo on the side door reading Fluff 'n Cut Dog and Cat Grooming. "You want me to put him through a little boot camp training?"

"Something like that."

"I'd be happy to."

She looked away from him, watching the easy strides of the Thoroughbred on the far side of the track, his forelegs marked with distinctive white socks. "He's beautiful."

"I've got him entered in a claiming race next week. I think he's got a chance."

They were both leaning on the fence now, their arms inches apart on the top railing, his darkly tanned skin a stark contrast to her fairer complexion. A slight breeze teased at the ends of her hair that she'd pulled back with a ribbon and she shivered in the cool air. Or maybe it was Jack's nearness that had her trembly.

"Aren't you afraid if he wins you'll lose him to somebody's claim?"

"If I do, I'll get more than a fair price for him and be able to buy an even better horse."

"Good business."

"Yep."

"You've done a lot around the place since you've been back."

"I saved every dime I could while I was in the service and plowed most of it into turning this into a horse farm."

As the horse loped past, Jack called to the rider, "Work up to some wind sprints, Alberto."

The jockey waved his crop in acknowledgement.

"I didn't know you had an employee," Lindy said.

"Actually Alberto is more like a partner. I didn't have enough money to pay him a salary so I gave him quarter ownership of the horse. We both have a vested interest in My Family Jewels being a winner."

"I was, well, surprised that you came back to

Goodfellow after the Marines. I would have thought you'd have had enough of this town."

He slid her a glance, his lips quirking into a half smile. "Two reasons. For one thing, I've got something to prove to myself as well as to the good folks of Goodfellow."

"You don't have anything to prove to me. I knew you weren't like your father."

"Or my brother," he added a little more grimly. "But the fact is, Ma owned this bit of land. There was actually some insurance money when my stepdad died. She paid off the mortgage and I inherited when she died a couple of years ago. On the open market as a tobacco farm the place wasn't worth selling. But with some sweat equity..." He watched the jockey pick up the pace and the horse's stride lengthen. "And some luck."

Lindy had the distinct feeling Jack was a man determined to make his own luck. She had no doubt he'd succeed. And that any child of his would be proud to call him father.

Her throat constricted with that realization and her chest filled with a powerful emotion.

Hesitantly, she placed her hand on his sun-warmed arm. "I don't know quite how our, uh, situation will work out but I've made one decision." In her heart she knew she couldn't make any other choice, even at the cost of her own dreams. "I plan to have your baby, Jack. I won't terminate the pregnancy."

His shoulders visibly relaxed but he didn't look at her. "Some folks would say that's not a smart thing to do, that you'd just be passing on bad blood."

"They'd be wrong," she said staunchly. "There's nothing wrong with your blood, Jack Colby. There never has been." Which didn't change the fact that marrying him might well be a more foolish mistake than the one she'd already made.

Turning, his dark eyes focused on her with laser intensity. "I'd say there's as much spunk in you as any Derby winner."

His compliment sent a flutter of warmth rippling through her veins.

"Come on," he said, looping his arm around her shoulders. "I want you to meet another lady with plenty of spunk."

Her eyebrows shot up and her stomach dropped to somewhere around her ankles. It had never occurred to Lindy that there might be another woman in his life. A girlfriend. Someone waiting in the wings who wouldn't be thrilled with the news that Jack had gotten Lindy pregnant.

Or that he had volunteered to marry her.

"SHE'S PREGNANT!" LINDY said with a gasp, the heat of embarrassment flooding her cheeks. "It must be something about the water in this town."

Chuckling, Jack stroked the mare's muzzle affectionately. "Salty Lady should foal in the next week or so. With luck she'll produce a fine animal that will be the start of Colby's Breeding Farm."

"I feel so foolish. When you said you wanted me to meet a lady, I thought…" Her words trailed off.

He cocked one brow. "What?"

"That you, I mean…that you had a girlfriend."

"Not me. Lady here has been the only woman in my life since I got back to town. Until you, that is." He shot her one of his wickedly sexy grins.

She should have known Jack wasn't the kind of man to cheat on a woman. He was too honorable for that.

"What happened to her?" she asked, noting the scars on the mare's rump.

"She was in a stable fire. The owners were going to put her down, but she's got great lines and a pedigree better than any other mare I'd have a chance of buying. I made them a better offer than the glue factory and bred her with My Family Jewels.''

Shuddering, Lindy couldn't help but picture the exquisite chestnut mare being slaughtered. She reached into the stall to pet the animal. Salty Lady danced away from her.

''She's still pretty skittish around people,'' Jack said. ''When I first brought her back here, she'd hardly stand still while I put ointment on her.''

''She doesn't object to you petting her now.''

With a few soft words, he coaxed the mare back to him. She lowered her head, accepting his touch once again and he scratched her between the ears. ''It takes most women some time to develop trust in a man. Lady wasn't much different. She'd been through a lot.''

Lindy suspected Jack could entice any female he met into trusting him with only a smile and a few softly spoken words. Certainly she hadn't put up much of a fight. Now she was going to have to pay for her indiscretion.

Tootsie, who'd followed them into the horse barn, cocked her head and whined.

''What is it, girl?'' Lindy asked.

''I think we've got company.'' Giving the mare one last scratch, Jack headed toward the open end of the barn where sun cast a bright column of light through the open doorway.

"Yoohoo! Anybody here?" came the call from outside.

Lindy rolled her eyes and groaned inwardly. How on earth had Marcie tracked her down here?

She followed Jack outside.

"Well, there you are," Marcie said, waving. "I just happened by and I saw your truck parked over there. Couldn't help but wonder what in the name of peace you were doing at Jack Colby's place at this time of day." She glanced up at Jack with open interest. "Not that it's any of my business, of course. But a girl's got a right to a little friendly curiosity now and then."

"And we all know what curiosity did to the cat," Jack said pointedly, a sexy smile stretching his lips.

Lindy scurried to reach Marcie before Jack did anything to start more rumors—like mentioning he'd proposed to her.

"Hi, Marcie, aren't you the early riser for a Sunday morning?" She tucked her arm through her friend's. "Or are you just on your way home from Jasper's place?"

Marcie's blush started on her creamy-white throat and rose like a spring flood, practically turning the roots of her dark hair to red—if that were possible.

Saving Marcie any further need for explanation, Lindy said, "I was just asking Jack if he'd help me out with Petey."

Marcie looked confused. "Petey?"

She ushered her friend toward her truck. "You

know, Mrs. O'Toole's parrot. I discovered sort of by accident that Petey speaks Marine lingo, except I can't seem to get him to say anything besides that 'heads up!' business. I thought Jack could help me out since he's a former Marine."

Marcie nodded dumbly.

"Isn't that right, Jack?" Lindy said over her shoulder. Why in the world had her voice gone all breathy and nervous, like she'd been caught naked in the front pew at church.

"Be happy to do what I can."

She opened the truck door and reached for the parrot's cage.

"He's the one, isn't he?" Marcie whispered.

"This is Petey, all right."

"No, I mean Jack! Jack Colby's the one who got you pregnant."

Lindy exhaled deeply. She wanted to deny the truth. But Marcie was like a tick determined to burrow under her skin. The only way she'd back off was if Lindy lit a highway flare under her rear end.

"Well, shoot a bug!" Marcie chortled.

Lindy wheeled on her friend. "If one word of this leaks out—one word, mind!—I swear I'll tell your mama you've been sneaking out to see Jasper. She'll fry your toast, that's for sure."

"Lindy, honey, I wouldn't say nothin'. You know that." She crossed her heart. "But Jack Colby? My sakes! You sure picked yourself some stud muffin! What are you gonna do?"

She yanked Petey's cage out of the truck. "I don't know yet, okay?"

"Heads up! Heads up!"

"Oh, shut up, Petey!"

"I stand corrected!"

She eyed the parrot with dismay. How was Mrs. O'Toole ever going to cope with this crazy bird?

Covering her hand with his, Jack eased the cage away from Lindy's grasp. "I'll get him."

"Thanks." The word stuck in her throat. Whenever Jack touched her, she seemed to forget how to breathe. Or to think rationally.

Marcie backed away. "Well, you two, I've got to be going. Don't you know Mama expects me at church. Good to see y'all."

Lindy couldn't respond. She had the desperate feeling within hours the entire congregation of Goodfellow Methodist Church would know the rumors about her pregnancy were true.

And would know exactly who the expectant father was.

BY SUPPER TIME she knew her worst fears had been realized.

"Chad?" she questioned, opening the front door to Chad Hollingsworth's knock. "What brings you here?"

"I, uh, I thought maybe..." Self-consciously, he gazed at the tips of his shoes, his feet so big his high school graduating class had named him Captain Ant Killer and voted him the one they'd call if they needed a grass fire stomped out.

Lindy's shoulders slumped. "You've heard, haven't you?"

He nodded. "I thought you could use a friend."

Pushing open the screen door, she let him inside. Chad Hollingsworth was probably one of the sweetest guys in town, in contrast to his father, who was all bluster. Chad hadn't taken to the family business of horsebreeding. Instead, after graduating from college, he'd become a junior stockbroker in Lexington.

He stopped in the middle of the room to give Tootsie a pat. When he glanced up, his expression looked more determined than Lindy had ever seen him, despite the blush that colored his chubby cheeks.

"I just wanted you to know, if you need somebody to marry you, I'll do it."

"Chad, that's so—"

"Or if you'd rather, I'll get Daddy's shotgun and make Jack do right by you."

"You don't have to do that," she said softly, touched by Chad's offer. "He's already said he would."

He hung his head again. "That's too bad. I was kinda of hoping you'd pick the first choice and marry me."

"Chad, we've never even dated. Why would you—"

"I almost asked you out once. But I got cold feet. I knew my Daddy wouldn't, well, you know... approve."

"And I'm sure he'd love the idea of you marrying me."

"I've got a job now, my own place, and I'm real good at what I do. In another year, I'll be partner in the brokerage firm and my personal investments are growing by better than ten percent a year." He spoke in a rush as though he were trying to sell himself before she slammed the door in his face. "I could take care of you. Or if you wanted, we could live in the big house with Daddy."

She shuddered at the thought. But as she looked at Chad, she realized he was prosperous. His slacks were a fine wool, his shirt hand-tailored silk. From all appearances, he was well on his way to outstripping his father in terms of wealth.

Moved as Lindy was by Chad's proposal, she knew she'd never be able to accept it. She couldn't imagine spending the rest of her life with him. There was simply no chemistry, no spark there. And she'd be danged if she'd kowtow to the senior Hollingsworth or spend her time golfing at the country club just to please Chad's father. She'd never fit in with that set and wasn't about to make a fool of herself trying.

"I really appreciate what you're trying to do, Chad. But you need to find a woman who thinks of you as her own special hero. Not someone who's gotten herself in a fix and needs a husband.''

"I'm not exactly sure I'm good hero material.''

Standing on tiptoe, she kissed his cheek and smiled. "You will be, when the right girl comes along.''

He seemed mollified by that hopeful thought. "If you decide you need the shotgun—''

"You'll be the first to know.''

But first she had to figure out exactly what she wanted to do. From her current vantage point, none of her choices looked good. But it was nice to know she had one gentleman friend in town. A rich one at that.

JACK KNEW HE had to give Lindy some time. That didn't make it any easier for him to stay away from her. The longer they put off the decision to marry, the harder it would be on Lindy's reputation. Not that marrying him was likely to enhance her standing in the community. But in the long run with a baby to think about it'd be better for the child to be legitimate.

He gave her one day.

After he finished his chores Tuesday morning, he left Alberto to handle My Family Jewels's training and headed into town to Lindy's grooming shop. Although no cars were parked out front, he made it a point to park his truck in the back. No need to advertise his presence.

Roseanne was sitting on a wooden crate by the back door staring gloomily off into space.

"Hi," he said.

Her eyes red and puffy, looking as happy as someone who'd been eating a green persimmon, she gave him a watery smile. "Hi."

He figured nobody had enough liquid in their bodies to cry for four straight days. The poor kid must have the world's worst allergy problem.

He didn't find Lindy in the back room, and there was only one white-haired poodle in the shop for grooming. Slow day. All the better for them to have a chance to talk.

And for Jack to avoid getting drenched in the process.

Lindy was at the front counter talking on the phone. "I'm sorry you have to cancel, Mrs. Davis. What other day would be good for you and Arnold this week?" She listened a moment, her hand idly rubbing along the back of her neck. "Yes, of course I understand. But regular grooming is important for a—"

Crossing his arms, Jack leaned against the doorjamb waiting for her finish. She definitely had hips worth admiring. Her long braid, like the mane on a palomino, he'd prefer to see hanging free and loose so he could comb his fingers through the silken strands.

"Thank you so much for sharing your opinion,

Mrs. Davis,'' she said tautly. ''And I do hope you'll be happy with your new groomer.''

She slammed the phone down hard and made a sound of primal disgust.

''Problems?'' he asked mildly.

She jumped and whirled, her hand covering her heart. ''Do you have to sneak up on a person?''

''Sorry.''

Visibly trying to get herself back under control, she shoved the phone aside and used a thick pencil to cross out a customer on her appointment book.

''What's going on?'' he asked.

''Oh, nothing very important.'' She tugged her braid to the front of her shoulder. ''It's just that the high-minded folks of Goodfellow have decided, in their combined wisdom, that I now have some sort of contagion that would infect their pets if they should bring them in for grooming. Which they've been doing for years and I never so much as scratched one of their precious, spoiled animals with my clippers. Much less had an impact on their morality.''

Jack got a very uncomfortable feeling in the pit of his stomach. ''That cancellation was about me?''

''*That* cancellation plus the others I've gotten that practically cleared out my shop both yesterday and today are about a bunch of bigots in this town and a *friend* with a very big mouth.''

He swore. ''I'm sorry, Lindy. I was afraid—''

"No need for you to take all the blame. I was certainly a willing participant."

"Yeah," he said softly, closing the distance between them. "But neither of us expected the price you'd have to pay. Including your business."

Closing her eyes, she leaned her head against his chest. "You may yet have to pay a price, too."

He wrapped his arms around her. "I'd do it all over again in a minute, sweet sugar. In a minute."

Tensing, Lindy tried desperately not to enjoy Jack holding her, not to feel the pleasure his words gave her, or to inhale too deeply his masculine scent, a mixture of leather, sunshine and a note that was distinctively his own. Not since she was a child had she leaned on anyone. She was her own person. Prided herself on being strong. Now she simply wanted to weep.

It must be the hormones, she thought grimly.

Jack lifted her chin, his dark brows furrowed, his eyes gentle. "We can get married anytime you say. That ought to quiet the gossipmongers."

"Not likely." She swallowed a nearly hysterical sob. "And wouldn't you know, I went twenty-five years without so much as going steady much less getting any proposals. Now, in less than a week I've had two men offering to make an honest woman of me."

Like a fast-approaching storm, his expression clouded. "Who else wants to marry you?" he demanded to know.

"Chad Hollingsworth offered marriage—or, as an alternative, the loan of his Daddy's shotgun to use on you."

"What'd you tell him?"

"Pretty much the same thing I'm telling you. I refuse to let anyone *force* me into a marriage, even the man who got me pregnant. We hardly know each other, Jack." A lifelong crush on her part didn't actually make them bosom buddies.

"I'll understand if you decide not to marry me. Hell, in your shoes I'd think twice, too. But either way you won't need a shotgun." His fingers skimmed gently over her face. "You know, we were damn good in bed together. If you want us to get better acquainted…"

Shaking her head, she made herself step out of his embrace. "That kind of temptation is exactly what I'd like to avoid."

"Seems to me that's like worrying about closing the barn door when the horse is already gone."

She glanced toward the back room to make sure Roseanne wasn't privy to their conversation. Bless the poor child's heart, the girl hadn't been worth a lick of work in nearly a week—assuming Lindy had had any work for her to do.

"I hardly think feeling forced to wed and basing our marriage on—"

"Great sex," he inserted.

She scowled. "—lust would improve our chances for an enduring relationship."

"It'd be a great beginning." Grinning wickedly, he boosted himself up to sit on the edge of the counter. His long legs encased in tight-fitting black jeans dangled nearly to the floor, his worn boots a testament to his hard work. "But if you'd like to spend more time getting to know each other, why don't you come to the races Friday, see My Family Jewels run?"

Seeing a horse race wasn't a bad idea. It was the temptation of another kind of family jewels that had her resisting. "Friday's a workday for me. I can't close the shop—"

"Unless you don't have any customers."

That was a low blow but all too true. "I'll have to wait and see."

"Fair enough."

The phone rang. Jack picked it up and handed her the instrument.

Her eyes locked on his, she used her most cheerful voice, dreading that the call was another cancellation. "Good morning. Fluff 'n Cut Grooming."

"Now you gone and done it, girl," her mother's voice accused her.

She frowned. "Done what, Mama?"

"You gettin' mixed up with that Colby boy is costing *me* customers."

"You haven't done anything wrong. How can—"

"Hazel Bingham canceled her appointment today, that's what she did."

"Mama, Hazel isn't a customer. She's your cousin. The only thing she pays you in is jars of pickled watermelon rind and chicken gizzards. Even if she doesn't get her hair done—"

"That's not the point, missy. She's registering her disapproval of what you're doing and she's blood kin. When one block tumbles you know what happens to the rest of house, don't you? My whole business is likely to fall down."

So was Lindy's. But she wasn't going to blame it on Jack. The whole dang town was at fault.

"I allow as how it wouldn't be so bad," her mother continued, "if you'd gotten caught short with one of them fancy bluegrass families. But to get caught with that no-account—"

"Mama! I'm tired of hearing you talk ugly about Jack Colby. He's a fine man who's making something of himself—"

"Well!" she blustered. "His kin stole the mayor's car. A Cadillac! Folks around here don't forget things like that."

"That was his brother, not Jack! The worst he ever did was get into fights. It's not like—"

"The Colbys have always been bad. Even stealing from the racetrack. Round here, that's like stealing from church." Her mother lowered her voice. "All I ever wanted was the best for you, Lindy."

"I know, Mama, but I have to go. We're real busy here," she lied, hanging up on her mother.

Jack was silent for a while and Lindy didn't meet

his gaze. Instead she fussed with the phone, poking it with her finger to clear out the dust that had settled between the numbers, wishing he hadn't heard her end of the conversation.

"I'm half-surprised you didn't move out of Goodfellow long ago," he said quietly.

Her head snapped up. "My family's been here for seven generations. I have as much right to stay in town as you do."

His lips twitched into a half smile. "And you're just about as mule-headed as me. Quite a pair, aren't we?"

A pair? Not really. But if things were different, if Lindy hadn't been so determined to prove herself to those who had spoken ill of her family, maybe she would have moved away years ago. Or maybe she wouldn't mind so much that of all the men she knew, only Jack Colby touched her heart in an inexplicable way that made him so hard to resist.

He hopped down from the counter. "You don't have to defend me, you know. I've been taking care of myself for a long time."

"And more times than not, you got a bloody nose for your efforts."

"I handled it."

"It always galled me that the guys in school had it in for you."

"You knew about that?"

"I watched you fight a couple of times."

He lifted his brows. "Who were you rooting for?"

Embarrassment heated her cheeks. "You."

"Guess I should have paid closer attention to who in the crowd was on my side." Leaning forward, he brushed a kiss to her lips, lingering for a heated instant longer than necessary. "Thanks, sugar. I'll see you at the racetrack."

Lindy knew for a fact that showing up with Jack would only confirm everyone's suspicions. But if she was going to have Jack's baby, she ought to at least spend a little time getting to know her child's father.

Coaxing Roseanne back inside the shop, she left the teenager in charge of what little business they had, and used the lull to run some errands.

Her first stop was the post office, the most solidly constructed building in town, built during the WPA era. Her granddaddy had worked on the project. Rumor had it he'd operated a still out of the basement until the feds actually took possession of the building and closed him down. Until that happened, it was said her granddaddy's work crew set the best attendance record of any WPA gang in the entire country.

That kind of family history was exactly what kept Lindy from moving away, from not turning her back on her roots—and made some of the townspeople look down their collective noses at her.

She started up the wide stairs to the post office

only to be met at the double doors by Marge Salter, who was dressed for a tennis date. Despite the warning that no dogs were allowed in the building, she led her Irish setter on a short leash.

Colleen wagged her tail in recognition. Spotting Lindy, Ms. Salter cocked a faintly etched brow in disapproval.

Lindy stopped long enough to pet Colleen.

"I suppose I should know more than most how a virile man can turn a woman's head," Ms. Salter said, now smiling almost smugly. "My Asa still has what it takes after all these years."

"Yes, ma'am." Her virile husband was fast approaching seventy and was happiest posing with one of his Thoroughbreds in the winner's circle—when he wasn't ogling a woman young enough to be his daughter.

"Of course, at my age I do have trouble envisioning both you and I attending the same PTA meetings with our little kiddies. Naturally I'll expect your support when I run for president. It will be my third term, you know, one for each of my sons." With that pronouncement, Marge Salter marched down the steps, her dog at her heel, her blue breeding veins visible in her muscular legs.

Lindy stared after her dumbstruck. Marge Salter pregnant? Is that what the woman had been trying to tell her? So far as Lindy knew, there were only two Salter children, both of them boys with an eye for anything in skirts.

Lord, if Marge was going to have a baby, it *had* to be something bad in the water!

6

MY FAMILY JEWELS was running at a small track west of Lexington where untried horses had a chance to test their abilities. The venue drew a crowd of devoted racing fans, gamblers, and owners and breeders looking to pick up a good horse cheap.

Given her slow grooming business and a decided urge to see Jack, Lindy hadn't come up with any reasonable excuse to stay away from the races. Absence definitely made her heart grow fonder when it came to Jack. Though that wasn't necessarily a smart move on her part.

She parked near the owners' entrance and sweet-talked her way through the gate.

A gray cloud cover had dropped a mizzling rain earlier in the day, but now the sun was out, the grounds surrounding the racecourse were abloom with brilliantly colored, fragrant irises, snapdragons, peonies, daffodils and lilac bushes. She'd scarcely gone a hundred feet before a large, male hand closed around her arm.

"Well, hello there, sweetie. Didn't expect to see you slumming around any ol' racetrack."

Turning, her eyes clashed with those of A. C. Salter, the ne'er-do-well second son of Marge Salter. Just the sort of full-of-himself bluegrass royalty her mama had hoped Lindy would one day wed.

"Free country." She shrugged out of his grasp.

"It surely is that, honey. And from what I hear, I've misjudged you all these years."

A leer, that was definitely what he was giving her, and the expression didn't do a thing to enhance his almost too-handsome appearance. In his silk shirt and spotless, dove-gray slacks, plus slicked-back hair, he looked like a character out of *The Great Gatsby*.

"No misjudgment, A.C. I'm still not interested in what you're offering." Which wouldn't be a wedding at all.

"But maybe you're not so high-'n-mighty these days, what with you showing your true colors with Colby."

Ladies shouldn't spit. Lindy wanted to. "*Excuse* me." Furious, she brushed past him.

He didn't let her go but snared her again. "Come on, honey. We could have some fun. Remember, I'm the one with the juice. I can electrify you, if you give me a chance."

She bristled. Only her basic sense of dignity prevented her from clobbering him with a good right hook. "That's an old joke, A.C. It didn't work in seventh grade and it still doesn't."

"I'm hurt, baby. I'm really hurt. We Salters are damn fine-haired fellows when it comes to the ladies."

"So your mother says of your father."

His faux sexy grin faltered. "What's Mama been saying?"

"Let's just say I hope you enjoy having a baby brother or sister."

Shock widened his eyes. "My God, did Mama find out about Daddy's girlfriend?"

"Look, I was just..." She was getting in way over her head, and it served her right for speaking out of turn. Some secrets were better left unspoken, as she well knew. "I was looking for Jack."

"Right here, sugar."

Like magic, Jack appeared beside her, slipping a thoroughly possessive arm around her waist. Jack, casually dressed in jeans, a T-shirt and a cowboy hat, looked as powerfully male as always, and made A.C. appear overdressed and effete by comparison.

"Thanks for looking after my girl, A.C."

She almost had to press her thighs together in response to the heat of her reaction to both his words and his touch. But her mind rebelled against his stamp of ownership. "I'm not *anybody's* girl." Not yet.

He tugged her a little closer, his hat shading his eyes.

A.C. looked at him smugly. "I've always had a fondness for a woman who knew her own mind."

"Yeah, well, mind your own business, A.C."

Twisting away, Lindy escaped from Jack's hold. "I'm not some old bone to be fought over by you two Kentucky cowboys."

The two men continued to glare at each other, the people entering through the owners' gate sidestepping the confrontation, eyeing the scene with open curiosity. If Lindy had meant to draw attention to her visit to the racetrack she couldn't have arranged it more effectively.

Clenching his hands, Jack fought the urge to punch A.C.'s lights out. That's what he would have done in high school. The Marines, however, had taught him power wasn't limited to the strength of his fist. A man could successfully face down an enemy without ever lifting a finger—and win.

A schoolyard bully, A. C. Salter had always been his enemy.

"Why don't we let our horses duke it out on the racecourse," he said tautly. "My horse against yours. A side bet."

"Jack, you can't risk—"

"Deal!" A.C. smiled smugly. "But let's make it interesting. How does a thousand dollars sound?"

Like more money than Jack could afford to lose. But he'd seen A.C.'s horse run in a race last week— and finish dead last. The animal didn't have the speed or stamina of My Family Jewels or any other horse in the field. The early betting had Salter's horse a fifteen-to-one long shot. Jewels was almost even money.

Jack could sure use an extra thousand bucks.

He extended his hand. "Deal, A.C. I'm even willing to take a check." Horsebreeders didn't dare renege on their bets or the news would spread that their word wasn't worth diddly-squat.

Jack knew he was a pretty darn good judge of horseflesh. It was a no-brainer that Jewels would beat the Salter Farm's entry, Randy Boy. Even so, Jack didn't like the way A.C. swaggered off toward the stables after making the bet. He was just a little too confident for Jack's peace of mind.

"You still can't resist a fight, can you," Lindy said with a shake of her head. "And now you've started taking risks with money you can't afford to lose."

"I didn't hit anybody, and no way is Jewels going to lose the race."

"So you say." She huffed, but he loved the way she was so vexed by what he'd done. At least she cared.

Wearing her Sunday best, she looked good enough to eat in a peach-colored summery dress and a wide-brimmed, floppy hat to keep the sun off her face. He definitely wanted to take a nibble. But when he'd spotted her talking with his high school nemesis, he'd been torn between staking his claim on Lindy and taking a swing at A.C.

"You've just made *three* mistakes in the course

of about *two* minutes," Lindy amended with angry sparks flaring in her jade-green eyes. Turning, she marched toward the viewing stands.

Suppressing a grin, he caught up with her. "How's that?"

"First." Halting, still angry enough that her cheeks were bright pink, she tilted her head back and held up one finger. "I'm *not* your girl. We don't have an understanding between us."

"You're carrying my baby," he said in a low, determined voice. "That's understanding enough for me."

"Two." Ignoring his response, she jutted up a second finger and her chin came up another notch. *Adorable*. "You've got no call to be jealous of A.C."

He choked on a laugh. "I've never been jealous of any man in my life. I'm sure not gonna start by being jealous of A.C. He's never been anything more than all-vine-and-no-taters unless he had a bunch of his buddies around to back him up." He wasn't even going to think about how his stomach had burned red-hot when he'd seen the two of them talking together.

"And three," she said pointedly, "you haven't got good sense risking your hard-earned cash on a side bet you can't afford to lose. Money we...I mean, *you* could use."

He heard her slip of the tongue and knew she'd been thinking seriously about marrying him—

whether she realized that or not. He swallowed down an unfamiliar taste of panic. He was willing to do the right thing. He just hoped the decision would be *right* for Lindy and the baby. "I won't lose, sugar. The Salter horse is spindly-legged and ready for the glue factory. That bet's a sure thing."

Whirling, she tossed her head like a high-spirited filly, making the brim of her hat bounce. "Right, that's what all the gamblers say on their way to the county poorhouse."

He caught her hand before she could get away, and threaded his fingers between hers. So delicate. Almost fragile. A sudden urge to protect her—from A.C. or any other predator—surged through him. Or maybe *he* was the one she needed protection from. "Hey, don't be mad. I'm glad you came to the track."

Lindy couldn't quite suppress the shudder of pleasure that rippled through her. She made a throaty sound of dismay. *Darn him* for being the only man who made her feel this way.

"Come on," he coaxed in his sugarcoated drawl. "Jewels doesn't go till the third race. I'll give you the grand tour of the stables."

"I can't recall a sweeter invitation," she said tartly. But, in fact, she knew she'd be tempted to go with Jack anywhere he wanted to take her. She simply wasn't quite sure she was willing to give up all of her own dreams in order to marry Goodfellow's most obstinate bad boy.

SHE WAS A HEAD taller than Alberto and probably outweighed him by more than she'd care to say. But she'd never seen a more dazzling smile.

"Jewels, he's gonna win," he said proudly. The jockey wore the Colby silks—red, white and blue. "A little nervous now, I think, so much noise and confusion 'round here, but he'll be okay once he's on the track."

She stroked the horse's shoulder and soothed her hand down his foreleg, his sleek muscles rippling beneath her palm. "You'll do just fine, won't you, boy," she crooned.

He shook his head, then shifted his weight to lean into her, settling immediately.

Standing behind her, Jack said, "You're good with animals."

"It's my job." Dogs, cats, goats and horses—even parrots—she loved them all. The smell of the animals, their basic honesty, appealed to something earthy within her, an elemental response not unlike her primal reaction to Jack.

She definitely didn't want to dwell on that last thought, so she changed the subject. "How's Petey getting along?"

Giving My Family Jewels a gentle swat, he said, "If he were a real recruit the DI would have him doing pushups from now till Christmas."

"That bad, huh?"

"Worse. Now the darn bird has taken to grabbing anything within his reach and ripping it to pieces. I made the mistake of leaving a cereal box near his cage. He didn't eat the cereal, just chewed up the cardboard.''

Lindy expelled a discouraged sigh. "Maybe I ought to tell Mrs. O'Toole to take him to a psychiatrist.''

In a tender gesture, Jack placed his hand at the back of Lindy's neck, massaging the tense muscles there. Unfortunately, if he'd intended to help her relax it wasn't working. Her reaction to his touch was the exact opposite.

The remainder of the stable tour was brief, and despite his attentiveness, Lindy could tell Jack was distracted. The race was important to him, and not just for the thousand dollars he'd recklessly wagered with A.C.

By the time the horses for the third race began their parade to the starting gate, waves of tension were coming off Jack. His only instruction to Alberto was to beat Randy Boy at all costs. Then he took Lindy to the stands to watch the race. Her nerves were as tangled in her throat as she imagined Jack's were.

Lindy marveled at the colorful silks the jockeys wore and the sleek beauty of their spirited mounts. The festive atmosphere of the racetrack, the risks people were taking, energized everything and everyone around her.

"You want to place a bet?" he asked absently. He removed his hat, ran his fingers through his short, damp hair, his gaze never leaving the horses, measuring both his own and the competition.

"I work too hard for the money I earn to throw it away." And with her shop closed today, she was already losing money.

He settled his hat again. "I'm not normally a gambler either."

"Except when your ego gets in the way."

His lips quirked and he shrugged, but his study of the horses remained so intense Lindy wondered what he was seeing that she couldn't.

The first horse went into his gate without a fuss; the second one balked, and the jockey had to circle around to try again. The other Thoroughbreds danced nervously, the added wait making them anxious.

Jewels went willingly into the third gate. Randy Boy eased into the gate beside him.

The instant the final horse was in position, bells rang and the gun sounded. Over the P.A. system the announcer shouted, "They're off!"

Lindy's stomach took a dip. It felt like her money was riding on Jewels, not Jack's. It didn't help a bit to have him squeezing her hand so hard she thought her bones might break.

"Out of the gate, it's Beefcake showing his stuff on the outside..." the announcer's voice blared through the loudspeakers. "...with Curl Up tight on the inside rail. At the first turn, Randy Boy is squeezing My Family Jewels hard to the inside."

"Ouch! That doesn't sound good," Lindy said. The horses moved so fast, the pack so tight, it was hard to see who was ahead. Dirt flew up from their hooves; their feet pounded on the track.

"Don't worry," Jack said. "Jewels will get through the pack."

"At the back of the field, Tube Steak is lagging behind the field. Oohs 'n Aahs is trying to slip through the center of the field but is being blocked by Beautiful Noise, who won't give way."

"Come on, Jewels," Jack said through his teeth. "Let's move it, Alberto."

The fans in the standing-room crowd surged forward to get a better view, pressing Lindy against Jack and the guardrail. Excitement rose, curling through Lindy both from the heated press of Jack next to her and escalating cheers of those around her. The thrill of the race contagious, Lindy added her voice to the crowd.

"Come on, Jewels!"

"At the three-furlong point, My Family Jewels and Randy Boy are neck and neck with Beefcake challenging on the outside. Missed My Widget is fading fast."

"I thought you said Randy Boy was ready for the glue factory," Lindy shouted over the noise of the crowd.

"Yeah, I did." Jack had gone very still. He wasn't shouting his encouragement as the horses rounded the last turn. Instead, a muscle flexed in his jaw and his eyes had narrowed.

"Jock Strap can't stretch it out enough and is losing ground to Curl Up on the rail," the announcer said. "It's Jewels and Randy. Now it's Randy and Jewels. Randy by a half length."

The lump that had been in Lindy's stomach rose to fill her throat. Poor Jack! He never should have—

"It's Randy Boy by a length at the end and pulling away. My Family Jewels is second by a neck and Beefcake took the show over Oohs 'n Aahs."

The crowd murmured its pleasure—or displeasure—depending upon how their favorites had done.

Jack cursed.

Lindy felt sick that he'd lost money that would be hard to replace. "I'm sorry—"

"There's something wrong. Last week A.C.'s horse lost by three lengths to the whole damn field, including Jock Strap. Now he blows past every horse as if they were running in knee-deep mud." Tugging Lindy away from the railing, he said, "Come on, we're going to the winner's circle. I want a closeup look at that horse."

THEY COULDN'T GET within twenty feet.

A.C. was holding court with racing officials and his cronies from the country club set but he wasn't letting anyone near his horse.

In his gut, Jack knew there was a damn good reason why. He'd be willing to bet the farm the

Randy Boy that ran last week—and lost—was no relation to the horse who'd run today.

"You're not exactly acting like a good loser," Lindy commented.

"That only applies when the other guy plays by the rules."

She tipped her head back, making the brim of her hat flare. "What?"

"That horse is a counterfeit."

"Aren't you going a little far with that kind of an accusation? A.C. wouldn't—"

"Oh, yes, he would. A.C. has been trying to prove to his old man for years that he had an eye for horseflesh. His pa gave him one more chance. A.C. blew it, so he had a ringer shipped in. Probably from South America."

"You can't be sure—"

"Trust me, sugar. That isn't the same horse that wore Salter Farms' colors last week."

Doubt clouded her expression. Jack didn't blame her. There weren't many in Goodfellow who'd believe him if he made his suspicions public. But it hurt that Lindy didn't have a little more faith in him. It hurt a lot more than it should.

"Let's get outta here before A.C. decides to collect on the bet," he muttered.

But A.C. had already extricated himself from his crowd of fans and was striding toward him, a smug grin plastered on his face. Jack would have given a month's pay for a chance to wipe it off by voicing his suspicions. Without proof, sticking his neck out in front of all these people wouldn't serve any point.

"I surely do like to see a man eager to pay his debts," A.C. said, then waggled his brows at Lindy. "Why don't you 'n me spend the money together? We could have a high ol' time."

"No, thanks. I want no part of ill-gotten gains."

A.C. hooted a laugh. "Now don't that beat a stinkbug! I'll just have to spread all that pocket change around with somebody else."

"You do that, A.C." she said.

A.C. looked at Jack expectantly, practically holding out his hand waiting to be paid off.

"I don't have my checkbook with me. You'll have to give me a day or two."

"Now you wouldn't be the kind of man who welshed on a bet, would you?"

"I've never in my life welshed on an *honest* bet, and I don't intend to start now."

Jack walked away and, after a moment, Lindy followed him, half-running to catch up. She looked more suspicious now than she had before.

"You're up to something, Jack Colby. I know you are."

He kept on walking. "I'm going to go check on My Family Jewels. You got a problem with that?"

For an instant her glance slipped to his jeans, and he almost had to laugh.

"I know you better than that," she said, her cheeks glowing red because he'd caught her.

"You've got that look in your eyes that says you're about to invite some big trouble down on your shoulders."

"Hey, and I thought you said we needed to get better acquainted. If you can read me that good, then we can move on to the interesting stuff." Halting in an area between two rows of stables where not many pedestrians traveled, he pulled her to him. "Like taking up where we left off after our night together." He bent down to brush a kiss to the fluttery pulse on her neck, the quick taste of her skin sending a rush of arousal through him.

"Stop that, Jack! Somebody will see us." She shoved at his chest though not forcefully enough to push him away. "And don't you think for a minute you can distract me. You're planning something foolish that's likely to end with you in jail."

He nipped on her earlobe, closing his lips around the tiny gold stud she wore. God, she tasted good and smelled like heaven. "As long as you're over eighteen and willing, nobody'll put me in jail for what I have in mind."

"Jack! I'm not—" She gave a low, throaty sound, her voice shaky. "You're going to sneak into Salter Farms, aren't you?"

"You don't need to trouble yourself, sweet sugar, 'bout anything I'm gonna do except take you to bed the moment you say the word."

The sound of an approaching horse convinced Jack to let Lindy go. Just as well. He was close to bursting and was so hot he wanted to take her in the nearest stack of hay. She deserved better than him and he shouldn't forget that no matter how much he wanted to bed her again.

She stepped back, waited until the horse and rider passed, then planted her fists on her hips. "Why are you so butt-headed determined to prove A.C. cheated you? Why don't you just let it go?"

"He didn't just cheat me, sugar. He cheated every race fan at the track today, most especially those who bet on My Family Jewels. I take powerful exception to anyone who does that."

She glared at him, her cute little stubborn chin cocked up at an angle, her eyes glistening with pure conviction. Their embrace had unsettled her hat, leaving it cockeyed, and the clip that had been holding her hair back had come loose, releasing strands to feather her resolute jaw.

Something stirred in Jack. He wasn't much good at naming emotions. Most of the time he tried to ignore them. But this feeling broadsided him. It was more than sex, more than the simple urge to mate with a fiery woman who'd match him stroke for stroke.

This was damn serious…and scared him half to death. Both for her sake and his.

"All right, if that's how it's going to be," she said. "I'm coming with you."

He gaped at her. "You can't."

"You just try and stop me, buster, and you'll get a fair idea what running into a buzz saw feels like."

7

THE CLOCK ON THE Blazer's dashboard read eleven fifty-five—five minutes before the witching hour.

Chill bumps sped down Lindy's spine as she drove the dark country road toward Jack's place. Periodically the shadowed outline of trees marked the roadway like ominous sentinels. No way could she let Jack go to the Salter farm on his own. And she didn't doubt for a moment he'd try going alone.

Or that he'd try to stop her from coming with him.

Stubborn man!

Dressed in jeans and a dark jacket, she'd scrunched her blond hair up under a navy blue baseball cap—a perfect fashion statement if you happened to be planning a breaking-and-entering caper.

Her headlights picked up the dinged mailbox that marked the driveway to the Colby farm, and she turned into the lane. A startled rabbit dashed in front of her truck, forcing her to slam on the brakes. Darn! Her nerves were as bristly as the fur on a cat who'd gotten his tail stuck in an electrical outlet!

She pulled up beside Jack's truck, relieved he

hadn't already left on his mission, and shut off the engine. She'd been pretty sure he'd wait until the quiet part of the night and he had.

Climbing out of her truck, she'd barely started for the house when the back door opened.

Lord, he was a big man. Silhouetted by the kitchen light, he nearly filled the doorway. Broad shoulders. Narrow waist. And long, long legs. He was capable of intimidating the most powerful foe, yet Lindy knew he could be gentle, too. With his animals.

And with her.

Something squeezed tight in her chest. Her head told her she shouldn't be falling in love with Jack Colby. Apparently her heart was determined to send an entirely different message.

"Evenin', Jack," she said brightly, reaching the back stoop.

"You shouldn't have come."

"What? And miss all the fun? Not on your life."

"What if you get caught? That would hardly be good for your business."

Trying not to dwell on that possibility, she marched up the steps and brushed past him. In the process, she caught a whiff of his scent, the subtle mix of horses and hard work. "You need a witness to whatever you find. Nobody's going to take a Colby's word over a Salter's." Which was exactly why she shouldn't get involved with him, a niggling voice reminded her. "Besides, you need someone as a lookout."

His scowl deepened. Lindy didn't worry about it. She didn't intimidate easily.

"So what time are we leaving?" she asked. The kitchen was as tired looking as the rest of the house, the round table marked with use, the appliances old and worn. But the room was large. With new curtains and a collection of dofunnies scattered about, it could be cheerful. A place where a family could gather—

"You're not going."

She whirled to face him. "Sure I am. If you don't take me, I'll simply drive there myself. And two trucks are gonna make a lot more noise than one."

"You've got it all figured out, don't you?"

"I figure A.C. shouldn't cheat you out of a thousand dollars. We may need that money later."

His dark brows shot up. *"We?"*

"Well, I mean… You might…" She backpedaled as fast as she could. She had no business even thinking about how to redecorate his kitchen—or any other part of his house. "But if we do decide to…I'm not saying we will. I mean…"

In an action so quick she barely realized it was happening, she was in his arms, and his mouth claimed hers. The kiss was hard and fast, deep and lingering. In moments she was breathless. His tongue toyed with hers and she forgot where she was, forgot why she had wanted to avoid this very thing.

Kissing Jack Colby was like running smack-dab into a potent natural force. He was irresistible.

She gave up the battle. Of their own accord, her hands plowed through the thickness of his short hair, loving the way the strands parted for her fingers. She pressed her body against him, nestling between his hips, his arousal making her excitement soar.

She moaned deep in her throat.

From the other room, Petey squawked. "Heads up! Heads up!"

Like he'd been dashed with cold water, Jack broke the kiss. His arms that had been wrapped so tightly around her, eased. Slowly his breathing returned to normal.

"I don't know whether to give Petey a medal," he said. "Or haul him in front of a firing squad."

"I've always appreciated a decisive man. Let's give him a medal, *then* shoot him."

His lips slid into a smile of surrender, his calloused hands framing her face. "You're determined to go with me, aren't you?"

To the ends of the earth, she almost said, but was afraid the free fall at the final step would hurt too much. "Tonight, yes. I'm going with you."

"Don't say I didn't warn you we might get caught."

"I won't."

He tucked some loose strands of her hair back under her cap. "Okay, let's get ready. Those pretty little cheeks of yours are going to need some grease-paint."

"Greasepaint?" she gasped.

Letting go of her, he stepped across the room to the tile kitchen counter and picked up a tin of shoe black. "Camouflage. If we don't, we'll stand out like neon in the starlight."

For a moment, Lindy entertained serious second thoughts about hanging around with an ex-Marine. Oh, well. In for a penny, in for a pound.

JACK CLIMBED OVER the pasture fence and helped Lindy follow him. He didn't think they were in any real danger. No one was likely to take a shot at them, or at least he hoped not. Still he wished she'd stayed at home.

He wished he could take her back to his house and do more than just kiss her.

Except for his buddies in the Marines, no one had ever been willing to stick his—or her—neck out for him. Until Lindy. That made her the most coura-geous woman he'd ever met—or the most foolish. He hoped it wasn't the latter.

Keeping to the shadows, he led her toward the horse barn. Her hand felt small in his. Trusting. If she wasn't so mule-headed stubborn...

"What are we actually looking for?" she whis-pered.

"All Thoroughbreds are branded inside their lip when they're born. A registration number. Counterfeits have their numbers changed."

"You're telling me there's a clandestine factory somewhere cranking out counterfeit horses?"

He shot her a look. "South America. Now, can you keep quiet long enough for us to get in and out of this place in one piece?"

She wrinkled her nose and waved him along.

Maybe she was just nervous. Jack knew he was. He'd been on night patrols in Kuwait when he hadn't felt this big a knot in his gut. His horse losing in that claiming race had cost him more than the thousand-dollar bet to A.C. Without a good racing record, offspring sired by My Family Jewels would be worth far less than Jack had hoped.

The individual stall doors were locked tight, the horses inside quiet. Not knowing which stall belonged to the phony Randy Boy, Jack didn't dare pick a lock at random. Too much chance of the horses making a fuss one of the groomers would hear.

He reached the end of the building. A beaming floodlight made the area as bright as day. Now came the tricky part. The only thing to do was to brazen it out as if he belonged here.

"Wait here," he ordered Lindy.

"What are you going to do?"

"I'm going to check the barn door. When I get inside, you wait to make sure nobody heard me.

Then, and *only* then," he emphasized, "you come running. If I rouse someone, you get the heck out of here. No sense for us both to spend the night in jail."

She nodded. "Got it."

Jack had the feeling she'd have made a helluva Marine—assuming she really was going to follow his orders.

Giving her hand a final squeeze, he marched out into the area, full strut. A workman on an important errand. Except his mouth was dry and a fine sheen of sweat covered the shoe polish on his face.

He grabbed the door, gave a tug and it slid open. He ducked into the footwide opening. Keeping his breathing even, he let his eyes get accustomed to the faint light inside.

Lindy appeared at his side, gasping for breath. He started down the aisle between the double row of stalls. The horse barn was huge compared to his, holding as many as twenty horses, and impeccably well cared for. He had to give the Salters credit. They didn't pinch pennies when it came to their animals. Their ethics, or at least A.C.'s, he suspected, didn't come up to the same standard.

The horses were mostly dozing, their eyelids heavy, their long lashes fluttering closed even as he passed by. They reminded him of a well-satisfied woman, the way he'd like to see Lindy after he made love to her.

He'd almost reached the end of the row before

he spotted the stall with a nameplate that read Randy Boy.

"Hiya, Boy," he said softly.

The horse nickered in response.

"Is that him?" Lindy asked. "He's beautiful."

"Yeah." He rubbed his hand over the animal's nose, scratching the white blaze on his forehead. "The poor guy deserves better than to be a stand-in. He's got great lines."

Pulling a penlight from his pocket, Jack coaxed the horse to let him pull down his lower lip to take a peek. What he found was troubling, to say the least. The registration number belonged to Randy Boy, and it didn't look like it had been altered.

"Damn," he muttered. His heart sank. Maybe he'd been wrong.

"What?"

"The number hasn't been changed."

"Well, his markings sure have. That blaze on his forehead came directly from a bleach bottle and a healthy application of dye, or my mama isn't no hairdresser."

His head snapped around. "You're sure?"

She shrugged. "Look at his roots."

He flashed the light across the horse's head. "Sugar, you are one smart lady!"

At that precise moment, the overhead lights came on, making Jack squint against the sudden brightness. From the doorway an angry voice shouted,

"Move a muscle, you clowns, and you'll get a belly full of shot!"

Freezing right where he was, Jack closed his eyes. Damn! He'd never wanted to get Lindy in this kind of trouble. And by the time the whole of Salter Farms had been roused out of bed, it was going to be trouble with a capital T.

Lindy shot her hands up and her knees went trembly. A young groomer had a shotgun pointed right at her, and from the look of his shaking hands, he was more scared than she was.

"Don't sh-shoot," she stammered.

Jack stepped in front of her, his hands raised, too. "You can lower your gun, son. We're not armed."

Another figure appeared in the doorway. "I'll take it from here, Tomas," A.C. said. "The police will be here any minute."

The young man stepped back, but he didn't lower his gun. He kept pointing it at Jack's middle.

Seeing A.C. swagger toward them so smugly, Lindy found her voice. "Good, I'm glad you called the police. I'm sure Chief Pickles will be fascinated to learn how you tried to cheat Jack. The racing commission ought to be interested, too."

A.C.'s too-pretty face turned ugly. "You look fetching in shoe black, my dear, but you really ought to learn not to stick your nose in where it doesn't belong."

Beneath her camouflage, Lindy's face grew hot with anger.

"Let's keep this just between you and me." The threat in Jack's voice vibrated low in his chest. "Call off the cops."

"Not likely, Colby. You and your kind don't belong in this town. If I had my way, Chief Pickles would escort you to the county line and dump you there."

Jack took a step forward. The kid with the gun raised the barrel. And in the distance the approaching sound of sirens grew closer.

Lindy gritted her teeth. By dawn the whole dang town would have another juicy morsel of gossip to chew on. She and Jack were the lucky ducks they'd be talking about. Again.

"OH, TAKE ME hoooome, Kathleen, take me hooome…" Luther Hayes, the drunk in the adjacent cell crooned a poor imitation of the Irish ballad, out of tune, the lyrics not quite right.

Lindy winced. The town of Goodfellow only had two jail cells. Understandably, she'd opted to room with Jack rather than Luther. Even Chief Pickles had agreed that was a good choice.

Staring glumly through the bars to the barren corridor, Jack said, "Maybe A.C.'s right. I should have kept the hell away from Goodfellow."

Using a damp paper towel the guard had provided, Lindy took another swipe at the black on her face, probably only smearing the gunk around. "Did I hear someone sounding retreat?"

"More like a reality check."

"Nonsense. Marines don't retreat."

Turning, he jammed his hands in his jeans pockets. His brooding eyes were as dark as the clothes he wore. "I didn't even have enough cash to bail us out, Lindy. You had to call Chad."

"I didn't think my mother would be a good choice."

"Tura lura lural. Tura lura lieeee..." Luther's voice cracked on the long high note.

Crossing the narrow cell, she went to Jack and wrapped her arms around his waist. "Chad didn't seem to mind I'd called him, even at such a gawd-awful hour."

"That's an Irish lullaby..." Leaning against the bars that separated the two cells, Luther studied them through watery eyes.

"That's because he wants to marry you," Jack said.

"What I don't need is another pity proposal." Despite her strengthening feelings for Jack, he hadn't made any reference to love being a part of their relationship. Doing the right thing, was what he'd offered. Lindy wasn't at all sure she could settle for that.

"Ain't you Thad Montgomery's little girl?" Luther asked.

She glanced his direction. "That's right."

"Well, now, ain't that a coincidence, you 'n me being locked up right next to each other like this?"

He hiked up his trousers that had slipped below the barrel of his belly. "He was a fine ol' boy, your daddy was. That's for sure certain."

She smiled weakly. "Thank you." If Luther had known her father it was probably because he was a regular moonshine customer.

"No, I mean it, missy. One time I was down to my last two bits." Swaying on his feet, he held on to one of the cell bars so he wouldn't fall down. "Your pappy loaned me a hundred bucks so's I could pay the rent, that's what he did. 'Course, my Maybelle was alive then and... Yes, sir, knowed your mama, too. Fine woman." Tears filled his eyes and he broke into another voice-cracking version of "Take Me Home, Kathleen."

Under his breath, Jack said, "How long do you suppose before Chad gets here?"

"He said he'd come as soon as he got dressed. But I don't know how far away he lives." Meanwhile, she wondered where her father had gotten a spare hundred dollars. Had that been why they'd always been so broke? Was it somehow a result of a generous spirit, not laziness? Deep inside, she hoped that was the case, and maybe why her mother had held her head so high despite their distressed circumstances.

Resting her head against Jack's chest, Lindy listened to the strong, steady beat of his heart, a counterpoint to Luther's poorly sung ballad. Chester Pickles had seemed downright tickled to lock up the former ice-cream shoplifter for the more serious crimes of trespassing and unlawful entry. And he'd all but gloated over the chance to arrest yet another Colby.

The town of Goodfellow had a long community memory.

And no one seemed interested that A. C. Salter was a crook, his winning horse a fraud.

His song coming to a blessed halt, Luther directed his blurry gaze at Jack. "Now let me think… You're one of them Colby boys, ain't you?"

Jack tensed as though ready to do battle. "I am."

"Yes sirree, I thought so. I can see it in the both of you. Good, solid Kentucky stock what came through the Appalachian gap with ol' Dan'l Boone, hisself. The best most, they were and all their kin. None finer no matter what folks say nowadays. I reckon the two of you will raise up a fine lookin' passel of kids. Fine lookin'."

Lindy almost laughed at Luther's high praise. But truth be told, when she imagined Jack's child, she pictured a baby with his dark eyes looking up at her, his cheeks dimpling when he smiled. The image nearly took her breath away it was so vivid— so exactly what she wanted her baby to be.

Good, solid Kentucky stock with the inborn gumption to cross mountains to settle a wild, untamed land. When you got right down to it, that combination was hard to beat.

She hugged Jack, grinned and whispered, "He's

right, you know. Our baby is going to be the strongest, smartest, most beautiful baby in the entire county.''

He looked startled. Then with a low growl, half laughter and half mocking, he kissed her.

He was still kissing her when Chad arrived to bail them out.

"THANKS FOR BRINGING us home, Chad.''

Jack held open the Cadillac's passenger door for Lindy. In spite of the fact it made good sense, he was galled he'd been relegated to the back seat of Chad's fancy car while Lindy sat up front. He'd wanted her back there with him. Where he could hold her. Kiss her.

His adrenaline had been pumping hard since the break-in of the horse barn and the discovery of A.C.'s fraud.

Then with the arrest, being dragged into jail, and not being able to protect Lindy from his own tomfoolery, he was fit to be tied.

He wanted her. Now. All to himself without a drunk—or a rival—hanging around.

Chad leaned his elbow on the open driver's side window, looking like a stockbroker in his white shirt and jacket even though dawn had just begun to show on the eastern horizon. The guy had even taken time to shave before he'd picked them up at the jail.

"I'd be happy to follow you home, Lindy," Chad said. "Make sure you get there safely."

"She'll be okay," Jack assured him, barely able to keep from shoving the car back out toward the road by his own brute strength. "Before she leaves, I need to talk to her about—" About making love. About wanting to feel her legs wrapped around him again. Being inside her again. "—Petey."

"Is there something wrong?" she asked.

"We'll talk." He gestured toward the back door. "Inside."

Cocking her head, she gave him an odd, confused look. Her face was still smudged with shoe black, her hair had streamed loose from the twisted braid she'd formed hours ago. Her clothes were rumpled, bruises of sleeplessness underscored the green of her eyes.

From Jack's perspective, he'd never seen a sexier, more desirable woman. Even though he knew it might not be smart, he was determined to make love with Lindy again. Now. The memories of their one night together were too powerful to ignore a minute longer. The desire he felt for her this instant was so compelling he'd willingly run a gauntlet of fire and swords to reach her. If he was crazy to want her that much, so be it.

Grabbing her hand, he all but dragged Lindy toward the house. "Thanks again, Chad," he called over his shoulder. "I'll pay you back as soon as I can."

"No hurry."

He didn't acknowledge Chad's response. Instead, he shoved open the door, pulled Lindy inside and slammed it behind him. He yanked the shade down on the door window.

"Jack?"

"Sugar, your kisses in that jail cell nearly drove me crazy. If you don't want me to make love to you now—*right* now—you'd better tell me in no uncertain terms because in about thirty seconds there'll be no way I can stop."

He held his breath as he heard Chad's car drive away.

Lindy's tongue swept out to dampen her lips, the gesture so visceral it made him ache all the more.

"I want you, Jack, as much as you want me." Her arms slid up his chest, her hands linking around his neck. "Your thirty seconds are already up."

She'd wanted this every day—every night—since the last time Jack had made love to her.

She wanted his big, calloused hands all over her, arousing her to a feverish pitch, abrading her flesh with his gentle caress. She wanted his lips teasing her, his tongue tasting her—everywhere.

She wanted him inside her.

With few wasted motions, he stripped her jacket off and lifted her T-shirt over her head, trapping her against the kitchen counter as his mouth closed over her lacy bra. He tugged and sucked and her nipple pebbled.

"Jack…" She yanked at his shirt, pulling it from his jeans. She had to get closer, needed to touch him.

There was a frenetic quality to the way they undressed each other, strewing pieces of clothing through the kitchen and down the hallway to his bedroom. It had been too long. Delaying this another minute, another second, was pure torture.

They fell onto the bed, their bodies tangling, the rumpled sheets cold on Lindy's back, the bedding lumpy beneath her hips. The room smelled of him, masculine and earthy. The dawn light creeping through the window gave the room a surreal feeling in contrast to the wild beating of her heart, the raspy sound of his breathing.

He kissed her lips, her jaw, her breasts. His hands stroked her inner thighs and explored her most private places. Hot chill bumps covered her flesh.

"You are so beautiful, sweetheart. So beautiful."

His endearment swept through her, warming a lonely part of her heart, and she arched up to him. "Now, Jack. Please."

Automatically, he reached into the drawer of the bedside table, retrieving a silver packet.

She caught his wrist. "We already left the barn door open. I want to feel you this time. All of your family jewels."

"Oh, baby…" he groaned, his smile strained. "They're in your hands. Take good care of 'em."

"I will," she whispered.

He covered her with kisses again. She nipped at his shoulder, threaded her fingers through his hair. She burned with a need only he could fill. And when he rose above her, slipping inside her with one long thrust, he did just that.

She sobbed his name, a joyous cry of pleasure.

He withdrew and entered her again, torturing her.

She writhed beneath him, explosive need building until they were one person, no beginning, no end. He took his time, tension visible in the tightness of his strong jaw, the cant of his brows, his eyes as black as midnight.

And then she couldn't watch any more as the explosion shook her from deep inside. She burst with pleasure and release, shattering like a fine crystal glass breaking on a tile floor, catching the light of a rainbow in the reflection of sunrise.

The sensation went on and on yet was over too soon. Then she felt him come apart in her arms. She reveled in his rough shuddering, the low moans that racked his body, his weight pressing her into the old mattress.

And she knew deep in her heart this was where she belonged. With Jack.

SHE BARELY HAD time to get back home, showered and to the shop before the first customer arrived with an Airedale that was overdue for a bath and a good combing. Only one other dog owner came in, obviously a lady who was unconcerned about the latest gossip in town.

But two dogs on a Saturday did not a grooming business make, Lindy thought grimly.

Roseanne bounced in the back door, her smile so wide she almost couldn't keep it on her face. "Sorry I'm late, Lindy."

"I can't afford to pay you when you're not here, Roseanne." Not that she even needed an assistant with business so slow.

"I know. I'm really sorry." She didn't look at all remorseful as she checked the two dogs in their cages. "I'm gonna have to take next Saturday off, too."

"Oh?"

As if it were possible, Roseanne's smile broadened. "I'm getting married."

Stunned, Lindy tried to keep her surprise hidden. She knew Roseanne had a boyfriend but she didn't think they'd been dating long. "That's wonderful. But isn't it a little, well, sudden?"

The adolescent's cheeks turned pink. "Truth to tell, I got caught short. But Billy decided it was okay. We love each other."

"You're pregnant?"

She nodded.

Goodfellow High School class of 2018 was going to be huge! And no doubt the unintended pregnancy had been the cause of the teenager's weeklong fountain of tears.

"I'm happy for you, Roseanne. Really, I am. And I hope you and Billy will be very happy together."

"Then can I have next Saturday off?"

"Of course." Woe be it for Lindy to interfere with young love.

The phone rang and she didn't have time to dwell of the implications of Roseanne's pregnancy or impending marriage. What she needed to worry about was getting her business back on track.

And what she should do about Jack.

"Fluff 'n Cut," she said cheerfully.

"Good morning, Lindy, dear. It's D'Arcy here."

Lindy checked the poodle clock on the wall behind her. It was 6:00 a.m. California time. "You're up early, D'Arcy," she said to the owner of the grooming shop.

"I've been hearing some troubling news."

Closing her eyes, Lindy marvelled at the long reach of the Goodfellow gossip machine. "Oh? What's that?" As if she couldn't make a dang good guess.

"I remember those Colby boys all too clearly, dear. The whole family. They're just not *our* kind of people. Robbing and fighting, the whole lot of them."

Lindy bristled. "Are you saying a man who risked his life in the uniform of our country, is as hardworking as any man I've ever known, isn't *your* kind of person?"

"What I'm saying," D'Arcy said with a huff, "is

that if you decide to marry that boy I will have to rethink our business arrangement. I won't have *my* reputation ruined by being associated with the Colbys in any way whatsoever. Do you hear me, young lady?''

Lindy heard her all right, and her heart sank to somewhere near her big toe. She'd been so happy this morning in Jack's arms, in knowing that's where she belonged.

Now it could cost her the dream she'd so carefully nurtured for most of her life. And every dollar she'd paid on the lease would go up in so much smoke.

8

LINDY SPREAD OUT the Sunday edition of the *Good-fellow Appalachian Sentinel* on her kitchen table. The biweekly newspaper, affectionately referred to by the locals as the *GAS*, trumpeted such notable community happenings as the Masonic Hall Paint-and-Clean-Up Day and the Red Raiders Little League team winning ninth place in a tournament in which ten teams had been entered. Last year, the article noted, when Richie Zettleman pitched a game they'd lost 27-0, the team had placed tenth. The players were applauded for their marked improvement.

But Lindy wasn't interested in the earth-altering news of the day. It was the business ads in the *GAS* that held her attention.

Tootsie nudged her knee and whined.

"I know, sweetie." Absently she petted her dog, rubbing her hand over Tootsie's pregnancy-swollen midsection. "I haven't been giving you nearly enough attention lately, and I know you're probably feeling all fat and miserable." Exactly like Lindy would be feeling in about eight months. "But right now I've got to figure out how to generate more business for Fluff 'n Cut."

Dang it all! Having her own business had always been her dream. Despite all that had happened, Lindy had no intention of giving up her ambition easily.

The fact that the whole town was gossiping about her, and that D'Arcy had threatened to take the shop away from her, simply meant Lindy had to work harder. Desperately she tried to suppress the knowledge that if she hoped to succeed in her quest, marriage to Jack was impossible.

He'd proposed only out of duty. He'd wanted to do the right thing.

Studying the *GAS,* she discovered that Graham's Grocery was offering discount tickets for a senior citizen tour. The day trip included a visit to a bourbon chocolate candy factory in Frankfort founded by two sisters during prohibition. Free samples would be available.

At Annette's Coffee Shop the owner was selling five-dollar raffle tickets for two seats at the Derby, proceeds to go to Boy Scout Troop #267, which Annette's grandson just happened to belong to. She'd throw in a free cup of coffee for every ticket a patron purchased.

Even the *GAS* had a coupon offer. Residents could get a month's free home delivery of the *GAS* by mailing the coupon in. Of course, everyone in town already received the newspaper because it was tossed on their lawns twice a week. Some folks had a pile of *GAS* two-feet high moldering in the grass, no doubt generating toxic vapors.

Lindy didn't have anything she could give away, but she could work more cheaply in the effort to regain her regular clientele and attract new customers. To cut expenses and make ends meet, she'd have to eliminate the bows she provided for freshly groomed dogs and cats, and the perfume she spritzed on them—and forget about eating steaks herself. Not that she'd bought one in a month of Sundays, anyways.

Sighing, she pulled out a sheet of lined notebook paper and began to jot down ideas for a two-for-the-price-of-one grooming promotion.

The phone rang, and she shot a glowering look in that direction. Didn't people know she had work to do? Forget it was Sunday; forget the quick flash of hope that the caller might be Jack.

She crossed the room to pick up the phone. "Hello."

"I need Isabel right now."

She blinked at the sound of Jack's terse demand. "Hi, how are you?" would have been a nice greeting. "I had a great time the other night" would have done just fine. "I love you" would have been too much to expect, she supposed, but wanting *Izzy*, the goat?

"Dare I ask what you have in mind to do with Isabel?" she asked cautiously.

"It's Salty Lady. She's gone into labor. She's agitated as hell and I can't calm her down. I've read goats and horses, 'specially mares in labor, are good for each other. At this point I'm willing to try anything. Can you bring her?"

Lindy straightened immediately. "Sure. I'll be there as quickly as I can."

"Thanks, Lindy, and…" He hesitated, a Marine sounding like he'd landed on dangerous ground filled with land mines. "I appreciate your help."

Lindy wasn't all that sure of her footing either. There'd been no expression of love on Jack's part— or on hers, either. At least not out loud. She still wasn't willing to force a man to marry her, however much she might love him. That sort of arrangement could only be filled with strain and very likely lead to failure.

No, Lindy wouldn't marry Jack unless she was convinced he loved her. Truth be told, that decision had nothing to do with her business prospects.

It had to do with not risking her own heart.

RISKING HER BODY was a whole different matter, however, when she tried to load Isabel into the Blazer.

The goat did not go willingly. Anywhere. Particularly into the rear end of a vehicle.

Isabel nipped at her. Butted her. Stomped on her toes with her sharp hooves. She had Lindy hopping out of the way like a jumping jack on a pogo stick.

Breathless, finally Lindy grabbed the goat by her floppy ears and gazed into those stubborn rectangular eyes. She set her jaw. "I don't care if you're pregnant and cranky. I know a butcher in town who would be happy to substitute ground goat for a little fresh ground beef," she warned. "And if you don't do exactly as I say, you're going to be his first experiment in customer satisfaction. Got it?"

Isabel's head bobbed.

"All right, then. Get into the truck. Jack needs you." Would that he'd also need Lindy, she thought as she tugged and shoved the goat into the vehicle. Tootsie bounded in without any encouragement, and Lindy closed the door behind them both. And there they were, three pregnant females en route to help yet another expectant female.

She desperately hoped Jack knew what he was doing by requesting a goat to join his delivery team.

SALTY LADY HAD forgotten everything Jack had taught her about trust. Her ribs heaved and she skittered away from him whenever he got close. And she wouldn't lie down to let nature do its work.

Meanwhile, My Family Jewels was pacing his stall like an expectant father.

Expectant father.

Even the thought of being a father brought beads of sweat to Jack's forehead. What did he know about parenting? He sure as hell hadn't had much of a role model. His real father hadn't been around long enough to count, and his stepdad had beat the tar out of Jack just for the sport of it. Not that Jack and his brother Alec hadn't deserved a good walloping from time to time.

Like the time when they'd taken apart the high school principal's Ford Model T automobile and reassembled it on the gym roof, he recalled with an unrepentant grin.

Lady blew what sounded like a disapproving raspberry.

"It was a harmless stunt," he said defensively, as though he'd read the horse's thoughts. "Besides, the auto shop teacher gave us both A's. I don't think he liked Blotto any better than the kids did."

Unfortunately Alec's pranks grew increasingly mean-spirited, his drinking bouts more frequent, until he'd totally lost track of the difference between right and wrong. Their stepfather seemed to think that was fine. The result was Alec being in and out of jail for most of the past ten years, including his current stint in an Ohio prison.

Jack had made different decisions. He'd joined the Marines, promising himself he wouldn't follow in his brother's footsteps. Or their father's.

None of which meant Jack was equipped to be a decent father himself.

Stroking Lady's nose, he wondered if he and Lindy ought to take parenting classes. Probably a good idea—at least for him. Hell, he hardly knew what a diaper looked like much less how to deal with a rebellious teenager.

His mental gears came to a grinding halt.

If Lindy didn't agree to marry him, Jack might not have any say in how their son was raised. Or their daughter. Eventually Lindy would find someone else to marry. Jack would be left out in the cold.

An icy sense of dread filled his gut. Why would she want to marry him anyway? As much as he wanted to succeed at the horsebreeding business, he could still make a blue fist of things. Fall flat on his face.

He wouldn't want to drag Lindy down with him. Or their child.

And he'd already gotten her arrested. They could both be fined—or go to jail—for trespassing.

If Lindy had good sense, she'd stay the hell away from him.

With a practiced eye, he studied Lady. Her muscles tense, the mare was fighting the delivery of her foal. If something didn't happen soon Jack would have to call the vet. Or get in there and deliver the foal himself. And Lady wasn't about to let anyone get that close.

"Come on, Lady. Relax. Women do this all the time."

"Easy for a man to say."

He turned and grinned at the sight of Lindy. For a moment, he only saw her. Not the goat she led on a rope or the dog that was trotting beside her.

Just the woman he wanted to spend the rest of his life with and was scared spitless that getting his wish would be the worst thing that could happen to her.

"Thanks for coming," he said.

"No problem."

Her green-eyed gaze swept over him, caressing him like the softness of spring grass, making him want to lie down beside her in a sheltered pasture and make love to her there.

As though she could read his mind, her cheeks flushed and her gaze slid away to the mare. "How's our patient?"

"Still nervous."

As if to emphasize the point, Lady's sides heaved and she whinnied, tossing her head.

"You sure Isabel will help? She hasn't been in a very friendly mood this morning."

He shrugged. "We'll keep the goat on a short tether. If Lady seems upset, we'll pull Isabel out of there."

Lindy handed over the rope and Jack walked the goat into the stall. Lady backed up to the far wall, the two animals eyeing each other with open curiosity, their nostrils flaring.

"It's okay, Lady. Isabel's here to help you out."

"Why do I think Goat Lamaze for Expectant Mares won't be a big seller?"

Momentarily distracted, he shot Lindy an amused look, and his grip on the rope eased.

Isabel bolted. She butted Lady in the side, then stood straddle-legged, challenging the mare to throw her out of the stall.

"Izzy! Stop that!" Lindy shouted.

Swearing, Jack made for the goat. She turned on him and lowered her head. Her whole body shook.

Lady pawed the ground.

Jack grabbed for the rope just as Isabel shot forward. Like a drunken bullfighter, he tried to dodge out of the way but the goat clipped him on the shoulder. The bedding straw was slippery beneath his feet. He lost his footing and his feet went flying.

Tootsie barked. Isabel bleated.

Lindy shouted, and she tried to catch Jack before he fell.

No such luck.

Arms and legs akimbo, Jack twisting in the hope of breaking Lindy's fall, they both landed in a heap on the hard concrete floor. The air was driven from his lungs. He cracked the back of his skull, saw stars and sucked in a mouthful of dust.

Across the way, My Family Jewels reared and snorted.

Bits of hay drifted down, lodging in Lindy's hair like confetti. Her eyes were wide with shock and surprise.

Coughing, Jack tried to clear his lungs. "You okay?"

She nodded. "Dogs and cats are easier."

"Unless you're the one who has to chase them up a tree."

"You're right. We're both in a dangerous business."

The most dangerous thing was how Lindy's smile, her sweet honeysuckle scent, made Jack want things he had no right to possess.

The moment lingered, the air filled with the elemental power of earth and animals. Male and female. Jack's gaze focused on her lips. Vaguely he was aware this wasn't the time or place, but he wanted to kiss her. Make love to her. Now. Urgently.

A subtle yet unfamiliar sound nearby drew his attention.

In unison, he and Lindy glanced toward the goat only to discover Isabel standing over a mottled-gray kid she'd just given birth to, licking him and looking pleased as punch about her accomplishment.

"Isn't he adorable?" Lindy said, stifling a giggle.

With mama's encouragement, his coat still damp from the birthing, the kid struggled to his feet and stood on wobbly legs. Salty Lady lowered her head, welcoming the kid to the neighborhood with her own lick of greeting.

"I've never seen a horse do that," Lindy whispered. "Mother a goat."

"Neither have I."

And then, as if having observed Isabel accomplish the amazing feat of giving birth, Lady lowered herself to the floor, apparently deciding she could give birth, too. Almost immediately, the foal's fore-feet appeared, one slightly ahead of the other.

Sitting up with Lindy still in his lap, Jack held his breath and together they watched the miracle happen—the future of Colby Farms unfold. By measured inches the foal appeared. A well-shaped head with big, brown eyes framed by long lashes. Chestnut like his daddy. Long, spindly legs.

In an odd way, Jack felt as proud as if he'd been watching the birth of his own child. This was the birth of his breeding farm. His future...and that of the baby Lindy carried in her womb.

Instinctively, he rested his palm on her flat belly.

She covered his hand with hers. Their eyes met in silent communication and she leaned forward to kiss him.

Jack hadn't experienced much tenderness in his life. Lindy's was the sweetest, most loving touch he'd ever known. He wanted to keep her with him forever; for her sake, he ought to let her go. Let their baby go.

His head swam in a sea of confusion.

With a sigh, she nestled more comfortably into his lap. At least she seemed comfortable. Her weight, her softness, was putting a serious strain on his family jewels.

"It looks like Isabel got herself a billy goat. Can you tell if the foal's a boy or a girl?" she asked.

With the foal still trying to gain its feet, Isabel

and Lady appeared to be taking turns licking and drying the two newborns without respect to which baby belonged to which mama. And the two babies were investigating their opposite half with as much curiosity as their mamas had demonstrated when earlier introduced.

"Looks like a colt to me." Jack shifted Lindy's position, helping her to her feet, then levered himself upright. "A real humdinger. If he's got his daddy's spirit, he could be a winner."

"I'm sure he will be. Have you thought of a name yet?"

"Nope. I didn't want to jinx anything."

She brushed back strands of flyaway hair from her face, catching bits of hay with her fingers. Her eyes twinkled. She looked slightly wanton, as though she'd enjoyed a quick tumble in the hay. Jack wished they had.

"Superstitious, are we?" she teased.

"All horsebreeders are to some extent."

They stood together, his arm around her shoulder, her arm looped around his waist, and he was aware that their easy camaraderie could shift to mind-blowing sex in an instant. That it was the spark between them that had created a link neither of them had asked for nor wanted. A baby of their own.

"Where's Tootsie?" she asked, looking around.

"Maybe all the commotion scared her off."

Lindy felt a prickle of unease raise the hair on the back of her neck. Tootsie, ever protective of her, rarely wandered far from her side. Particularly in an unfamiliar environment.

Slipping free from Jack, she strolled down the line of empty stalls. Jewels had quieted since the birth of his offspring, content to munch oats from his feed bag.

"Tootsie!" she called. When there was no response, she asked, "Where's Alberto?"

"It's his day off. He's visiting his family."

Feeling increasingly anxious, she went from stall to stall, searching the shadowed corners of each one. At home she'd made up a box lined with blankets for Tootsie to use when her puppies were born. She'd placed it in a quiet spot on the back porch where the new mother and her babies wouldn't be disturbed. With Tootsie so close to her time, maybe Lindy should have left her at home this morning.

Peering into the last stall, Lindy spotted a subtle movement and caught a glimpse of golden fur.

"Tootsie, are you all right?" Approaching cautiously, she squatted down about three feet from her dog. "Well, would you look at that. How many babies have you got, sweetie?"

Tootsie busily tended to what looked to be four little balls of fur, any one of them no larger than a handful.

Lindy's heart filled with love for all of them. She owed one puppy to the breeder whose dog had mated with Tootsie, and she almost wished she hadn't planned to sell the rest of them. But the money would build her bank account and make her dream of her own grooming shop a reality that much sooner. Her resolve weakened. Maybe she could keep just one for herself...

Jack came up behind her, crouching and resting his hand on the back of her neck, kneading gently. "I'd say Goodfellow is experiencing a serious population explosion."

Tipping her head back, she let him ease her tense muscles, although other parts of her body were mindful of his intimate caress and were anything but relaxed. "Wait till all the pregnant women in town deliver their babies. We'll be able to bottle the tap water and sell it as a fertility potion."

"Great. That means if the horsebreeding business flops, we'll have a fallback position."

"You aren't going to fail, Jack. You're too stubborn." And that was the essence of why she loved him. Against all odds, Jack wasn't a quitter.

He stood, bringing her to her feet, too. Automatically she turned into his arms and gazed up into his eyes. She'd never considered herself particularly pretty, certainly not petite, but with Jack she felt...feminine. His potent masculinity brought out her womanly side. She wanted to be his match, his opposite half. To be soft where he was hard, to give what he wanted to take. To love and be loved in return.

He brushed a tender kiss to her lips. "Outside of the Corps, nobody's ever had much faith in me."

"I do."

Dipping his head, he kissed her more fully, crossing her mouth with his, his tongue testing the seam of her lips. With a sigh, she welcomed him, her body humming with desire.

The quiet sound of animals tending their young created an elemental rhythm that reverberated deep inside her. In time it would be her turn to nurture a child. *Jack's child.* She would cherish those moments just as she relished this time with him, loving him.

A thought occurred to her and she smiled.

"What?" he asked, frowning.

"I just thought of a name for the colt." Purposefully, she rubbed her hand across the ridge of Jack's arousal.

He groaned, the ring of brown around his pupils almost vanishing into the black iris. "We can do the christening later. I've got other things on my mind right now."

"So do I." She brushed up against him again. "But I'll have to run a taste test just to be sure my memory's accurate."

"Memory?"

"I'm thinking Salty Jewels would be a perfect name for him. Want me to check it out?"

"Lindy, I—"

She cupped him, whispering, "How 'bout we go inside and I'll test my memory for accuracy."

In a strained, husky voice, he uttered exciting,

erotic words that thrilled her, made her want to be as bad as possible with Jack. The man she loved.

"Hey, Colby! You in there?"

Like they'd been shot, she and Jack burst apart.

Jack swore an earthy, distinctly Marine curse. "One thing you can say about our chief of police—he's got rotten timing."

Lindy allowed as how Chief Pickles had an uncanny knack for messing up an otherwise beautiful moment, a talent he'd demonstrated early on when he'd threatened to haul her off to jail in that ice-cream incident. She'd never quite forgiven him. Gritting her teeth, she knew she wasn't in a forgiving mood now, either.

Lindy and Jack met the chief at the open double doors to the barn.

During his high school years, Chester Pickles had won a state wrestling championship—in the hundred-and-three-pound weight class. No one was allowed to forget that. He still strutted like a bantam rooster, his khaki uniform shirt buttons straining across his more recently acquired potbelly.

"I'm here," Jack said.

Pickles's hand slid to his holstered gun and he eyed them both as though he'd come across a ring of dangerous thugs. "I checked out your story about A.C.'s horse being a counterfeit. Randy Boy's as legit as can be. Got the right markings and brand. His papers are in order, far as I can tell."

"The horse that beat Jewels was a phony,

Chief,'' Jack insisted. "The racing commission needs to investigate.''

"They'd dyed the blaze on his forehead. A.C. wouldn't do that unless—"

"You two'll have to tell it to the judge. That's what I came to tell you. Your case is on the court calendar for Wednesday morning, first thing. You both had best be there or I'll have to haul you in.''

Jack's expression turned as grim as Lindy felt.

"We'll be there,'' he said.

Pickles gave them his beady-eyed look, then turned and marched toward his police cruiser. When all the bars of red, yellow and blue lights on the car flashed, it looked like a one-man Christmas parade. The built-in electronic bullhorn was capable of producing more volume than a rock band at an outdoor concert. Pickles loved to use all his toys to scare the bejeebers out of the teenagers who lingered after dark in the parking lot near Mill Creek. That's when he was at his best, as the local bully with a badge.

Fortunately he'd never caught Lindy necking in the back seat of some kid's car. She'd always been too afraid to go along with the crowd.

She imagined Jack hadn't been so cowardly.

He ran his fingers through his hair. "I don't get it. Even Pickles should be able to tell a counterfeit horse from the real thing.''

"Maybe A.C. switched them back after the chief took us to jail.''

"If only he'd had enough sense to listen when

we—'' He seemed to shake off his morose mood, shooting her one of those wicked smiles of his. The one that put a gleam in his eyes and meant trouble.

He caught her hand, tugging her close. ''Seems to me we were on our way inside when that ol' sourpuss showed up.''

A jolt of awareness skittered along her nerve endings and her breath caught. ''I do seem to remember something like that.''

''Good. I think the ladies in the maternity ward can get along without us for a while.''

Lindy hoped so. Because she really wanted Jack to make love to her again, wanted to lose herself in his arms and not worry about going to court and maybe to jail, or having D'Arcy take the shop away from her.

They walked toward the house, his fingers linked with hers. The afternoon air was warm, though not nearly as heated as the blood pulsing in her veins. The sun cast speckled light through the ancient walnut tree onto the narrow driveway, mottling the weeds that grew between the tire tracks. Clumps of purple irises at the side of the house lifted their heads to drink in the sun's warmth; the scent of honeysuckle drifted on a soft breeze.

No question about it. Lindy was in love. The intoxicating feeling made her giddy. She'd waited so long. It didn't matter that she'd fallen for the wrong man, one who could still disrupt her life. Her heart simply wasn't willing to listen to that small voice of reason.

Jack held open the back door and she stepped inside.

"Hit the deck! Hit the deck!"

Jack dived for cover under the kitchen table, dragging Lindy with him.

"What the hell!" he muttered.

Lindy gasped for breath. "It's only Petey."

They both peered up at the parrot's cage—the empty cage that was sitting on the kitchen counter.

Jack scrambled out from under the table. "I swear, I'm gonna wring that bird's neck. In about two seconds, he's gonna be Sunday supper!"

"Now, Jack," Lindy soothed. "Remember, Mrs. O'Toole left Petey in my care."

"As far as I'm concerned, she can have him back anytime she wants. I've had it up to here with—"

"Ooh-rah! Ooh-rah!" Petey chanted as though he'd just finished a cross-country march.

Trying to follow the sound of the bird's voice, Lindy looked around. "Where is he?"

"Damned if I know."

Bits of feathers and cardboard drifted down from a high shelf over the counter.

Jack picked up some of the cardboard. "That stupid bird got into my six-pack of beer."

"You mean he's drunk?"

He looked up at the source of the falling debris. "I don't think so. As near as I can tell, Petey's not an alcoholic. He's got a cardboard fetish. Not that that isn't weird enough.''

Using his arms, he hefted himself up onto the counter and half stood, peering onto the shelf where Petey had ensconced himself. ''Well, I'll be—''

Yelling, Jack leapt back off the counter and fell to his knees on the floor, his hand covering his nose.

''What happened?''

''That...that bird bit me!''

Lindy pulled his hand away from his face. The tip of Jack's nose sported a red welt. ''I'm so sorry, Jack. You must have frightened him—''

''I've got big news for you, sweetheart. Petey is definitely not a *him*.''

''He's not?''

''That bird has turned every bit of cardboard in the house into a nest. Which is exactly where *she* laid her egg.''

Lindy sat back on her haunches.

Petey a girl?

Another in a long line of pregnant Goodfellow females? It boggled the mind.

''Definitely the water,'' she mumbled. ''We'll make a fortune.''

Jack stared at her stupidly. Then slowly his eyes crinkled and a smile appeared, dimpling his cheeks. He barked a laugh that became a rolling, deep-throated chuckle, warming Lindy's heart in ways she'd never expected. Forget sex and lust. This man was simply wonderful to be with. And with every passing moment, she loved him more.

Soon they were all but rolling around on the floor together, laughing so hard they both had tears in their eyes. Above them, Petey...well, Ms. Pete, she supposed, squawked and complained. But neither of them cared.

Until someone pounded on the back door.

Sobering, Jack staggered to his feet. "I swear, if that's Pickles, I'm going to make a present of that damn bird to him."

Lindy choked back another laugh. "You wouldn't."

He winked at her. "Not a chance, sweetheart. She's a Marine Corps pin-up, if I ever met one."

Trying to right herself, Lindy swept back her flyaway hair and tried to straighten her blouse while Jack opened the back door.

Marcie burst inside. "I've been looking all over for you, Lindy. I called and you weren't at home. Then I called your mother—"

"You didn't." Lindy wasn't yet ready to face her mother about Jack and what she intended to do, despite her mother's dire warnings.

"I didn't tell her why I wanted to talk to you. I'm not that big a fool."

No, but her dear friend was the talkingest woman in the county.

"So what do you want?" Lindy asked.

Her dark eyes taking in the scene, Marcie said,

"I heard it on GAB. It even made the national news."

"The radio station?" Jack asked.

Marcie nodded, her pixie haircut bobbing.

Lindy grimaced. WGAB was the local radio station—the *GAS*'s only competition for area news—twenty-four hours of country music and gossip. Lindy didn't often listen.

In contrast, her friend was addicted to every little tidbit that GAB broadcast and had a real talent for dramatizing every event. "What did you hear, Marcie?"

"Well, it seems there's a pregnancy test kit out that shows false positives. There's a huge national recall going on because everybody who took the test came up pregnant, even when they weren't."

The burning sensation started in the center of Lindy's chest and spread outward. "Were some of those tests sold locally?"

"Sure. That's why I needed to tell you." She glanced from Lindy to Jack and back again. "Goodfellow Pharmacy is right smack in the middle of the whole recall business. It's the only kind of pregnancy test kit they carry. And none of the kits were any good."

Lindy got a sinking feeling in the pit of her stomach. Half the women in Goodfellow thought they were pregnant.

Maybe it wasn't the water after all.

9

MARCIE'S CAR BACKFIRED as she accelerated out the driveway and onto the county road. Lindy winced.

She wasn't pregnant.

Somehow she'd known that from the beginning. But then the test Jack had purchased had come up positive... Out of duty, wanting to do the right thing, Jack had proposed. And she'd fallen in love.

Her stomach roiled; tears stung at the back of her eyes and she shivered in the cool afternoon air, watching Marcie's car vanish out of sight around a bend in the road.

Dear heaven, when had her outlook changed? When had she started to *want* Jack's child? *And* Jack?

Standing beside her under the old walnut tree, he tucked his hands in his jeans pockets, and stared at a spot about a foot in front of his feet. "You figure I bought one of those bad test kits?"

"I think there've been a lot of false alarms lately in Goodfellow." She recalled Roseanne who was going to marry her beau but maybe wouldn't now. And Ms. Salter who was really too old to be starting all over again. And Addie MacKenzie who would be brokenhearted if she wasn't pregnant when she and her husband were so eager to have children. How many others would there be? How many would be relieved? Or filled with the same regret that ached in Lindy's throat?

How did Jack feel?

"I guess this means you're off the hook," she said, swallowing hard.

He didn't look at her; his body language told her little. "Not necessarily. You still could be—"

"We were careful, Jack. You know that. And I'd had a period."

"You'll take another test? Marcie said—"

"I'll be at the Goodfellow Pharmacy tomorrow morning along with half the women in town. That's when Marcie said they'd have new test kits available."

"You'll let me know the results?"

She shrugged. "Sure. But it'll be negative, Jack. You know that." And there'd no longer be a reason for him to do the noble thing and marry her.

He kicked at a rotten walnut that had fallen to the ground last fall. It split apart and age-blackened pieces skittered across a weedy stretch that used to be a lawn. "Well, I guess that's it then."

"Jack, I—" What could she say? That they could get married anyway even though he didn't love her? She couldn't do that to him, or to herself. They both had their dreams. Their own goals—hers to operate her own grooming shop, his to be a successful horsebreeder. Marriage and having babies hadn't been a part of their plans. It didn't matter that her heart was splitting into as many pieces as the rotten walnut had.

This time she had to swallow twice before she could speak past the lump in her throat. "Could you help me get Tootsie and her puppies into the Blazer? I think I ought to take her home."

"Sure."

"You might want to keep Isabel here till—"

"I'll keep her." Abruptly, he turned and went striding off toward the barn.

Well, hell's fire and tarnation! She was a little grumpy at the moment, too. He didn't have to go all ugly on her. Or maybe he was just happy to see her gone, to no longer feel obligated to marry her.

For her part, Lindy planned to have a good cry over this whole mess. Then she'd be fine. Just fine!

She drew in a shaky breath. Yeah, right!

JACK GRABBED A cardboard box and some empty burlap feed bags from the tack room. Damned if he wasn't back to square one.

He'd talked himself into believing it'd be okay for him to have a kid. With Lindy, all of her good qualities would offset the influence of his "bad blood." And now it wasn't gonna happen.

That was fine by him. His mama had taught him

to chew his own tobacco. He'd never relied on any-one except himself. Nothing had changed.

Except it felt like somebody had rammed a bay-onet into his chest up to the hilt, and it hurt like hell to draw even a shallow breath.

Tootsie eyed him warily when he entered the horse stall where she'd given birth to her babies. "It's okay, girl. Lindy's taking you and your pups home now."

Gingerly he placed the puppies in the box one at a time, cushioning them in the rumpled burlap, none of them bigger than he could hold in the palm of his hand. Two of the four had slightly darker fur than Tootsie. A contribution from the father's gene pool, Jack imagined, and he wondered what a baby would look like that he and Lindy had created to-gether. Or if they had four babies, would two have her fair complexion and the other two his deeper hue?

Sure as hell he'd never find out, and he hated the useless spear of regret that sliced through him.

"I opened up the back of the truck."

He drew a steadying breath before turning to Lindy. "Great. We're set to go here."

The minute Jack lifted the box of puppies, Toot-sie was on her feet. She wasn't about to let her babies out of her sight and needed no urging to follow them into the back of Lindy's Blazer.

Jack closed the tailgate behind her.

"Guess that's it, then," Lindy said. She fussed

with her hair, flipping it into a loose knot that Jack had an urge to comb free again.

If it hadn't been for Marcie's lousy timing, he and Lindy would be basking in the afterglow of their lovemaking by now. Or maybe they'd be working on a second round.

"I'll see you in court Wednesday, right?" he asked.

Her expression clouded over. "Do you think we ought to have an attorney?"

Hell, he didn't have money to hire a lawyer. But he didn't want Lindy going to jail either. "I'll get somebody."

"Okay. Thanks." She seemed to hesitate, to have something else to say but apparently thought better of it and got into the truck.

Jack moved out of the way. She started the engine, backed up. Like a fool all he could think to do was wave. Hell, there wasn't anything left to say anyway.

Unless the second test came out positive.

THE MINI-MOB outside the drugstore looked like a bunch of day-after-Christmas bargain hunters at the biggest sale in town. Two dozen women jostled each other, elbowing their way to the front of the line that had formed waiting for the store to open.

As the minutes ticked by, the tension rose, and Lindy sensed things could get ugly.

Lindy was in no hurry to get a brand, spanking

new pregnancy test kit. As she saw it, neither a positive or negative result would be entirely satisfactory. If by some miracle she was actually pregnant, she'd be putting Jack back in the position of feeling he *had* to marry her, noble man that he was. And if the new test proved she wasn't pregnant, which she was sure was the case, then the hollow sensation in her chest would never go away.

Someone shoved by her, practically taking her shoulder off.

"Whatever is taking those people so long to open the doors?" Marge Salter complained. "Don't they know some of us have golf dates and we don't want to be late?"

"It's not quite nine o'clock, Ms. Salter," Lindy pointed out.

A scuffle broke out nearer the door, two young women nearly coming to blows. A third woman stepped between them, gaining a better place in line.

"Well, it wouldn't hurt them to open early just this once."

Lindy was going to agree, even back away so Ms. Salter could go first, and then decided she was tired of kowtowing to the woman simply because she was a grooming customer and had tons of money.

"Golf date or not, you'll just have to wait your turn, Ms. Salter."

The woman "humphed" at her and tried to use her shoulders—well developed by a thousand golf swings—to push past Lindy.

"And while you're at it," Lindy continued, not giving an inch, "you might want to think about A.C. running a counterfeit horse in place of Randy Boy last week."

A mother in a housecoat and slippers confronted her teenage daughter in line. "I knew you'd be here, young lady!" She grabbed her child by the ear.

"Mama!" the girl wailed.

Ms. Salter said, "He'd never do any such thing—"

"But he did. Jack Colby and I caught him red-handed before he could switch the horses back again. Then, to cover his tracks, he had Chief Pickles arrest us."

"You broke into our property. That's criminal—"

The irate mother was shaking her finger in her daughter's face. "You're never going near that boy again, do you hear me? I don't care if you're pregnant or not. I will not have you embarrass me like this again."

"Your son cheated," Lindy said, trying to ignore the battles raging at the head of the line. "You know yourself A.C. couldn't pick a winner in a one-horse race. How come he got so lucky last week?"

Ms. Salter sputtered, "I don't believe you," and was prepared to argue further, but movement inside the drugstore distracted her.

The crowd surged forward.

The clerk was slow as molasses unlocking the door.

From out of nowhere, Roseanne dashed to the front of the line, shoving the door open and knocking the hapless employee on his keester when he didn't get out of the way quickly enough.

Never in the two years she'd known Roseanne had Lindy seen the girl move so fast. Obviously until now adequate motivation had been lacking.

Marge Salter's competitive spirit took over. She charged ahead, practically knocking down Addie MacKenzie, who'd always been a little fragile. But Addie fought back with a pointy elbow right to Marge's ribs and the back of her hand to Marge's nose.

Marge staggered to a halt. "Hey…" she complained, but Addie and the crowd had swept past her.

Rufus Pettigrew, the owner of the drugstore, had held sway behind the pharmacy counter for as long as Lindy could remember. Over the years, his hair had thinned and gone gray, his bland face wrinkled and his complexion had grown more sallow. As the mob descended on him at a full run, his eyes widened.

"Now, ladies, if you'll just be calm. For the pharmacy's record, each of you will have to fill out one of these forms." He held a pad of paper aloft.

The women complained vocally.

"I'm not going to fill out—"

"If the manufacturer hadn't screwed up—"

"Just give me a new kit—"

At the head of the line, Roseanne took matters into her own hands. She sprang up onto the counter with the agility of an Olympic athlete and dropped down to the other side, snatching up a handful of test kits.

"Who needs these?" she cried.

"Now, young lady, you can't come in here—"

"I do! I do!" the women shouted.

Blue-and-white boxes of pregnancy test kits flew out from behind the pharmacy counter like butterflies startled into flight. Lindy snared one in midair, then had to wrestle it away from Sallyanne Nadeen, who wasn't even dating anyone as far as Lindy knew. But then, the world had been full of surprises lately.

By the time Lindy looked around, the crowd had moved en masse to form a new line at the rest-room door.

"Hurry up, will you?" someone complained. "I really have to pee."

The other women booed her.

Lindy decided she could wait until she got home to take the test. She could wait till a month from Sunday, for that matter. She wasn't pregnant. Confirming it would do nothing to raise her spirits.

Her hand slid to her midsection and she palmed her mostly flat tummy. How was it possible to miss something you'd never had?

The door to the ladies' room burst open and Addie appeared, pumping her fist in the air. "I'm pregnant!" she shouted. "A big pink plus!" Tears of happiness began to stream down her cheeks.

Lindy's heart constricted. Despite her best efforts, envy gnawed at her. Until the past few days, having her own grooming shop had been enough. Her future. Her biggest ambition.

Now she wanted more.

Now she wanted Jack's baby.

She started to turn away but before she could, Marge Salter appeared. Her face had gone gray; hunching over, she walked through the crowd like an old woman, her golfing outfit incongruous on her suddenly aging frame. She shuffled down the aisle of vitamins, ignoring the displays.

"Marge?" Lindy stopped her. "Are you okay?"

The older woman jerked her head up. "Leave me alone."

"No, I won't. You look terrible. What can I—"

Her eyes filled with tears. "Asa's going to be so disappointed."

"That you're not pregnant?" she asked softly. "You already have two—"

"That I'm... The big *M* isn't so terrible, you know."

Lindy blinked, unsure what Marge meant. "Big *M*?"

In a hushed whisper, she said, "That's why I

haven't had my flow." Her voice dropped even deeper. "Menopause. The big *M*."

Lindy nodded. "Oh, no, that's not so terrible. Of course not."

"It doesn't mean Asa needs to go looking for a—" Marge threw herself into Lindy's arms, sobbing. "A younger woman. He expects so…so much of me. I've tried so hard to be…"

Lindy stood there stupidly in the aisle between the vitamins and cough syrup, holding Marge as she cried, having no idea what to say. She suspected the hope of a new pregnancy had been Marge's search to regain her youth, to give her a competitive edge over her husband's mistress. And that made Lindy mad.

Getting old wasn't bad. And menopause didn't mean *old* old! By this time in her life, Marge ought to have the confidence of her husband's love—even if she couldn't break a hundred on the golf course or conceive a child. And she shouldn't have to worry about her husband's infidelity.

Gently she ushered Marge down the aisle, skirting the ever-so-tempting chocolate candy display, and out the front door. The fresh air appeared to revive her.

"Well, my dear." Straightening her shoulders, Marge scrubbed her eyes with the heels of her hands. "My golf partner is probably wondering what on earth has happened to me."

"Yes, ma'am."

She took a step toward her top-of-the-line sport-utility vehicle, then stopped and turned back. Her jaw tightened, all signs of vulnerability vanishing. "I'll have a chat with A.C., but I truly can't believe he'd do anything dishonest. Not when it comes to his horses. His father would never permit it."

"Look around for a bottle of hair coloring that matches Randy Boy's blaze."

Marge narrowed her eyes. "And I think *you* ought to keep your distance from that Colby boy. He's always spelled trouble." Tossing her head like one of the high-strung horses at the Salter stables, she marched away.

Lindy snorted in disgust. No way was Marge Salter going to admit her precious son had violated the horsebreeder's code of honor. That would be worse than admitting she was getting old!

As far as Lindy was concerned, Jack Colby was worth a dozen Salters, or any of the other bluegrass families that ruled the community of Goodfellow. Not that anyone cared.

Women drifted past Lindy as she walked toward her truck, some with smiles of relief, it seemed to her. Only a few appeared disappointed by the new test results.

"Hey, Lindy." Roseanne sidled up beside her. "I'm gonna be a little late for work, okay? I've gotta call Billy and tell him what happened."

"So, ah, are you pregnant?"

The girl gave her a sheepish grin. "No, I guess

not. But Billy says that's all right, too. It'd be good if we put off a family for a while, save our money, you know."

"But your wedding—"

"Billy's glad this whole mistake kinda forced him into thinking about us being together forever, you know? He loves me a whole lot. But now we can plan a fancy wedding with bridesmaids and everything, just like I've always dreamed about."

"You're a lucky girl, Roseanne."

"I know." With a wave of her hand, the girl trotted off toward the pay phone in front of Graham's Grocery.

Sighing, Lindy got into her truck. She was trying very hard not to envy Roseanne's good fortune, to have found a man who loved her and wanted to marry her, pregnant or not.

Lindy hadn't been that lucky.

Until Jack had come into her life, she hadn't realized that had been her dream, too.

SHE REACHED THE shop to discover Roberta Fawlty and her spaniel, Miss Bee, waiting for her. Opening the front door, Lindy said, "I'm sorry I'm late, Mrs. Fawlty."

"Oh, that's all right, dear. I know how it is when you're pregnant. Sometimes the mornings can be so difficult."

Lindy took Miss Bee's leash. "I'm not pregnant, Mrs. Fawlty."

"Of course you are, dear. I heard you myself ages ago telling a friend on the phone the good news." Her cheeks flushed slightly. "Of course, I didn't mean to eavesdrop but I was standing right there by the counter. I couldn't help but overhear you."

"Ages ago?" Lindy searched her memory. Mrs. Fawlty brought her dog in for grooming about once a month but Lindy couldn't remember discussing... "Do you mean when you saw Jack Colby here?"

"Oh, no, not then. Long before that. I heard you very distinctly say 'Our pregnancy is going along just fine.' I was ever so happy for you."

But the day Jack showed up had been the first day Lindy learned the whole world thought she was pregnant—and she wasn't. It had been nothing more than a terrible rumor started by...

It dawned on her what Roberta was talking about. "Mrs. Fawlty, what you heard was me talking to a breeder whose dog we'd mated with Tootsie. The breeder was checking on *Tootsie's* pregnancy, not *mine*."

"Isn't that sweet. So your dog's pregnant, too?"

"She had her puppies yesterday. And you misunderstood. I've never been pregnant." Though a part of her had been desperately pleased with the prospect of having Jack's child and she'd adjusted to the possibility.

Mrs. Fawlty looked terribly perplexed. "I was so sure you said—"

"Mrs. Fawlty, after you overheard my conversation, did you just happen to mention to anyone that you thought I was pregnant?"

"Well, I don't exactly remember and I certainly didn't say anything right away. But maybe I did mention it later to a few people. But only to close friends I knew would be happy for you."

"Would that have included Mrs. Murdock and Betty-Jane Fetzer?" A couple of the talkiest women in town?

"Well...I suppose it's possible..."

Lindy rolled her eyes. At least now she knew where the rumor had come from and why.

But that knowledge did little to ease the ache in her heart.

THE NEXT AFTERNOON, Lindy was admiring her grooming shop, the spotless cages, towels neatly stacked, her clippers freshly sharpened—and the total absence of any animals to groom—when the phone rang.

With her luck it would be a telemarketer.

"Fluff 'n Cut," she announced with little hope it would be a customer on the other end of the line.

"A.C. admitted to his father what he'd done," Marge Salter announced without preamble. "Neither of them were going to fess up till I found that horrible bottle of hair color."

Lindy sighed with relief. "Does Chief Pickles know?"

"He does, and the charges against you and that Colby boy have been dropped."

"Thank goodness." Neither she nor Jack would be going to jail. She'd call to let him know the good news.

"Yes, well...I've also made it clear to Asa that if he so much as looks cross-eyed at a younger woman, I will make the racing commission aware of this incident. In which case, he will be toast!"

Lindy swallowed a smile. "Yes, ma'am."

"And for heaven's sake, stop calling me ma'am. It makes me feel ancient."

"Of course...Marge."

"That's better. Furthermore, I'd like to make an appointment for Colleen for a grooming session. In fact, I believe I'd like to set up a regular appointment, say once a week."

"That would be wonderful, yes, of course." Lindy started scribbling Colleen's name on her appointment sheet.

"And I believe I have a few friends who've been taking their dogs to Lexington for grooming. Snobs, you know, who don't think you can get high-quality service right here in Goodfellow. I think I'll mention how pleased I am with your tender loving care of Colleen. That's terribly important for a dog owner, you know. That the groomer cares about her animal."

Lindy had trouble not stumbling over her tongue in her eagerness to agree. Bless her, with Marge's approval and support among the country club set, Lindy's business would blossom. She'd be a success.

Too bad she felt as though she'd lost something even more important in the process.

10

MY FAMILY JEWELS reached the finish line a full length and a half ahead of the second-place finisher. It had been a week since the stallion lost to the counterfeit Randy Boy. Every day he was gaining more strength, more speed.

Jack should have been more excited about his Thoroughbred's success. Not only did it mean money in his pocket now, it meant Salty Jewels would increase in value. Colby Farms was well on its way to being a profitable operation. He was damn proud of that.

But as he made his way to join Alberto in the winner's circle, he swore under his breath.

Without Lindy in his life the joy had gone out of him, and made his accomplishments seem like fool's gold.

He went through the routine of being congratulated by race officials for Jewels's win and claiming the substantial check for first-place purse, but his heart wasn't in it.

After making sure My Family Jewels was safely cooled down and rubbed down, Jack headed back to the farm to check on Salty Jewels and the mare. The colt was growing like the proverbial weed. In three years there'd be a new Jewels running in the Kentucky Derby. He could feel it in his bones.

Jack wished he cared more. It had taken him nearly a week to figure it out.

The only way any success he achieved would matter was if Lindy was at his side the day his horse won the Derby—at his side as Mrs. Jack Colby.

AT A LOSS FOR words, Lindy stared at the hamster in the cage on the counter, then looked at the ten-year-old girl who'd brought her prized pet into the shop.

She'd been busier than a cat with his fur on fire all day; she had been since Marge Salter had taken it on herself to spread the word about Fluff 'n Cut to her country club friends. Lindy had already sent Roseanne home and had been ready—thankfully— to close for the day.

Now she had one last customer. A hamster.

Lindy didn't really have the energy to deal with the child's problems. But the youngster looked so...forlorn, how could she refuse?

"Millie, honey, I don't usually groom hamsters. They can take care of that for themselves."

"My mama says you're real good with animals, better even than the vet. Everybody says so. And Mercury doesn't exactly need grooming."

"What does he need, honey?" At the moment he

was shivering in a pile of wood shavings in one corner of the cage, scared out of his wits, and looked like he could use a blanket.

"When he gets on his wheel, he runs backwards. All the kids laugh at him." She hung her head, her braids drooping forward. "And they make fun of me."

"I see." Lindy reached across the counter to stroke the top of Millie's blond head. Could there be anything worse in the world than to be laughed at? "I'm not too sure what I can do—"

"I've got money." From her jeans pocket she dragged up several crumpled dollar bills. "I know it isn't much—"

"Why don't you keep your money till we see if I can—"

The bell on the shop door tinkled.

Not expecting anyone, Lindy looked up in surprise and her jaw dropped. She felt as if a trap door had opened beneath her and she'd fallen a thousand feet down a mine shaft. Her blood roared in her ears; she couldn't catch her breath.

Jack Colby. Wearing his Marine dress uniform, his chest filled with medals. Carrying a covered birdcage in one hand and a huge bouquet of flowers in the other.

It had been a little more than two weeks since she'd seen him and she drank in the determined set of his strong jaw, the flash of I-won't-take-no-for-an-answer in his dark eyes, and her heart suddenly took flight. He was a Marine on a mission.

At the very first opportunity, she intended to surrender.

"So do you think you can fix him?" Millie asked, wide-eyed as she glanced from Jack to Lindy and back again.

"He's perfect just the way he is," Lindy said on a sigh, her thoughts focused far more on Jack than her young customer.

Jack grinned his wicked, there's-trouble-coming-your-way grin.

"But he does it *all wrong*," the child wailed.

Jack coughed to cover a laugh, and Lindy yanked her attention back to Millie. "Honey, I'm not entirely sure—"

"What seems to be the problem?" Joining them, Jack placed the birdcage on the counter, the flowers beside it and studied the hamster. There was a flutter of wings inside the birdcage and a soft cooing sound.

"Her hamster runs backwards on his wheel," Lindy explained, amazed at how breathless her voice sounded.

"That's bad?" he asked.

Folding her arms on the counter, Millie leaned her chin on them and stared into the hamster cage. "Everybody thinks it's dorky."

"I see." He met Lindy's gaze and winked. "Why don't I see what I can do?"

Millie lifted her head. "You think you can fix him, mister?"

"Marines may not always get it right the first time, but then they regroup and try again."

A flush stole up Lindy's neck. "They do pretty good the first time, too."

"That a fact?" A smile playing around the corners of his sensual lips, he bent over the hamster cage and removed the top. Reaching inside, he lifted the wheel, fussed with it and settled it back in the cage.

"You know how to get him onto the wheel?" he asked Millie.

"Sure. I just put him there. He makes it go." She gave a discouraged twist of her lips. "Backwards."

"Give him a try now."

Not looking at all confident that Jack's minimal effort had solved the problem, Millie did as ordered. She picked up her hamster, gave him a little kiss, and put him on the wheel.

Immediately Mercury began spinning—in the right direction.

"You did it!" Millie threw her arms around Jack's waist, hugging him. "Thank you, thank you! Now the kids won't make fun of me anymore."

A little awkwardly, Jack patted Millie's back. His deeply tanned complexion flamed an embarrassed red. "You listen to me, young lady. Anybody who cares as much as you about your, uh, hamster is a pretty terrific person. Don't let the kids at school put you down for any reason. You got that?''

Hero worship glowed in the girl's blue eyes. She nodded.

"Okay, then," Jack said. "Get on outta here. I got something special to say to Lindy."

Her back a little straighter than when she'd arrived, her eyes a little brighter, Millie hurried to do Jack's bidding. She scooped up the hamster cage, setting the wheel into furious motion, and scooted out the door. And Lindy was struck by what a wonderful father Jack would make.

When the door closed behind the child, Lindy asked, "What did you do?"

He shrugged, but he looked pretty tickled with himself. "There was a catch on the wheel, like a stopper. I released it so the wheel would go both directions. Not a big deal."

She laughed. "Millie thinks you walk on water."

His expression turned serious. "I'm more worried about—"

"Polly want a cracker! Polly want a cracker!"

Lindy's gaze shot to the birdcage. "Ms. Pete?"

"See for yourself." He lifted the cloth cover.

"Good morning! Good morning!" Ms. Pete stood, flapped her wings and settled down again on her shredded cardboard nest, carefully tucking her incubating egg under her body.

"That's wonderful, Jack. How on earth did you—"

"She look the same to you?"

Frowning, Lindy studied the parrot. Same green feathers and yellow beak. "I guess so…"

"Pretty baby," the parrot purred.

From his inside jacket pocket, Jack retrieved a chunk of birdseed pressed into the shape of a cracker.

Delicately, Ms. Pete took it from his fingertips and murmured something resembling thank you.

"That's amazing. You must have spent hours teaching her—"

"She's a counterfeit."

Lindy stared at him stupidly. "You mean that's not a real parrot?"

He laughed. "No, not that counterfeit. But A.C.'s antics gave me the idea. It took me more than a week of phone calls but I finally found a breeder in Raleigh and swapped him even. Do you think Mrs. O'Toole will mind?"

The bird dipped her head. "I love you," she cooed, more mourning dove than parrot.

Laughing, Lindy said, "I think Mrs. O'Toole won't be able to resist her. What's her name?"

"Esmeralda."

"We'll have to tell Mrs. O'Toole the truth but I'm sure she'll be delighted."

"The breeder said he'd trade me back if this bird didn't work out. And he knows a retired Marine Master Sergeant who used to be a DI. The breeder figures Ms. Pete will find a good home."

"I can't believe you went all the way to Raleigh." Smiling and shaking her head, she reached across the counter and took Jack's hand. "Thank you for going to so much trouble for Mrs. O'Toole."

"You're welcome." He cleared his throat, looking like he was about to speak again, then uncharacteristically, thought better of it.

She glanced at the flowers on the counter—roses mixed with lilacs, gladioli, birds of paradise plus other blooms Lindy couldn't identify. Their scent sweetened the air, making it smell like springtime—and love.

"Did you have something else on your mind?" she asked hopefully. Surely spending that much money on a floral arrangement meant something was up.

"I've been thinking..."

She waited.

He cleared his throat again and straightened his shoulders. "Just because a person is raised in a certain town isn't a good enough reason for that person to stay there forever."

All the air left her lungs, replaced by an ache that expanded to fill her entire chest. "You're leaving?"

"It seems like the right thing to do." Placing his hands on the counter, he hopped up and over the barrier between them. "Jewels won a nice purse this week. With all that I've done to the farm, it'll bring a good price now. I can start over somewhere else."

"I see." That was a lie. She could barely see at all. Her eyes had glazed with tears. Any second now they'd spill down her cheeks and Jack would know what a fool she was. *He meant the flowers as a goodbye present.*

"I don't give a damn for myself but I don't want our kids to go through all the stuff I did growing up. Being told all the time they've got bad blood."

Numbly, hardly able to hear his words of goodbye, she said, "No, of course not."

"I figure I'll have enough for a down payment on a small place, maybe north of Lexington, and I can rent time on a practice track for My Family Jewels."

Practice with her would be more fun, and she wouldn't charge his family jewels so much as a nickel.

"That'd be far enough away so nobody would know us," he continued.

So far away Lindy would never see Jack again...and she'd always live with a broken heart.

"I'm not sure what to do about a grooming shop for you. I'm hoping I can find a big enough house that maybe you could run your grooming business out of the horse barn or from the back porch."

"Sure. Mama has her beauty shop—" Lindy's head snapped up. "What on earth are you talking about?"

His forehead furrowed. "Where we'll live after we get married. What did you think?"

Her mouth opened and closed several times but she couldn't get out a single sound.

"I'm not in any big rush," he assured her. "I plan to court you right this time. That's why I brought the flowers."

"F-flowers?" Her mind reeling, her gaze slid to the colorful bouquet. *This wasn't goodbye.*

"I didn't know which kind you liked, so I got something of everything they had."

"They're..." She swallowed several times. The exquisite flowers on the counter took on a new vibrancy in the same way his words gave her new life, new hope. "Married? Us?" An impossible dream come true?

His lips twitched. "You and me. I think that's how it's done."

He really meant it, didn't he? Surely her imagination wasn't making this up. Her ears weren't deceiving her simply because she wanted him so much. Loved him so much. "You're proposing?"

"I thought it'd be a good idea." His smile grew less confident. "You don't?"

"No. I mean yes, I do think it's a good idea. A wonderful idea." Excitement bubbled in her like someone had popped the cork in a bottle of champagne—an effervescent combination of desire and joy that was instantly intoxicating. The fine vintage made her head spin.. "But you can't give up your horse farm. It's your dream."

"You're wrong. You're my dream. And in time,

My Family Jewels will start a dynasty, and I'll have the breeding farm I want. Plus you...the woman I love."

"Oh, Jack..." Her tears did fall then, and she threw her arms around him, kissing him until she was breathless. He tasted of all she had ever wanted, strength and nobility, a special kind of courage that made him battle bullies when most would have looked the other way. Her heart filled with pride that he had chosen her to be his wife, that he loved her. Finally drawing back, she took a shaky breath and gave him a watery smile. "I love you, too. So much."

"Good." He grinned at her, feathering her face with his fingertips, wiping away her tears of happiness. "You had me worried there for a minute, sweet sugar."

"I thought you only wanted to marry me because I was pregnant, and then when we found out the test was part of a bad batch—"

"I want you to have my children, Lindy. We can start a family now or a year from now. But I want you to be the mother of my children." The way he looked at her, with such depth and intensity, she felt as though he was reaching inside her, caressing her soul to soul. Long ago she'd recognized in him a kindred spirit. Now she knew it was true.

She palmed his dear face, so rugged and masculine, she'd never stop wanting to look at him. Stop loving him. Every day she'd find something new to admire, a facet of his personality that would speak to her heart and make it sing. "Oh, Jack, you're going to be such a good daddy."

"I don't know about that but I'm willing to take parenting classes if you think it will help."

"Didn't you see how Millie adored you? You're great with kids...and with animals." Her forehead tightened. "But I don't think we ought to leave Goodfellow. Our ancestors earned the right to be here. Remember what Luther Hayes said when we were in jail?"

"He was drunk."

"He also said our people came across the mountains with Dan'l Boone." She lifted her chin. "I think that's something our children can be proud of. And we ought not to let anybody run us out of town."

He pulled her close again and she rested her head on his chest, his uniform fabric rough against her cheek.

"What about your business? D'Arcy's going to have a fit if you marry me. She was always the most stuck-up woman in town, putting on airs almost as bad as Ms. Salter."

"Let her have a fit. She can even lease Fluff 'n Cut to somebody else, if that's what she wants. You've got a big back porch at your house and an even bigger horse barn. I can run my business there where I can be close to you and our children. I'm dang good at what I do," she said seriously.

"D'Arcy may not like me marrying you but my customers won't mind. And so what if they do?"

With his fingertip, he tipped her head up. "You sure?"

"Positive." Her dreams had changed, too. Some things were more important than a fancy grooming shop. Like the love of a good man.

"I swear, I'll do everything in my power to make you happy."

"You already have, my love."

He kissed her long and deeply. Nothing else mattered except that he loved her. They'd build their life together right here in Goodfellow. Sooner or later the townspeople would accept them. Between them they carried the *best* bloodlines in the state. Their children would grow up knowing that.

The bell tinkled on the shop door.

Jack and Lindy jumped apart like they'd been goosed.

"Mama?" she said. Her mother rarely came to the shop, and now she was all dressed up like a country bride, her hair dyed a shocking shade resembling the color of table squash.

Her mother shot a look at Jack, her eyes narrowing.

"It's a pleasure to meet you, Mrs. Montgomery." Deftly, Jack plucked a pink rose from the bouquet on the counter and handed it to Lindy's mother. "Now I see where Lindy got her beauty."

Her mother's cheeks colored with a blush that matched the rose.

Dumbfounded, Lindy looked at both Jack and her mother.

"I want you to be the first to know, Mrs. Montgomery, that your daughter has done me the honor of accepting my proposal of marriage."

"She has?" She blinked her heavily mascaraed eyelids.

Steadying herself for whatever objection her mother might raise, Lindy said, "Yes, Mama. We plan to get married as soon as possible."

"Well that's…fine, dear. Perhaps you and your gentleman friend would like to come to Sunday supper. I'll have pot roast."

Something was wrong. Her mother was taking her marriage to Jack way too calmly, as though she had better fish to fry.

"We'd be happy to come, Mrs. Montgomery," Jack said, slick as a greased pig.

"I just may invite a gentleman caller myself," her mother said coyly.

"Who?"

"Well, now, dear, I just came by to tell you Luther Hayes and I are on our way to Lexington to take in a movie. I didn't want you to worry if—"

"You're dating Luther?" Lindy gasped.

"He's an old family friend."

"He's a drunk, Mama!"

"Pshaw! He may indulge a little but what man worth his salt doesn't now and again?"

Lindy rolled her eyes. "Just be sure if he's drinking, you do the driving."

Straightening herself to her full five feet, three inches, her mother said, "I'm not a child, Lindy."

Of course not. But it was hard to imagine her mother *dating* anyone after all these years...and Luther Hayes? It boggled the mind. Then again, Lindy realized with a frown, her mother's name was *Kathleen!* And the Irish ballad Luther had been singing...

Oh, my, who would have guessed?

AFTER HER MOTHER left, Jack reached for Lindy again. "Now where were we?"

"Hang on a minute." Reluctantly she pressed herself away from him. "With all this excitement, I've got to visit the ladies' room."

"Want me to come with you?" he asked with a wicked gleam in his eyes.

"No," she laughed. "But you can lock up the shop. I'll be right back and we can finish what we started at the house."

"I'll be waiting."

Happier than she'd been in what seemed like forever, Lindy headed for the back room and the miniscule rest room there. When she turned on the light, her eye caught sight of the unopened pregnancy test kit she'd gotten from Goodfellow Pharmacy two weeks ago. She'd never taken the test. She hadn't wanted to know the result, which she was sure would be negative. But now...

She read the instructions one more time. It was silly, really, to think about... But they had made love that one time...and they hadn't been exactly careful...there'd been no reason...

JACK PACED THE floor at the front of the shop. How long did it take a woman to go to the bathroom, for God's sake?

He guessed he'd better get used to the idea of waiting for his woman. *His wife!*

Grinning at the idea, he peered outside at the traffic passing by on Second Street. Not much of anything happened in Goodfellow, but it was his hometown. And Lindy's. She was right. They'd do just fine here, and so would their kids. Just because things got a little tough, a Marine didn't retreat.

He turned when he heard her coming back. If he'd had to wait much longer, he would have gone after her.

Her eyes were wide, her cheeks radiant with high color.

"What's wrong?" he asked.

"Nothing. It's just that..." Self-consciously, she grabbed the braid from behind her back and brought it forward in front of her shoulder. "Remember when I took the pregnancy test you brought me?"

"I remember." The results had been a helluva

shocker for Lindy…and for him, too, though the rumor had prepared him.

"And after we heard about the false positives everyone was getting, we figured I wasn't exactly pregnant?"

"Yeah," he said slowly. His forehead tightened. "What are you trying to tell me, sugar?"

"I finally got around to taking the replacement test the pharmacy passed out."

"Just now?"

"Right."

"And?" A nervous flutter turned his stomach inside out, like a part of him knew what the answer was going to be.

She grinned. "I got a pink plus. We're going to have a baby, Jack."

Jack felt the blood drain from his head and his stomach did another terrifying header. "But if you weren't pregnant before, how—"

"I guess when we thought we'd already left the barn door open, we should have closed it—just to be on the safe side." She tugged her lower lip between her teeth, her green eyes filling with concern. "Do you mind?"

Recovering from his momentary shock, Jack swept her into his arms and hugged her tight. His spirits soared. Everything he'd been afraid to hope for, to dream could come true, was going to be his.

"No, sweetheart. I like it this way—you and me and our baby, too. I love you, Lindy. I always will."

As his mouth covered hers and the sweet feel of her body molded against him, Jack realized he'd come home. At last.

PLAY THE
Lucky Key Game
and get

HOW TO PLAY:

1. With a coin, carefully scratch off gold area at the right. Then check the claim chart to see what we have for you — **FREE BOOKS** and a **FREE GIFT** — **ALL YOURS FREE!**

2. Send back this card and you'll receive brand-new Harlequin Duets™ novels. These books have a cover price of $5.99 each in the U.S. and $6.99 each in Canada, but they are yours to keep absolutely free.

3. There's no catch. You're under no obligation to buy anything. We charge nothing — ZERO — for your first shipment. And you don't have to make any minimum number of purchases — not even one!

4. The fact is thousands of readers enjoy receiving books by mail from the Harlequin Reader Service® months before they're available in stores. They like the convenience of home delivery and they love our discount prices!

5. We hope that after receiving your free books you'll want to remain a subscriber. But the choice is yours — to continue or cancel, any time at all! So why not take us up on our invitation, with no risk of any kind. You'll be glad you did!

YOURS FREE!
A SURPRISE MYSTERY GIFT

We can't tell you what it is...but we're sure you'll like it! A
FREE GIFT—
just for playing the LUCKY KEY game!

FREE GIFTS!

NO COST! NO OBLIGATION TO BUY!
NO PURCHASE NECESSARY!

PLAY THE
Lucky Key Game

Scratch gold area with a coin.
Then check below to see the gifts you get!

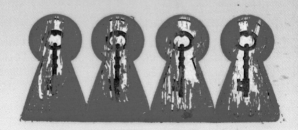

The Harlequin Reader Service® — Here's how it works:

Accepting your 2 free books and gift places you under no obligation to buy anything. You may keep the books and gift and return the shipping statement marked "cancel." If you do not cancel, about a month later we'll send you 2 additional novels and bill you just $5.14 each in the U.S., or $6.14 each in Canada, plus 50¢ delivery per book and applicable taxes if any.* That's the complete price and — compared to cover prices of $5.99 each in the U.S. and $6.99 each in Canada — it's quite a bargain! You may cancel at any time, but if you choose to continue, every month we'll send you 2 more books, which you may either purchase at the discount price or return to us and cancel your subscription.

*Terms and prices subject to change without notice. Sales tax applicable in N.Y. Canadian residents will be charged applicable provincial taxes and GST.

If offer card is missing write to: Harlequin Reader Service, 3010 Walden Ave., P.O. Box 1867, Buffalo NY 14240-1867

BUSINESS REPLY MAIL
FIRST-CLASS MAIL   PERMIT NO. 717   BUFFALO, NY

POSTAGE WILL BE PAID BY ADDRESSEE

HARLEQUIN READER SERVICE
3010 WALDEN AVE
PO BOX 1867
BUFFALO NY 14240-9952

NO POSTAGE
NECESSARY
IF MAILED
IN THE
UNITED STATES

LIZ JARRETT

Darn Near
Perfect

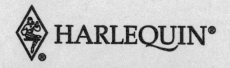

HARLEQUIN®

TORONTO • NEW YORK • LONDON
AMSTERDAM • PARIS • SYDNEY • HAMBURG
STOCKHOLM • ATHENS • TOKYO • MILAN • MADRID
PRAGUE • WARSAW • BUDAPEST • AUCKLAND

Dear Reader,

I just love romantic comedies. What could be better than falling in love and having fun at the same time? Of course, Michael Parker, my hero from *Darn Near Perfect,* sees nothing funny about his situation. He's not exactly the world's most adept volunteer. Boy, can I ever relate. Seems whenever I volunteer, I make more than my fair share of blunders. Still, I keep offering to help, figuring it's the thought that counts. And hey, no one's perfect, right?

Liz Jarrett

To my family, with love and gratitude
for believing in my dream
and
To Malle Vallik, thanks for making my
dream a reality

1

"THE OLD MAN'S LOST his mind."

Michael Parker looked up from his computer screen as his associate, Jeff Caitlin, tossed a memo on his desk, then flopped into a leather chair.

"Calm down." As always, Jeff was acting just like Chicken Little. The sky wasn't falling. Well, at least not yet. Of course, there was a distinct possibility things could turn messy. Calvin Desmond, President of Noress Electronics, did seem to be dancing damn close to the line that separated eccentricity from insanity. This last memo had been a shock to every senior manager at Noress. But Michael knew he would find a way around this problem. He always did.

"I can't believe we don't even get a choice in this," Jeff said. "I mean, how can he force all managers to volunteer at least ten hours a week at a community charity? He can't do that, can he?"

Michael rocked back in his chair, knowing Jeff wouldn't calm down until someone made him. "He just did, didn't he?"

"But it's ridiculous. Especially now. The company's got too many problems to deal with as it is." Jeff lowered his voice and leaned forward in his chair. "What happens if this blows the merger? Then we'll be the ones needing charity."

Michael couldn't argue. In fact, this memo made him wonder if Cal shouldn't retire now. Sure it sounded nice to set an example so the rest of the company's employees would get involved in the community. But in reality, the plan was probably just another one of Cal's attempts to buy his way into heaven.

"It could be a knee-jerk reaction because of his heart attack," Michael said. "Don't worry about it."

Jeff didn't seem reassured. He ran a hand through his thinning hair. "I'm starting to think my last promotion isn't such a great deal after all. All I've done is live at the office the past six months. How will I find the time to volunteer ten hours a week? Carol and the kids claim I'm home so rarely that soon they'll have to ID me at the door."

Michael bit his lip to keep himself from pointing out the obvious—you couldn't swim with sharks if you insisted on surrounding yourself with guppies. Michael had decided long ago he couldn't afford a personal life if he wanted to lead a company as prestigious as Noress Electronics. And if he didn't have time for a personal life, he didn't have time to volunteer.

Oh, he was all for charity and gave often. He knew firsthand what it meant to rely on strangers for help. But giving money was different from giving time. Money he had, time he didn't.

"We can probably give a few donations and that will make Cal happy," Michael said. He already was so buried in work he could hardly breathe. Too much depended on him at the moment. He was negotiating a major merger for the company, and if he pulled it off, Noress would be set for years.

And if he failed.... Ah, but he wouldn't. Failure was not an option. So he wouldn't fail. He wouldn't *allow* himself to fail. And once he pulled off this look-Ma-no-hands major miracle, it would be pretty much guaranteed that he'd be the next president of Noress. Then the years he'd spent dragging himself up through the corporation would have been worth it. At this point, one little memo wasn't about to throw a wrench in his plans.

Michael leaned forward, turning his attention back to his computer screen. "I'll talk to Cal. Don't worry about it."

"But what if you can't change his mind?"

Michael shrugged. "Then I'll find a way to turn this problem into an opportunity."

And he would. Nothing—and no one—was going to stop his climb to the top. Not Calvin Desmond. And certainly not some memo. He'd build a snowman with the devil before he spent ten hours a week playing saint for some charity. It just flat-out would *not* happen.

"SO WHAT ARE YOU going to do with him?"

Casey Richards hunkered under her ancient metal desk, trying to shove a piece of cardboard beneath the short leg. At the words, she rose to her knees and looked over the desktop. Elmira Ross, a dedicated regular at the Portersville Senior Citizen Center, stood in her doorway. Elmira was what the gentlemen called a looker. Even at seventy, she still turned heads with an irresistible combination of a devilish personality and the most unusual azure eyes.

"Do with whom?" Casey asked, refolding the square of cardboard.

"The new guy. Rumor has it we're getting a new man today."

Rumor would be Tommy Gilbert. Or Albert Terford. Or any of the other gentlemen who were infatuated with Elmira.

"The new guy, as you call him, is a volunteer," Casey said.

Elmira grinned, showing dimples that had probably broken more than a few hearts in her lifetime. "Oh, honey, you don't fool me. I know he's a young one. Why do you think I'm so interested? He could be perfect for you."

Casey didn't want to encourage Elmira, but she couldn't prevent herself from smiling. This was what she loved about being the director of the center—the regulars were a great group of people.

But she needed to be clear on this point, so Casey said, "Don't try to matchmake. This man is here to help the center."

The older woman shrugged. "You're part of the center."

"Not a part that needs fixing," Casey stressed.

"Oh, Casey, men are like hats. No woman really needs one, and on certain days, they're more trouble than they're worth. But if you're lucky enough to find the perfect one, then your life will be truly blessed."

Despite herself, Casey chuckled. "I don't want or need a hat. Moreover, Michael Parker is not a hat. He's a hotshot from Noress."

Just thinking about having a corporate exec here made Casey cringe. Sure, the center could use all the volunteers it could get. Heck, she encouraged companies to have their employees volunteer. But the senior vice president of Noress Electronics was the last thing she needed. Especially since she knew he'd been forced to volunteer. The man wouldn't want to be here. Men like him never wanted to be anywhere but at work. He'd probably end up being about as much help as using a thimble to bail out a sinking ship.

"I refuse to believe this man won't liven things up around here," Elmira said. "If he's an executive, then maybe he'll give us some help with financial planning."

As much as Casey would love Mr. Corporate Hatchetman to give the seniors financial advice, he probably would only know how to work with a budget in the billions. Plus, his own finances would be so convoluted with stock options and bonuses and incentives he wouldn't have a clue as to what life on Social Security and meager savings was like.

But she didn't say this to Elmira. Instead, she shrugged. "We can always hope for the best." With a final smile at the older woman, she ducked back under her desk and shoved the cardboard beneath the leg. It still wasn't enough. Groaning, she scooted around until she found a more comfortable position, then set about refolding the cardboard.

When she heard someone lift the phone receiver

and punch in numbers, she hollered, "That better not be a 900 number you're dialing."

"It's not a long-distance call," a man's voice said.

Casey frowned. Although male, the voice definitely belonged to a young man. He wasn't one of the seniors. She squirmed out from underneath her desk, bumping her head at the last second.

"Shoot." Half scooting, half crawling, she managed an undignified exit from under the desk, rocked back on her heels and looked up.

There was no doubt about the identity of the man standing on the other side of her desk. The custom-made suit gave him away. Very *GQ*. And very obsessed. He stood talking on her phone as if this were his office, not hers. She slowly rose to her feet, tried to brush off the dark smear across the front of her T-shirt, then gave up.

The man watched her with open amusement. He had great eyes. An interesting, almost warm, cerulean blue. Those eyes gave him a sincerity that had undoubtedly helped him in corporate takeovers and ruthless downsizings. He'd look across at his prey, and they wouldn't realize their days were numbered. They'd get suckered in by the twinkle in those baby blues, and before they knew what happened, kapow, they'd be history!

Yep, she'd give him this—he was a good-looking corporate shark. Easily over six feet, with midnight-black hair that was brushed back from his tanned face. A striking face with a square jaw and a tiny cleft in his chin.

Bet he pays more for a haircut than I pay for a

week's groceries, Casey thought, studying him while he rattled off numbers like a calculator.

When he simply nodded at her and continued with his conversation, Casey decided enough was enough. She leaned across her small desk and tapped on the phone.

"We only have one line. You need to end this call."

He raised his hand in an obvious signal asking for a few more minutes.

"I need those revised figures on my desk by five tonight, Glenda. I can't wait until morning." He looked at his slim, gold watch. "I'll be through here by four-thirty."

Annoyed, Casey tapped the phone again. "You can't tie up this line," she repeated, her voice louder this time. Okay, cute was one thing, but this big-business jock was about to turn into her worst nightmare. He'd only been here twelve seconds, and he'd already yanked her chain. *Sheesh.*

Sure, she'd admit that a man like Michael Parker could swing a lot of clout with other companies. And sure, he probably could help her rustle up donations. But there was also a really good chance he wouldn't help her at all. He might just spend all of his time on *her* phone doing *his* work if she didn't stop him. And she *would* stop him.

Without asking again, she calmly reached across the desk and depressed the button on her battered black phone. Then she waited for the fireworks.

"What the hell do you—"

She held up one hand, halting his words. "First off, we do not curse in this building. That will cost you a dollar. In the future, I expect you to find a more appropriate way to express yourself.''

''Who in the hell—''

''I mean it. You now owe me two dollars.'' She met his steely gaze with one of her own. Granted, her own five-seven height put her at a disadvantage. But she'd been raised by a corporate shark, so she knew how to stare down the best of them.

''I assume you're Michael Parker.'' She quirked one eyebrow and waited for his answer.

''Yes.'' From his expression, he was grappling with a lot of emotions, not the least of which she guessed was anger. This man needed to be hung up on. In her opinion, it was long overdue.

He motioned toward her phone. ''Look, I realize you've just got the one line, but that's a vital phone call. I'll only be a few minutes.''

A reasonable person would say yes, sure, he could use the phone. But Casey knew if she said yes now, he'd live on the phone, and she'd never get a bit of work done. And she needed to work. Someone had to do something about raising money for the new Senior Citizen Center. The Victorian house on Lake Hoffler was perfect for a new center.

But so far, the city was only willing to allocate two hundred thousand dollars, which would pay for the house, but not the renovations. She had to come up with the rest of the money before the lease ran out on this building in two months. If she couldn't come up with the money for renovations, then the whole project would go down the drain.

So even though refusing Michael Parker today

might seem petty, she needed every spare second she could find to hunt up donors.

"Why don't you just use your cell phone to make your call?" she asked.

He didn't seem surprised she would assume he had a cell phone. "Something's wrong with it." His hand snaked toward her phone. "So, if you'll just give me a couple of minutes."

The man was like a junkie needing a phone fix. She watched his fingers wrap around the receiver. "I'm afraid I can't do that. I need the phone. It's very important I round up donations."

He didn't relax his grip. "Well, my call won't hold you up for long." He lifted the phone a couple of inches. "I'll be off in plenty of time for you to make your own calls."

Casey's Irish temper flared. No way would she lose this fight. "You're here to help, not to use the phone."

He smiled, a smooth, no doubt well-used smile. Oh, it was a good one. Just enough sincerity and little-boy mischief in it to make Casey's pulse kick up a notch. Tiny lines fanned out from his eyes, making him even more attractive.

"I'm not trying to be difficult," he said.

Yeah. Right. And she had some swampland that would look great on a vacation postcard. "But you're succeeding, all the same."

That got him. His smile dimmed just a fraction. She could almost see him reevaluating her. He hadn't expected her to stand up to him.

"How about if I promise that the next time I come, I'll bring my own phone?"

Casey drummed her fingernails on the desk, the staccato pings unusually loud in her tiny office. Frankly, she was torn between wanting to be reasonable and wanting to stand her ground. She had enough goddess-warrior in her to want to win this battle, to be triumphant, to rule the day. A glance around her office brought her back to reality.

"Tell you what…you can use my phone today for exactly ten minutes if you make a donation to help renovate our new building."

Like a light being switched off, Michael's smile faded. "You're charging me to use the phone?"

"Not charging, exactly. Let's just say that during those ten minutes, I might have been lucky enough to find a corporate officer who would be happy to make a sizable donation to the center."

At the word *sizable,* a frown formed on Michael's face. "You can't be serious. Chances are, in those ten minutes, you wouldn't even have gotten beyond the receptionist."

He had a point, but she wasn't about to admit it. Truthfully, she rarely had luck getting help from local corporations. She tried, but usually all she got was a cool *no.* She smiled benignly. No sense telling Mr. Hotshot that.

"Actually, I've made quite a few good contacts in the community over the past couple of months," she said. "I'm sure I can get lots of donations. Now, about using the phone—"

"Ah, hell."

Casey shook her finger. "Mr. Parker, I've warned you about the language. The tally's up to three dollars."

For a split second, the manager mask on his face lifted, and she could see how thoroughly exasperated he was with her. Then the mask dropped back into place.

"Fine. You win. This phone call is dam—darn important, so I'll make a donation. How much?"

How much? Shoot, she hadn't thought that far ahead. She was winging this and hadn't really expected him to agree. She'd thought he'd just storm out.

So, how much? She studied his watch. Thin. Gold. Expensive. "Five hundred dollars."

He visibly blanched. "What? Are you crazy? I'm not giving you a damn cent."

That was it. Casey walked around her desk until she stood directly in front of Michael Parker. Then she straightened her spine to take advantage of what height she did have. Finally, she made eye contact with him.

"That makes it four dollars. And if you curse in this building one more time, I'm going to reject you as a volunteer. It's my understanding your boss, Mr. Desmond, specifically wanted you to work at the Senior Citizen Center. I imagine he'll be unhappy if you get fired your first day on the job."

As she expected, he didn't quail at her words. "I'm not afraid of Cal, so there's no point threatening me. I'm also a volunteer here, so you need me more than I need you."

"Not true. I don't need someone who's more interested in using my phone than in helping the seniors. We've been just hunky-dory without you until now, and we'll do just peachy-keen without you in the future. So, Mr. Parker, what will it be? My phone for five hundred, or shall I call Mr. Desmond and tell him things didn't work out?''

As he stood watching her, she noticed a slight shifting in his features. Some muscles tightened, others loosened. On another man, she'd say his expression was one of admiration. But as far as she could tell, Michael Parker didn't admire her. He viewed her as a small obstacle in his way.

But she knew, long before he reached into the inside pocket of his jacket and withdrew his leather checkbook, she'd won this battle. Inside, her stomach did a quick flip-flop. She'd actually won.

"Five hundred in exchange for using the phone whenever I want during the next two hours," he said, bending down to write the check.

Casey thought for a moment. A reasonable woman would take the check and run. But the little devil inside her wouldn't leave things alone. She opened her mouth before she could consider the wisdom of pushing a brick wall.

"Five hundred and you can use the phone for no more than thirty minutes while you're here today."

He paused, his hand frozen holding the pen above the pale green check. He didn't look at her. Didn't say a thing. Then, slowly, he lowered his hand and wordlessly wrote the check.

Casey felt like she'd won the lottery. When he finished writing, he tore the check out of the book and handed it to her.

"You can make it out to whomever you want. The center. The contractor." He tipped his head and gave her a pointed look. "Or maybe you'd just as soon make it out to yourself."

Casey smiled. "Why, Mr. Parker, we barely know each other, and you've already formed such a sweet opinion of me. I'm thoroughly delighted with all of your character traits, too."

His lips lifted at the corners just a tad. "How does anyone survive around you without cursing?"

"They use their imaginations." She glanced at the check and then held out her hand. "You still owe me four dollars."

As he reached for his wallet, he muttered, "Bass fishing."

Casey chuckled and snatched the four dollars from his hand. "See. I knew you'd find a way to stop cursing." She tucked the check and the dollars in an envelope. "Now, thanks to you, I've made a great start on the renovations fund."

Michael leaned against her desk, but when it wobbled, he straightened. "I'm only praying you're Casey Richards, the director here."

She extended her hand. "Yes. I can't tell you what a pleasure it's been to meet you, Mr. Parker."

He took her hand and shook it firmly. The handshake was swift and professional, but still, a tingle ran up her arm at the contact. Normally, that reaction told her she was attracted to a man. But in Michael Parker's case, she'd assume the tingle was static electricity. She'd never been attracted to a corporate shark in her life, and she wasn't about to start now.

Casey released Michael's hand and stepped back

a half step. "I hope you enjoy working here, Mr. Parker."

He picked up the phone. "Call me Michael. I like to be on a first-name basis with people who take me for that much money."

MICHAEL WATCHED Casey walk out of the office and felt like kicking himself. He'd broken his number-one rule—never underestimate an opponent. Hell, at first he hadn't even realized Casey Richards was an opponent. And who could blame him? When she'd crawled out from under the desk, she'd looked like a pushover. An incredibly sexy pushover, with wavy auburn hair that hung to the middle of her back, and large green eyes in a pretty oval face. Rounding out the tempting package was a gently curved shape in worn jeans. That shape made his mind wander off in dangerous directions.

Yeah, he'd underestimated Casey, all right. He'd figured the director would be some nice quiet woman he could convince to let him do his work while he was here. Not all the time, of course. He'd live up to his side of the deal and help out. But come on, he couldn't spend ten hours a week ignoring the office. He was tracking too many projects to waste a good part of each week playing bingo.

He glanced at his watch, then punched in the phone number of his assistant, Glenda Myers. Thank God she was back at the office keeping things running. He'd give this harebrained scheme one week at the most. Then Cal would see the huge hit to productivity the company was taking, and he'd have to rescind this order.

Michael knew all he had to do was survive a week or two. He'd been through worse—like the Kincaid takeover and last year's layoffs. This charity work would be a piece of cake.

While he waited for Glenda to answer, he glanced out the open office door and watched Casey working in the main room. She hadn't been what he'd expected, granted, but he had to admit he admired her. Not many people stood up to him anymore. He knew how to stare them down, but his best techniques hadn't worked with her. Which surprised him. The woman spent her days working with retirees. He wouldn't expect her to know the first thing about negotiating.

But she had. She'd negotiated him out of five hundred bucks. Although, to be honest, he'd probably have given her the money anyway, just to smooth things out over the next few days. In his experience, charity types loved you to pieces once you gave them a nice fat donation.

He continued with his phone call for quite some time before an odd sensation made him look out into the main room again. Casey caught his gaze. He expected her to smile, but she didn't. Instead, she frowned at him, tapped the chunky watch on her wrist, and then held up five fingers.

He glanced at his own watch, a present last year from Cal for the killer deal he'd worked on the Kincaid job. Damn if the woman wasn't right—he only had five minutes left.

Five hundred dollars sure didn't buy what it used to.

"HE'S A HUNK."

Casey spun around to find Elmira and her best friend, Dottie, directly behind her. The women stood watching Michael Parker through her open office door. Casey followed their gazes. These two ladies might be seniors, but there was nothing wrong with their eyesight or their judgment. Michael Parker certainly qualified as a hunk, but he personified everything Casey disliked in a man.

"He's okay," she admitted, knowing Elmira and Dottie wouldn't swallow a lie. "But if he thinks he's going to spend all of his time on the phone, he's got another think coming."

The two women trailed after her as she moved the chairs out of the way to make room for the birthday celebration due to start in a few minutes.

"My Bernie was that good-looking," Dottie said.

Elmira rolled her eyes. "Dottie, Bernie was barely over five feet tall. He didn't look a thing like that man does."

Rather than being offended, Dottie laughed. "Okay, so Bernie wasn't tall. But he was still great-looking. And he knew a thing or two about romance."

Elmira nudged Casey. "Do you think our hunk over there knows a thing or two about romance?"

Despite herself, Casey looked at Michael and pondered the question. He had the looks to make a woman's heart race. And the self-confidence. The question was whether he ever slowed down long enough to make the experience memorable. Would he linger over each caress? Hover over each kiss?

Her gaze dropped to his mouth, which currently

was in a tight, straight line. He wasn't happy about something. Casey watched his lips as he spoke. What would it feel like to have a man like that whisper seductive words in her ear?

"I think we've sent her into a tailspin," Elmira observed.

Casey blinked and looked at the two women, embarrassed by her daydreams. "I need to get back to work."

Dottie smiled. "Sure you do, dear. Don't let us get in your way."

Casey hurriedly pushed some of the tables together and replaced the chairs. She ignored the quiet conversation Dottie and Elmira held in the corner of the room and instead headed to the kitchen to put candles on the birthday cake. She didn't really need to hear them to know they were still discussing Michael. Dottie and Elmira had a long history of interfering in her love life. Both ladies thought it was beyond time Casey settled down. So far, they'd offered up all of their grandsons and one great-nephew, but to no avail. Casey had a specific type of man in mind, a home-loving man who adored children. The successful grandsons traveled all the time.

And the great-nephew disliked children.

But those failures hadn't slowed Elmira and Dottie down. If anything, the more men Casey rejected, the more the two women seemed determined to find a match. They felt by the advanced age of thirty-one, if Casey didn't marry soon, she'd die alone. And as Elmira liked to point out, the older Casey got, the smaller the fishing pond became.

Casey glanced back at her office. Speaking of fish, or actually sharks, there was a corporate shark who needed to be told a thing or two. No sense putting it off any longer. She had to get back in her office and settle the ground rules. Mr. Michael Parker needed to know straight out who was the boss here. He might be a bigwig at his office, but at the Portersville Senior Citizen Center, he was just one more volunteer to help during the birthday party.

OF ALL THE TIMES to not be able to cuss. Michael ran an agitated hand through his hair while Glenda related the latest disaster. He felt like a smoker stuck on an eighteen-hour flight. If he didn't vent some of his frustration soon, he'd explode.

Out of the corner of his eye, he noticed Casey Richards appear in the doorway. He wasn't halfway through his conversation with Glenda, but he knew better than to push his luck. He'd just have to stay at the office really late tonight to catch up on work.

"Look, Glenda, I've got to go. The warden is here." He glanced over his shoulder at Casey. She wasn't smiling, but she wasn't frowning, either. She met his amused gaze straight on, and then walked into her office and sat behind her desk.

With a couple of final words, he hung up the phone and took the chair across from Casey. The tiny desk put hardly any space between them, and it gave her no psychological advantage at all.

"You need a bigger desk," he observed, putting his day planner back in his briefcase. "Hel—" He froze, ignored her raised eyebrows, and continued, "Heck, you need a bigger office. This whole building, in fact, is way too small for the activities you have planned here."

She leaned forward. "Mr. Parker—"

"I already told you, it's Michael."

"Okay, Michael. I explained I'm in the process of getting a new building for the center. But the size of my office and desk is the least of my concerns. What does concern me is what you intend on doing while you're volunteering here."

Straight to the point. He liked directness in a business associate, and he appreciated it in Casey. He briefly studied her, noting again how attractive she was. Of course, Casey's appearance shouldn't concern him. She wasn't his type. He liked women who were equally intent on their careers. Women who knew how to handle themselves at a business dinner. Certainly not red-haired social-worker types with big green eyes.

"What did you think volunteering at the center would mean?"

He shrugged. "Helping do whatever it is you do, I guess." He shifted forward in his chair. "I suppose you know the purpose of my being here is to encourage other Noress employees to get involved with the community."

"Will these employees be able to volunteer during office hours like you are?"

He was pretty darn sure there was censure behind her words, although nothing in her tone backed up his suspicions. "Of course not. In my case, if I'm not asleep, I'm working. Basically, all of the hours in my day are office hours."

She watched him intently. Something about the

way she studied him told him she didn't like him much. Which was stupid, considering he'd just given the woman five hundred dollars for her new building. But he couldn't shake the feeling she viewed him as a distasteful pile she'd stepped in.

"Look, I certainly can use volunteers, but only if they're sincerely interested in helping. If you're just here to make your boss happy, then—"

"I plan on helping," he interjected. At her dubious expression, he added, "Okay, I'll admit I'd rather not spend a good part of each week here. Still, I'll do my best to help."

"Good," was all she said in a tight little voice that let him know loud and clear that she was still ticked off. Casey should never play poker—he could read her every emotion on her expressive face.

Leaning back in his chair, he considered her. People like Casey Richards baffled him. Why work so hard for something that personally got you nowhere? It didn't make sense.

"So, what can I do to help out while I'm here?" he asked.

"I don't know. What skills do you have?"

The way she asked, in short, clipped syllables, made him think she felt he had no skills. Or at least none that would be of use to her.

"I'm great at managing things."

She arched one eyebrow. "Things?"

"People."

She nodded. "So I gathered." She placed her arms on the wobbly desk in front of her. He looked at her hands. No rings. Short nails. A practical woman.

"This afternoon, please help with the birthday party. We have one for each senior every year. You'll find the decorations on the top shelf of the cabinet in the kitchen."

The idea of helping seniors with a party didn't appeal to him. Truth was, he didn't know what to say to the people here. He'd never known his grandparents, his mother had left when he'd been two, and his father had died years ago. Outside of work, Michael didn't know anyone over the age of fifty. What did you talk about to people who no longer worked?

This idea didn't appeal to him at all. "And after the party?"

"Then you can call some of your executive friends and *manage* them in the direction of their checkbooks. We need some serious donations."

With that, she left her office.

Michael watched her go. Great. Just great. Not only did he get to waste a large part of his week helping out around here, but now he got to hassle all of his associates.

No doubt about it—he had to get out of this place soon.

2

_____

MICHAEL DREW in a deep breath, bit back yet another curse, and blew up the twenty-third big, bright balloon in a pack of twenty-five. Two more after this. Only two more balloons to go and he'd be done. He shot a quick glance across the room at Casey, who was talking to some of the seniors. Of course she'd put him in charge of the party decorations. Especially balloons. She obviously thought he had hot air to spare.

"Your face is almost as red as that balloon."

Michael glanced at the older man who had come to stand next to him. "Yeah, I'm afraid I'm going to collapse a lung," Michael said.

The man chuckled. "I'm the birthday boy, Al Terford." Idly, he pushed some of the balloons across the table. A few tumbled with drunken abandon onto the floor. "Balloons. Now there's an odd touch. What are you going to do with these when you're done?"

Michael froze, some little internal gizmo dinging crazily inside his head. He turned and nailed Al with a direct gaze. "Don't you usually have balloons at these parties?"

Al chuckled again. "Well, no. We're kind of old for balloons. But I appreciate the gesture."

Michael looked at the balloon in his hands, replaying his conversation with Casey through his mind. She'd told him to put out the things for the party, indicated the cabinet where the supplies were stored, and explained he'd find everything he needed inside. And he had. On the top shelf, he'd found cups, plates and napkins.

Then two shelves down...balloons.

Ah, hell. Glancing up, he caught Casey looking his direction. She'd watched him blow up all these balloons and make an idiot of himself in front of the seniors. He should be mad. Furious, in fact.

But he wasn't. Instead, he found himself half admiring her. Okay, the lady was quickly becoming a personal pain in the butt to him. Still, he'd been at the center for what? Less than an hour. And the woman had already bested him. Twice.

The next couple of weeks should prove very interesting.

"You have to watch the women around here," Al pointed out. "They're sharp, so you have to be sharper."

With those words, the older man patted Michael's shoulder then wandered over to the table where Casey was lighting candles on a cake. Well, damn. When he finished knotting the last balloon, he settled back to watch the celebration. All of the seniors were having a great time. Casey was having a great time, too. Michael watched, fascinated, as she kidded around with the group. She really fit in here, but he couldn't help wondering why she wasn't working at a big company, making big bucks.

"Having fun?" Casey asked when she finally wandered over in his direction.

"I enjoyed blowing up all those balloons. Thanks."

Casey laughed. It was a teasing, light sound that ran across his skin like a touch. "Sorry. But I didn't tell you to do it. We used those balloons at our booth at the children's fair last September. I never thought you'd dig them out, but they do add a festive air. Now why don't you stop sulking and come mingle? No one's going to bite you."

"I'm not afraid," Michael said slowly, but the truth was, he'd never been too comfortable around older people. Cal knew that, which was no doubt why he'd been assigned to the Senior Citizen Center. In Cal's mind, it would be a real laugh to put Michael where he'd least fit in.

But rather than explain that to Casey, Michael changed the subject. "So you have birthday parties for everyone, do you?"

"Yes. It's vital to mark the major moments in the lives of those you care about."

Michael sensed there was more to what she was saying, but before he could press her on it, a loud squawking noise silenced the room. Every head turned toward him. Michael groaned and fished his beeper off his belt. Glancing at it, he saw Jeff was paging him. When he looked up at Casey, her frown told him how she felt about the interruption.

"I just need to make one quick call," he said.

Casey smiled at the group. "Nothing serious. Michael's got a hectic job." When the seniors resumed talking, she stepped forward until she stood directly in front of him. Then she said in a whisper, "Make your call. But next time you come here, please come without the beeper."

"Look, I'm not trying to—"

"You should respect the seniors enough to give them your complete attention while you're here. But you corporate jocks just don't get it, do you? You can't let go of your job for even a few moments."

Ouch. Where'd that come from? "I take it you don't like businessmen," he said.

She fixed him with a narrowed gaze. "I believe there's more to life than work."

He'd heard that song before, from a father who couldn't bring himself to show up for a job on a regular basis. But he knew Casey wasn't talking about goofing off to avoid work. No, she was smack-dab in the middle of her own personal anti-business agenda, and he needed to tread carefully here.

He scanned the amused faces assembled around the collection of tables. Everyone in the room was watching him. Now he knew how a butterfly stuck on a pin felt.

When he returned his gaze to Casey, he said, "Sorry." And he was. He didn't mean to give her flak, and he didn't mean to be disrespectful to the seniors. But this was a strange, new world he'd entered and adjusting would take some time.

Casey was silent for several long moments. Finally, she waved toward her office. "Go make your call. And after that, you might as well stay in there and make those calls for donations, too."

Deciding to leave well enough alone, Michael

nodded and headed toward the office. This was hard. He wasn't used to feeling uncertain, but he sure did around Casey and the seniors. His gut instinct told him the next couple of weeks were going to be bumpy.

AN HOUR LATER, Casey was still annoyed. She glanced toward her office repeatedly and watched Michael as he talked on the phone.

Wanting to postpone her talk with him, she headed toward the kitchen to count the hot lunches that had just been delivered. When the number was wrong the first time, she hoped she'd made a mistake. But when she got the same total once more, she was ready to chew out the delivery service. This couldn't have happened again. They were two lunches short.

She ran her hand through her hair. "Shoot."

The county supplied hot lunches to the center each day as long as she told them twenty-four hours ahead of time how many lunches she needed. The last couple of weeks, the number had been off more often than not.

Sheesh. How hard was it to count to twenty-seven? Heck, yesterday she'd deliberately phoned and faxed in the order to avoid any errors. Yet still it was wrong. Didn't the county understand that for many of the seniors, this hot lunch was the main meal of the day? How could they just flub the number?

Her head felt as if little imps were playing bongos on her brain. Idly, she rubbed her temples and looked for a place to sit. Her choices were limited.

The kitchen was ground zero, the worst area in the center. The counters were bowed, the linoleum was frayed, and two of the cabinets no longer opened. Boy, did the center need a new home. A bright, *modern* home with up-to-date facilities.

And a breathtaking view. Okay, so that wasn't absolutely necessary, but once she'd seen the old Victorian on the lake, she couldn't think of moving the center any place else. The seniors could sit and watch the sailboats, enjoy the cool breezes of spring and wander the manicured trails around the lake. Even the city council had agreed it made the perfect location, far better than anything else anyone had found. Except even with the family who owned it cutting the cost, the price was too high. The council would pay the two hundred thousand for the house if she came up with twenty thousand for modifications. Her share might as well have been a million.

Casey moved over to the door and looked across the main room to her office. She couldn't see Michael Parker, but she knew he was there. Working—probably doing his own work rather than making calls for the center. Objectively, he was exactly what she needed. He was a high-profile executive who could pull in large contributions and plenty of volunteers. Someone used to running big projects could come in very handy.

But she hated the fact that she needed him. Images of her father filtered through her mind. The missed birthday parties. The forgotten school plays. The never-ending stream of excuses. Until one day her father just stopped explaining. Or caring.

She glanced again at her office. Did Michael Parker care about anything? Would he help them even if he could?

Or was he like her father, a man who had lost interest a long time ago?

"WHY ARE YOU hiding in here?"

Michael glanced up. Two elderly women stood in the office doorway, giving him what could only be described as the once-over. He straightened in his chair.

"I'm not hiding. I'm raising money for the building." Some long-forgotten tidbit of protocol nudged at his brain and he rose. He never stood when a woman entered a room. If he did, he'd spend most of his days on his feet. Well over half of the employees he dealt with were women. But, admittedly, not women like the two standing just within the doorway. These women weren't associates and were making him feel awkward as hell.

"See, I told you he wasn't hiding." The woman on the left took a couple of steps forward. "I'm Elmira Ross, and this is Dottie Stevenson."

Neither woman made a move to shake his hand, so Michael stuffed his fists in his pockets.

"It's nice to meet you." He shot a glance back at the phone. Since Casey had left him here, he'd managed to scrounge up another four hundred in donations. Unfortunately, the donations had come from his attorney and his accountant, who would probably simply charge him more the next time he used them.

He didn't say anything else, mostly because he had no idea what to say. He didn't want to offend the women because they seemed nice. Still, he couldn't help hoping they would take the hint and leave him alone. Truthfully, they made him jumpy. Funny how he could speak to a convention center filled with employees but was struck mute by two elderly women. How ironic.

But rather than leave, Dottie moved over next to Elmira.

"Why don't you come out and meet some of the folks? Everyone is interested in you," Dottie said.

Michael's gaze darted beyond the women to the main room outside the office. After the party had ended, the tables had been shifted back into place. Now about twenty older people sat in small groups. Some were playing cards. Others were knitting. Everyone seemed busy, and no one seemed the least bit interested in him.

Except the two ladies standing in front of him now.

"I…promised Casey I'd make some phone calls." He reached for the phone, praying the women would finally leave. But they didn't. They stood firmly rooted and continued to study him with open curiosity.

"So, what does your wife think about you working here?"

This question came from Dottie, who immediately received a nudge and a stern look from Elmira.

"You don't have to answer that," Elmira said. "Dottie's nosy."

"Oh, and you're not interested?" Dottie asked her friend. Before Elmira could answer, Dottie turned and smiled at him. "A handsome man like you has to be married."

An unexpected smile tugged at the corner of his mouth. Dottie was buttering him like a Thanksgiving turkey.

"I'm not married." He lifted the receiver, but still, neither woman moved.

"Really? Not married." Elmira exchanged a look with Dottie that Michael didn't even want to begin to interpret. "Casey isn't married, either."

Her comment surprised him so much he had to struggle to keep his jaw from dropping. These women were here to matchmake? They didn't know a thing about him except he wasn't married, and yet they thought that information was sufficient to toss him in Casey's direction. He scanned the main room, looking for the subject of this discussion. He'd bet last year's stock options Casey didn't know these two ladies were in here trying to fix her up.

Suddenly curious about the red-haired director, he replaced the receiver, then leaned against the desk and smiled at the women. This information river flowed two ways. Maybe he could find out what made Casey Richards tick. In his experience, negotiations were easier if you understood your adversary. If he knew what mattered most to Casey, then he'd know what kind of bargain he could strike.

"Casey seems nice," he said, watching the women closely to see what reaction he got. As expected, their faces brightened and they moved forward, eager to share information.

"Casey's a doll," Dottie offered. "Simply a doll." Her smile faded a tiny bit. "But don't get on her bad side. She's no fool, and she doesn't take kindly to people who play games with her."

"That's right. Never mess around with our Casey," Elmira added. "She deserves only the best." Elmira shifted even closer. "Now tell us all about you."

Michael tensed. Good Lord. What had he gotten himself into?

MICHAEL FINALLY finagled his way out of the office and the inquisition Dottie and Elmira were conducting by claiming he'd promised to help Casey. In a way, his excuse was true. Especially since the women had warned him about getting on Casey's bad side. Life had taught him not to make an enemy out of a potential ally. He felt compelled to smooth things over with Casey before he created any more hard feelings.

He found her in the kitchen, stacking covered plates and muttering to herself. Unable to resist, he leaned against the doorjamb and watched her work. Casey Richards might be the thorn in his paw for the next few weeks, but she was also one hell of a sight. Especially her long hair. It cascaded like a waterfall down her back, swaying with her movements. From nowhere, a crazy desire hit him. He wanted to walk over to her, slide his arms around her trim waist, and bury his face in her glorious hair. He could easily see it in his mind. She'd lean back against him, sighing, her breasts rising to meet the palms of his hands. Then she'd turn and—

He must have made a noise because, startled, Casey jumped and turned to face him. "Holy—"

Michael blinked, torn out of his fantasy. "You'd better not be about to curse," he said, smiling at her. She looked flushed and flustered, her left hand resting just below her full breasts. Her eyes widened with surprise at first, but narrowed after she considered his comment.

"I was about to say 'holy cow.'"

He nodded, watching her closely. What was it about this social worker that drove his libido crazy? Normally, he wouldn't give a woman like Casey a second look. She wasn't even remotely his type.

But maybe that was the problem. He'd been working so much he hadn't dated in a while. Rather than having daydreams about this woman, he needed to call one of his regular companions. Jenny was always fun. Or maybe Denise.

Anyone but the redhead in front of him.

"So, did you finish all your calls?" she asked, turning slightly.

She was no less attractive in profile, he decided. The curve of her breasts, the swell of her bottom, were both entrancing. Heaven help him. He needed a date.

"I made a few. I got you another four hundred."

Casey stopped in mid-motion, turned her head, and rewarded him with a tiny smile. Or maybe it wasn't a smile. Her lips lifted a fraction of an inch. But at least it wasn't a frown.

"That's nice. I appreciate it," she said.

He nodded absently as she turned back to her task. The lady didn't like him. Not one bit. And

here he'd taken the plunge and navigated his way across the main room just to speak to her.

He cleared his throat. "It was no problem."

She pushed her hair away from her forehead, then turned to face him, wearing a distracted expression. "I'm sorry. What were you saying?"

"What's wrong with those plates?"

"We're two lunches short," she said. "I don't know how this keeps happening, but it does."

He glanced over his shoulder at the seniors in the main room, then back over at Casey.

"So just have whoever brings these things bring some more."

"They won't come back today," Casey said. "These meals have to be ordered twenty-four hours in advance. I'll have to whip something up. Unfortunately, we don't keep much food here, but whatever I come up with is better than asking two people to forego their hot lunch."

Now she was in his territory. Problem-solving was his life's blood. He grinned, oddly pleased he could help.

"Hold on a second," he said. "What are the rest of the people having?"

She regarded him with open suspicion, but she answered anyway. "Meat loaf, mashed potatoes, green beans and pudding."

"If I can use your phone again, I can solve this."

She moved toward him, her hands on her hips. "How?"

"I'll just call the cafeteria at Noress and tell them to send over some extra lunches."

"And they'll do it?" Casey asked.

"Sure."

"Great. Then do it. And after that, I guess your two hours today are done. Tomorrow, I'd like you to help with some repairs around the center." She hesitated a moment, then said, "Thanks."

With that, she brushed by him and headed out of the kitchen. But Michael had caught her expression before she'd walked away. She was surprised by his offer. Apparently, she hadn't expected him to help.

Feeling inordinately pleased with himself, Michael headed across the room to use Casey's phone. The woman mystified him. No doubt about it, she liked to be a helper. She probably wanted to have her hands in making the world better. Most people just wrote a check, but not her.

Was that why she was here? It had to be, because without even trying, she could be a big success working for a company like Noress. She projected a great image, managed resources well, and obviously knew how to hold her own in an argument.

Something she'd said finally hit him. Tomorrow she wanted him to do repairs around the center. Him? Repairs? Oh, no.

He glanced around but didn't see Casey. Well, he didn't have time to discuss this with her right now, but tomorrow he'd set her straight. There was no way he could do repairs. He was mechanically challenged. Hopelessly inept at things like that.

No way was he doing repairs.

No way.

IF TODAY WASN'T the worst day of her life, it ranked right up there in the top five. Sure, there had been

prom night when she'd turned out to be allergic to her corsage and spent most of the night with her nose running like Niagara Falls. And yeah, she had spoken at a city council meeting and found out later her slip was showing. But today was still pretty bad. Her feet ached, her head hurt, and she wanted Michael out of her life.

Groaning, she trudged up the stairs to her small apartment, her groceries in imminent danger of tumbling out of the over-stuffed bag. With effort, she shoved open the door to her apartment and headed to the kitchen. No two ways about it, Michael Parker stumped her. How could he live the way he did, always chasing promotions and raises? How could he feel fulfilled by just a job, especially one that didn't help people?

Her father used to say the best way to help other people was to help yourself. But Casey didn't buy his theory. She couldn't stand the thought of not working directly on a cause she believed in. The seniors at the center made her feel wanted and welcomed, and she knew she made a difference. Each time she improved the program, she had a positive effect. And as far as she was concerned, that was all that mattered in life.

The cross-stitched adage hanging in her mother's living room read: When I Go, I'm Taking My Memories with Me. That was what Casey wanted—memories, lots of them, of smiles and laughs, hugs and kisses.

After she put the last can of chicken noodle soup away, she tucked her canvas shopping bag in the cabinet and sat at the oak kitchen table.

How in the world could she come up with twenty thousand in just a few weeks? She'd have a better chance flying by flapping her arms. Still, she had to find a way. The seniors were depending on her.

Like a flash from a camera, an idea flared in her mind. Of course. A fund-raiser. It was the only way, especially since she was down to just twenty-six days to raise the money. Sure, putting together an activity that big in such a short time would take something close to a miracle, but what choice did she have?

The center could invite the citizens of Portersville, and the seniors could decide what sort of fund-raiser it should be. Then she'd move heaven and earth to make sure it happened.

She smiled. Now this was something Michael could really help with. Working at a major corporation had to have taught him how to pull together a huge project. He could also invite all of his business associates. And maybe the Noress employees. Heck, he could probably stock the fund-raiser with just the people he knew.

Suddenly, Casey felt very satisfied with herself. Her father had always maintained she didn't have a businesswoman's mind. Boy, was he ever wrong. She was about to prove she could multitask with the best of them.

"CAL, I NEED to talk to you." Michael moved farther into the President's office, carefully stepping over some errant golf balls. As usual since his heart attack, Cal was practicing his putting at ten o'clock in the morning. The older man called it his mid-

morning break, but personally, Michael called it a waste of time. He didn't need to take a fifteen-minute break every couple of hours. His mind stayed sharp no matter how long he worked.

Cal Desmond putted and then hooted when the ball went into an overturned plastic cup. "Damn, but I'm good. You need to take up golf, Michael. It clears the mind. Helps you sort things out."

Michael frowned and refrained from pointing out to his boss that he wasn't exactly playing at Pebble Beach. "No thanks. My mind is clear enough."

"Suit yourself. But if you want to take care of a company as big as Noress, you first have to take care of yourself."

Michael dropped into one of the leather chairs. "I work out, which keeps me healthy."

Cal raised one white eyebrow and gave Michael a pointed look. "Healthy in body, but not in soul."

The older man leaned against his golf club and studied his shot. Even though he was almost sixty-five, Cal bore little resemblance to an elderly man. His white hair was still thick. He stood almost six feet tall without a trace of a stoop, and could keep up with the best of them. Well, at least he had until his heart attack two months ago. But even that hadn't slowed him down for long. He'd been back at work in a couple of weeks.

Except now he wanted to save the world. Which was damn annoying and playing havoc with Michael's life.

"I think my soul's in good shape, too." Michael impatiently watched Cal make two more putts, both landing directly in the cup.

"I'm amazing," Cal said, smiling. He placed the putter against his desk and returned to the large leather chair behind it. "What can I do for you?"

"Cal, this volunteer work is impossible." Michael leaned forward, anxious to impress the seriousness of this situation on his boss. "Your managers all put in two hours yesterday at the charities, and Noress went crazy. Jeff and I were both here until after midnight. We can't afford to miss so much time from work."

When he finished speaking, Michael leaned back. Tension ran through his blood like a toxin. He desperately wanted to change Cal's mind. Seldom had he believed in something so strongly as he did in this. Cal was wrong. Pure and simple. Sure, in a perfect world, everyone would have time to volunteer for worthy causes. And he had to admit, what he'd seen yesterday had shown him the Senior Citizen Center was a worthy cause.

But the senior executives of Noress were the wrong ones to be helping out. They needed to be at their desks, doing their jobs, building a stronger company. Stronger companies made a stronger country, which helped everyone.

Just looking at Cal, though, didn't give Michael much hope. The older man's face had a resigned look to it.

"Michael, I know this seems like a lot to ask, but in the long run, helping others always helps oneself."

And a bird in the hand makes a mess on your palm.

"In this competitive market, Noress needs to

maximize its resources," Michael argued. "We need all of our employees working to their full potentials at all times."

Cal slowly shook his head. "Studies have shown companies with strong ties to their communities do better."

The tension in Michael grew to epic proportions. How could Cal, an incredibly intelligent man, not see he could ruin a great company? Michael ran through possible arguments in his mind, studying the older man closely. There had to be a way to make him see reason.

"Why don't we just make some sizable donations to the charities? I think cash would help them more. For instance, the Senior Citizen Center you assigned me to needs money for a new building. I can guarantee you the director would prefer you give her a big, fat check rather than send me down there every day. I'm in her way," he added. "She doesn't like it."

A wide grin graced Cal's face and did nothing to settle Michael's nerves. "Glad to hear you're fitting in so well," Cal said with a laugh. "When they gave me the list of local charities needing help, I knew the seniors' group was the right place for you."

A niggling suspicion ran up Michael's spine. "And why was that, Cal?"

Cal scratched the side of his neck and avoided Michael's gaze. "Oh, this and that."

Michael silently counted to ten. Then to twenty. Then gave up. One look at the self-satisfied face of his boss told him he was wasting his time. And time was a short commodity in his life these days.

"Are you going to reconsider this?" Michael asked, already knowing the answer.

"I'll make you a deal." Cal rose and picked up his putter. "I won't always expect everyone to donate ten hours a week, but I want my executive team to do it for at least a couple of months. At the end of that time, we'll talk."

For the first time since the memo had reached his desk, Michael saw a glimmer of hope. He stood and tucked his hands in his pockets. "Great."

Cal toed a golf ball into place, studied it for a second, then tipped his head and looked at Michael. "If that place needs money, I expect you to help them raise it."

"Why don't we just—"

"Raise it, Michael. Don't give it to them. People need your time more than they need your money." Cal's stern gaze didn't waver. No matter what his age, his faculties were in excellent shape. "Keep that in mind, son. Keep that in mind."

3

MICHAEL STUDIED the wooden shelf in his hand, then eyed the wall in front of him. How hard could it be to hang one tiny shelf? He could do this. Hanging a shelf wasn't like making repairs. Not really. After all, driving a couple of nails into the wall wasn't like performing brain surgery. He could do this. No sweat.

Just like he could pull off this volunteer gig for a few weeks. Sure, it would be difficult, but like they said at Noress: If You Can't Fix It, Feature It. That was his life philosophy. When faced with a negative situation he flat-out couldn't change, he found a way to turn it into a positive. The center was just such a situation, and he'd find a way to turn this negative to a positive.

Rummaging through the toolbox Casey had left him, he picked out a couple of nails. This would have been easier if Casey were here. But she was out picking up supplies and had left him a note asking him to work on the shelf. Still, he could do this, so he chose a spot and drove in the first nail. With only a tap, it flattened against the plasterboard.

"You need a molly."

Michael turned to find Al Terford standing behind him.

"Excuse me?"

Al chuckled and moved forward. "That nail won't hold squat if you don't anchor it. You need a molly."

"Who's Molly?"

"It's a piece of hardware, not a woman." Al chuckled again and dug around in the toolbox. "There aren't any in here. Tell you what, you pull that nail out of the wall while I go look in the supply cabinet and see if we have some mollies lying around."

Michael sighed. Of course he needed a molly. There was a good chance he could use a lobotomy, too, if they had one in the supply cabinet. Michael turned the hammer around. Maybe this wasn't as easy as he'd first thought. Well, he'd just pull the nail out of the wall, then ask Al to help him with the shelf. He had an M.B.A., for God's sake. What did he know about hanging a shelf?

The bottom line was, he should be at the office, not here playing Randy the Repairman for some Irish beauty. He pushed down the stress brewing inside him and forced himself to turn his thoughts back to the positive. There had to be an upside to being at the center.

An image of Casey automatically flashed into his mind like an unwanted response to an inkblot test. He grinned and dismissed the thought. Whatever Casey Richards was, she wasn't a positive in this equation. She was a distraction, a highly attractive distraction.

However, Cal's appreciation of his work for the center was a positive. If Michael made Cal happy, the older man would probably pick him as his replacement when he retired. Granted, Michael would have to work his butt off over the next couple of months to keep up with things at the office while still managing to make a significant contribution at the center. But he could do it. He didn't believe in half efforts. He'd seen his old man give up too many times to ever let that type of failure touch him.

With effort, he tried to push aside the errant, long-buried image of his father. Michael never thought about Burt Parker. Never. But that was what Casey and this place did to him. They made him think all sorts of crazy thoughts. Thoughts about his job. About his life.

About his father. It didn't take a psychologist to figure it out. Casey was disappointed in him, something that hadn't happened to him in years. Hadn't happened since the last time he'd spoken to his father.

Damn, if only Burt Parker could see him now. Here he was, Senior VP at Noress trying to hang a dumb shelf. His father had told him time and again to blow off college and take up a trade. That way, he could just work when the spirit struck him. But unlike his old man, Michael didn't mind hard work.

And he hadn't failed at anything since he'd left his father's apartment when he'd turned eighteen. No way was he about to start now. One way or the other, he would make this volunteer stint work. He wasn't going down in flames, no matter how hot it might feel at the moment.

"Hold on, Casey Richards," he muttered. "I'm

going to make some real changes around this place."

Using the claw part of the hammer, he tried to get the nail out of the wall. It took a couple of attempts, but eventually, he grabbed the nail and pulled. Hard.

A hole the size of his head appeared.

Damn.

CASEY LOOKED at the hole in the wall, then glanced at Michael. He gave her what could only be called a sheepish grin.

"Sorry about that. But I'm not really good at repairs."

"So I see," she said, not sure whether to laugh or cry.

"A dab of wood dough will fix that," Al offered.

"Are you kidding? My dog could fit through that hole."

Casey recognized the last speaker as Dottie. She bit back her own amazement at the mess Michael had made and turned to face the group.

"It's not so bad," she made herself say. "We'll get it fixed."

Before a huge discussion could break out, Casey headed to her office. She should have realized Michael wasn't the repair type. But hey? How hard was it to hang one simple shelf? *Sheesh.*

"I really do feel badly about the hole," Michael said. He'd followed her to her office. Now he came inside and shut the door. "I'll pay for the repairs."

Casey shook her head. "Don't worry about it. I can probably fix it. I'm good at fixing things."

He dropped into the chair facing her desk. "Well, apparently I have a real affinity for breaking things."

"So I'm noticing." She sat in her own chair and studied him. She still couldn't get used to how handsome Michael was. He was far too handsome for her own good. And the little bit of embarrassment still clinging to him only made him look cuter. Which was dangerous. Very dangerous.

Shifting her thoughts away from that Pandora's box, she forced herself to focus on the problem at hand. "I thought things over last night, and I've decided we're going about this all wrong."

"Going about what?" he asked absently, flicking plaster off his designer slacks.

"The donations. We need a lot of money quickly. To do that, we need to schedule some sort of major fund-raiser."

Michael looked at her and frowned. "That sounds like a huge effort. What about the money I raised for you yesterday?"

"It's great. Don't get me wrong. But unless you go on a swearing streak and end up giving me several thousand, we won't have enough." She waited, hoping he'd rise to the idea. Instead, he only frowned more.

"Do you have any experience with fund-raisers?" he asked.

She refused to let him dampen her enthusiasm. "No. But I'm a quick learner, and I'm sure the seniors have a lot of ideas." She smiled. "Plus, rumor has it you're good at managing things."

He finally returned her smile. "*Some* people don't consider that a positive."

Michael was teasing her, and she had to admit, he was appealing like this, relaxed and joking. "On further consideration, *some* people have decided your talent can be very helpful."

"So, what's in it for you if you raise this money?" he asked. "Will you get promoted?"

Scratch that appealing thought. The shark had sprung a giant dorsal fin. "It's not like that. Forget I brought the idea up. I should have known you wouldn't understand."

"Ah, hell, Casey—"

She glared at him. "One dollar."

He chuckled. "Okay. Maybe I'll learn. Eventually."

She didn't share his humor. "I'm starting to have my doubts."

"Look, Casey, I didn't mean that the way it sounded. I just think a fund-raiser sounds like a lot of extra work for you, especially if you aren't going to get anything out of it."

She leaned forward, placing her arms on the battered desk. "Not everything in the world revolves around the bottom line."

"Sure it does. Everyone wants something. It's human nature."

Disappointment washed through her at his statement. But what had she expected? Once a shark, always a shark.

Slowly, she studied him, taking her time. Michael never looked away. She knew she'd surprised him again. No doubt very few people could maintain eye contact with Michael Parker for long. But Casey never flinched. And after half a minute, she felt something new enter the equation. Something potent.

Something sexual.

The sensation settled around them, dancing across the room, making her skin tingle. Stunned, she blinked and broke eye contact. But the feeling didn't dissipate as expected. Instead, it became more noticeable. The air in the room felt thick, heavy with awareness. Loaded with anticipation.

She glanced back at Michael. It was obvious he felt it, too. He sat board straight in his chair, a half chagrined, half amazed look on his face.

They both spoke at the same time.

"Um, I guess—"

"Casey, why don't—"

They stopped talking and stared at each other. Sure, from time to time she'd meet a man who interested her. In those cases, if he was nice, she'd go out with him. But if he was in any way the wrong type, she'd just dismiss the feeling and that was that. No two ways about it, Michael was the wrong type with a capital *W*.

Unfortunately, she knew it wouldn't be that easy to ignore Michael. He was too intense. Too compelling.

Too sexy.

Shoot. As if her life weren't already complicated enough, now why'd this have to happen?

MICHAEL SAT staring at Casey, wondering what in the world had gone on here. One minute he'd been arguing with her, then the next thing he'd known, everything had changed. Of all the times to act like a teenager. He needed to get a grip on himself before he lost it completely.

After a few tense moments, he said, "You were telling me about the fund-raiser."

Casey fiddled with a red pencil on her desk. "Right. The fund-raiser. I haven't come up with any ideas yet, but I'm sure the seniors can think of something."

"You're going to ask the people here what they think you should do? That'll take a lot of time."

The soft, hazy look on her face evaporated like mist under a hot sun. Damn. He'd ticked her off again.

"The fund-raiser is for their new facility. Of course I'm asking them what they'd like to do." She leaned back in her chair. "I'm still not sure this is the right place for you. You seem so reluctant to get involved with the people. Yesterday, you hardly stepped out of the office at all."

Hey, he didn't deserve that. Okay, so he hadn't mingled. He wasn't a mingler by nature. But he'd been involved. He'd raised money. And he'd talked to Al. And to those two women, Dottie and Elmira. He hadn't hidden.

"I stepped out when I arranged for the extra lunches to be brought over," he pointed out, then felt more than a little childish for doing so.

The glimmer in her eyes faded a tad. "Right. Thanks."

He'd seldom heard "thank you" said with less sincerity. Hard to imagine that just moments ago, the air in here had crackled with sexual tension. Right now, Casey Richards looked as if she wanted to toss him out on his butt and lock the door behind him.

Which would suit him just fine.

"So, see, I mingled," he said. At her dubious look he added, "Okay. Maybe not a lot. I'll do better."

He could practically see the gears in her head turning. He knew she wanted to get rid of him. But since she hadn't yet, he was willing to bet she didn't have any more choice in his being here than he did. She depended on volunteer organizations for personnel and finances. Chances were she couldn't just pick and choose who she wanted.

Just like he couldn't walk away unless he wanted to risk his promotion. Whatever other differences separated them, maybe they were tied together in some sort of crazy way.

Lord, he hoped not. Working here felt like being in a maze. Every time he turned a corner, he thought he'd found the way out of this problem. Then he realized he'd simply run into another dead end.

A couple of months. Cal had said this crazy scheme could be renegotiated after a couple of months. Forty workdays at the most. Two hours a day. He could do that. Hell, he'd already made it through yesterday.

He only had thirty-nine days left. A new thought hit him.

"When do you need this money for the modifications?" Maybe, just maybe, luck would be with him, and she wouldn't hold this fund-raiser for a few months. He'd be long gone by then.

"I've only got twenty-six days left if we want to get the house. The owners were willing to hold it for us for a month. If we can't work out the finances, it will go on the market. Someone will snap it up in a second."

"How much money do you need?"

When she paused, he knew he wasn't going to like her answer. "Twenty thousand dollars."

Michael pushed out of his chair. "You're kidding, right? No way can you pull off a fund-raiser that big in such a short amount of time. Why didn't you start raising this money sooner? Casey, dammit—"

Casey looked furious. He knew he wasn't helping things, but instinct told him he was better off if Casey Richards kept disliking him. When she silently held out her hand, he groaned.

"I know. One dollar," he said. Before she could say anything, he pulled his wallet out of his inside jacket pocket, withdrew a five dollar bill, and placed it in her hand. "I'm sure I'll owe you more than that before the afternoon is over."

She rose. "No, you won't. I told you yesterday to stop cursing here." Placing both hands on her desk, she ignored the slight wobble and stared at him.

"If it's any of your business, I didn't know I needed this money until two days ago," she continued. "The city originally told me they would cover all the costs. But then they reexamined the budget and found out they didn't have enough money. One of the councilmen called me at five o'clock the day before last. You showed up yesterday. So as you can see, I started working the problem as soon as I could.''

He hated to rock her boat, but as far as he could tell, it was already sinking, so what the hell. ''No way can you put together a major event in a few weeks. There are too many details to take care of.''

''I will make this happen.'' She spoke slowly, clearly. Although the volume of her voice never changed, the impact of her words did. He didn't doubt for a moment that she believed what she said. ''And I'll do it without your help.''

''Fine.''

''Good.'' She nodded her head in the direction of the door. ''Since I'm going to be busy making plans, you can't work in my office today. Please go join the seniors. Several of the groups are playing pinochle. You can play, too.''

Pinochle? He swallowed past the tense knot in his throat. ''I don't know how to play.''

''They can teach you.''

Then, she smiled. Well, sort of smiled. Her lips pulled back, and he could see her teeth. But then again, you could see a mad dog's teeth right before he attacked. Michael shifted, uncertain how to act in this situation. Hell, it had been years since anyone had shoved him around like this. And even then, he'd only put up with it because he wanted to get ahead. Like he wanted to get ahead now.

''Pinochle isn't really my style,'' he said.

Her fake smile didn't waver, but he could read anger in her eyes. He was fairly certain she didn't like him. Which was a damn shame because he had to admit, he liked her a lot. Maybe too much. She had grit, even if she had chosen to waste her time working at a dead-end job. Casey also surprised him. Her personality didn't suit her soft, somewhat romantic looks.

He watched, fascinated, as she leaned forward and said, "Then change your style."

CASEY WATCHED Michael leave her office, wishing a giant anvil would land on his head. She should have expected him to balk at helping. In a way, she didn't blame him. They really didn't stand much chance of raising the money in such a short time. But she didn't want to admit that, even to herself. As long as even a few hours remained, she had to try.

Sighing, she leaned back in her chair, ignoring the woeful creak the worn metal made. Okay, so if she was going to do this, she needed to get moving. This afternoon, she could poll the seniors for ideas. She glanced at her calendar. The fund-raiser would have to be the last Saturday of the month. That gave her twenty-four days.

She knew it was a long shot, but then again so many things in life were. Even her father—who would hate what she did for a living—would admire her for trying to pull off the impossible. He'd always been involved in some crisis or other. Once or twice, he'd even slept at the office so he could be on hand to pull off a miracle.

He'd always said that nothing got the adrenaline pumping like accomplishing the impossible. And that's what she would do. She'd reach down inside herself, find a little magic, and get everything she wanted. All of it.

"You're either an incredible optimist or an incredible fool," she muttered to herself. She rose and headed toward the main room to survey the seniors for fund-raiser ideas. What was that saying? The only difference between a visionary and a madman was his advertising campaign.

She'd just have to make certain she had a terrific campaign.

"MIND IF I join you?" Michael asked Al and another man who were seated at the table farthest from Casey's office. The pair looked engrossed, so he figured he could sit for a while without them bothering him. Then in a half hour or so, he could go back and talk to Casey again. Maybe apologize.

Al looked up from his cards. "Have a seat."

Michael introduced himself to the other man, who shook his hand with a surprisingly firm grip.

"I'm Tommy Gilbert," the man said. "Nice hole you put in the wall."

Michael nodded. "Yeah. I try my best."

Both older men turned their attention back to their cards, and Michael pulled up a chair. For several minutes, he just sat quietly. Then he noticed Casey come into the room. He watched her move from person to person, speaking to each one. Her smile now was natural, making her even prettier than usual.

"She's a heck of a lady."

Michael turned and met the amused gaze of Tommy Gilbert.

"Yes. She is."

Tommy's brown eyes twinkled. "Not bad looking, either. If I were thirty years younger, I'd—"

"Still be too old for her," Al interjected. He chuckled for a moment at his own joke, then added, "Besides, even if you were her age, she wouldn't go out with you." He tipped his head down and looked at Michael over the top of his glasses. "She hasn't agreed to go out with *you*, has she?"

The question caught Michael off-guard. "I haven't asked her out," he said.

Tommy snorted. "Coward. Don't you know that you can't be shy around women? You need to ask 'em out before some other guy comes along and gets them first."

"Like you know anything about women," Al said. "You can't get Elmira to go out with you."

"Well, you haven't had any luck, either. And you've asked her a lot more than I have."

Michael relaxed a little, thinking that maybe the men had forgotten him. But before long, the pair exhausted their critique of each other's style and turned to study him.

"You do like women, don't you?"

Michael blinked. "Yes."

Tommy wagged a finger at him. "Then you need to get moving. I don't know how Casey's slipped by this long, but I'm sure sooner or later some lucky fella will come along and nab her. She'll make a great wife."

Al made a snorting noise again. "Women aren't

like that anymore. Don't you watch *Oprah?* Women have careers. They don't need to marry anymore.''

Tommy leaned forward. "I didn't say she needed to get married. But a lady like Casey will fall in love. Then she'll want to get married.''

"He'd better be special, because she sure is," Al said.

Michael nodded absently and glanced back at Casey. The men were right—she was special. But too soft. Too involved. She was a broken heart waiting to happen.

Or maybe it had happened already. Maybe that was why she wasn't married. Or maybe she just spent too much time worrying about this place. He still couldn't believe she expected to raise all that money in under a month. She could never do it.

But he admired her like hell for trying.

"So, you want to play?" Al asked, indicating the cards in his hand.

"No. I don't play pinochle."

Tommy and Al laughed. "Well, that's not exactly what we're playing."

Michael pulled his gaze away from Casey and looked at the men. "No?"

"No. It's just a friendly game of poker," Al said.

Michael was prepared to say *yes* when the door opened and Drew Charlin, the mayor of Portersville, walked in. Michael knew the man well, had attended many functions with him. Tall, with blond hair and a polished manner, Drew was a natural politician.

Drew Charlin didn't notice Michael when he flashed a smile at the crowd. He stopped next to

Casey and bent over to say something to her. The
sight annoyed Michael, so he forced himself to look
away. What did he care if Casey was friends with
the mayor? Hell, they probably dated. It was none
of his business.

Still, he had to exert a lot of self-control when
he glanced back and saw Casey rise and lead the
way to her office. When Drew shut the door behind
them, Michael muttered a curse.

"I'll second that," Tommy said, tossing a dollar
bill on the table. "Can't stand the man. He's not
right for her."

Michael couldn't stop himself from asking, "Do
they date?"

"Not as far as I know, but he's always coming
here and asking her out." Al carefully removed one
dollar from his wallet and then proudly denounced
Drew Charlin's parentage. "A man ought to know
when to leave a woman alone."

Michael refrained from pointing out that both
Tommy and Al had asked Elmira out several times.
Instead, he nodded. The thought of Casey with
Drew bothered him way too much to be good for
his own well-being.

"WHAT DO YOU MEAN, the city council may with-
draw the funding for the new center?" Casey asked,
pacing her small office. "You've committed that
money to us."

Drew shrugged his elegantly clad shoulders. "I
know, but some of the council feel the money could
be better spent elsewhere. Believe me, I'm trying
everything I can to put in a good word for you,

Casey. But let's face it—no one believes you can raise the money for the modifications. And if you fail, then the center might as well renew the lease here.''

"But this building is falling apart and it's too small."

"I'm sorry. The city just doesn't have enough money. If you can't come up with your share, then there's nothing I can do to help you."

Casey sucked in a tight breath. There was no sense arguing with Drew. If the city had the money, she knew he would help her. But the money didn't exist. Unless she raised it.

"Drew, tell the council to wait until the end of the month. I *will* have the money. I promise you."

Drew rose and smoothed his jacket into place. "You need to face facts—you can't do this. You're just one person. You can't raise all that money without any help. And as much as I'd like to help, at the moment—"

"I have help."

His look was dubious. "What help?"

"The seniors."

"I don't think so," Drew said, standing and laughing softly. When she frowned at him, he choked back the sound. "Sorry. Anyway, I wish you luck. But I did have another reason for stopping by. I also was wondering if you'd go to dinner with me on Friday." He opened the office door.

She'd rather dip herself in honey and sit on anthill, but the council wavering wasn't Drew's fault. He was nice enough, but he didn't get her pulse racing. "I can't."

Without meaning to, she glanced out her office and studied a group playing cards at a corner table, her gaze landing on Michael Parker. When she felt her heart rate increase, she silently groaned. Now why couldn't Drew have that same effect on her? Why did she have to be attracted to a shark?

Sheesh. She was a sad and sorry case.

THOROUGHLY EXHAUSTED by the time he left his office at eight, Michael unlocked his Mercedes and opened the door. He couldn't believe he still had to play a couple of games of racquetball with a potential client tonight. By the time they finished, he'd be too tired to move.

No way could he keep this pace up. He couldn't spend a large part of each day at the center, then work a full day at the office. And today, all he'd done at the center—well, besides make the hole in the wall—was play cards. After Drew left, Casey had remained shut up in her office. She'd invited several of the seniors in to talk to her, but she hadn't invited him. He'd left without saying another word to her.

Fine. Let her ignore him. Life would be a lot simpler if he could get Casey out of his life and out of his mind. Several times this afternoon, he'd found himself thinking about her while in a meeting. The extra demand on his time was turning him loony.

Shrugging off his jacket, he went to set it on the passenger's seat. Oddly, it felt lighter than usual. He patted the pockets, searching for his cell phone, and came up empty-handed.

"Ah, hell," he said when he remembered he'd left it at the center. He'd had his jacket off all afternoon and hadn't noticed it missing. Slipping behind the wheel of his car, he considered his options. The smart thing to do was to forget the phone and head on to the gym. The center would be closed by now.

But he wanted his phone. Crazy as it seemed, he felt naked without it. One of his girlfriends had once said he was a control freak and would probably surrender his favorite part of his anatomy before he'd give up his cell phone. She hadn't been too far off. He didn't like being out of the loop. With his phone, he could stay on top of the million fires he had to deal with on a daily basis.

Plus, these days, he sure as hell used his phone more than he used that body part.

Funny how he hadn't noticed the phone missing before now. But that was what the center did to him. What Casey did to him. She drove him nuts. He never forgot things. He kept a running list of important tasks in his head at all times. And he'd never forgotten his phone.

Until Casey had thrown him into a tailspin. Without stopping to analyze his motives, he turned right out of the Noress parking lot and headed back toward town. Even if it was a long shot, he wanted to try to get his phone. Maybe then, he could get some control back in his life.

When he pulled up in front of the center, the outside lights were on, but it looked fairly dark inside. Michael glanced around. A compact car sat in the far corner of the parking lot, but it could have been left overnight.

Michael walked to the front door and knocked, not really expecting an answer. But seconds later, the door flew open, and Casey stood on the other side. Except she didn't look like the Casey he knew. Her hair was a mess, she had smears of dirt on her face, and the front of her T-shirt was wet.

"What the hell happened to you?" Michael asked. Before she could answer, he moved past her.

Casey shut and locked the door behind him. "Look, I don't know why you're here, but I'm busy. So when you finish cursing, leave the money on my desk."

She turned and headed in the direction of the kitchen, with Michael right on her heels.

"Seriously, what's wrong?"

Casey entered the kitchen and then moved aside so he could see.

"The pipe under the sink broke tonight. Thank goodness I was here to turn off the water. As you can see, it made quite a mess."

Michael scanned the situation. "A mess" was an understatement. Water was everywhere.

"Have you called a plumber?"

Casey tipped her head and regarded him through narrowed eyes. "Yes. He'll stop by tomorrow to fix the pipe." She knelt and mopped up water with a sponge. "Why are you here?"

"I forgot my cell phone," he muttered.

"It's in the top drawer of my desk. I found it this afternoon."

He nodded absently. "Can't this wait until tomorrow?"

Casey shook her head. She'd pulled her hair into a ponytail, no doubt to keep it from dragging in the water. "No. I need to mop this water up tonight before it damages the floor."

He glanced toward the door. He really had to go meet that potential client. But an unnerving thought hit him—only a lazy bum like his dad would leave Casey stranded with this mess. His decision made, Michael headed out the door. When he reached his car, he got his workout clothes from the trunk. If he was going to spend the next couple of hours crawling on the floor, he wasn't going to do it in an Armani suit.

4

CASEY WATCHED MICHAEL walk away. Figured. Of course he'd leave her with this mess. He'd probably grab his expensive phone and hightail it home. A hotshot executive like him wouldn't think twice about deserting her.

Exasperated, she continued to sop up water, twisting the sponge roughly over the bucket. After another few minutes passed, she'd still barely made a dent. At this rate, she'd be here most of the night.

She heard the front door open again, and footsteps. For a second she thought Michael might have come back to help her. Instead, he walked in the opposite direction toward her office and the rest rooms. Peachy-keen great. Thank goodness she'd been here tonight so he could get his phone back and use the bathroom.

Casey wiped a weary hand across her forehead, pushing back some stray strands of hair drooping in her eyes. If only Michael had offered to help. She might've had a chance at finishing in time to go home and get a few hours of sleep.

"What did you expect?" she muttered, wringing the sponge into a bucket and wishing it were his corporate shark neck.

A few minutes later, she heard the sound of footsteps approaching the kitchen. Casey spun around, barely preventing herself from slipping on the wet floor, and froze. Before her stood an amazing sight. Not only had Michael returned, he'd changed his clothes. Casey rose slowly to her feet, wiping her wet hands on her jeans. Instead of a designer suit, Michael wore a faded red T-shirt and shorts.

He looked different. Less formal. Less forceful, but equally dangerous. Casey swallowed past a lump in her throat the size of a grapefruit. The man was gorgeous. She'd always thought he was handsome. But now he was a lonely lady's midnight dream and far too good-looking to be alone with.

"Thanks for understanding, Ted," Michael was saying into his cell phone. "I know, it's important we meet. Noress sure wants your business. How about tomorrow night?" After a moment, he said, "Great. See you then."

Michael pushed the Off button on his phone, then looked at Casey. She narrowed her eyes. "Why did you come back?"

"To help." He set his phone down on the counter. "Don't you have a mop?"

"We did. But I can't seem to find it." Stunned, she continued to stare at him. Had she heard right? Did he just cancel a business meeting to help her mop the floor?

"Your appointment sounded important."

Michael shrugged. "I managed to move it."

Warmth pervaded her at his words. Wow. He'd canceled his meeting. Would wonders never cease?

Michael headed toward the supply cabinet, slipping a little on the wet floor. With a chuckle and a grin to Casey, he deliberately slid across the room, stopping himself by bumping lightly against the cabinet.

"Don't I remind you of Tom Cruise in his underwear?" He shot her another killer grin.

"Um. I guess." Casey felt her heart rate kick into overdrive. Oh, no. Michael was much, much cuter than Tom Cruise. Unable to stop herself, her gaze skimmed down his body, landing finally on his feet. They were bare like her own. Even his feet were attractive. It seemed so intimate to be looking at his bare feet, so personal. With effort, she pulled her gaze away and looked at his face.

Michael met and held her gaze, the single bulb from the overhead light throwing his face partly into shadow. She felt his look like a touch as it skimmed her body. Her breathing increased. Her breasts swelled. She tingled with want.

Sheesh. She needed to get out more. She was acting like a dieter in a chocolate factory. Avoiding his gaze, she knelt and started sopping up water again. "You don't have to help."

A second later, he knelt next to her, a matching sponge in his hand. "Sure I do. I know you don't think much of me, but I wouldn't leave you alone with this mess."

Knowing it was risky but unable to stop herself, Casey turned her head so she could study him. This was a new and totally unexpected side to him. She would have expected him to pull out his checkbook and offer to pay someone to clean up. Anything but get down on his knees and help.

As if feeling her gaze, he stopped.

"What?" he asked softly, a quizzical smile gracing his handsome face.

"I'm surprised you came back," she admitted, finding it difficult to concentrate when he was watching her with those hypnotic blue eyes of his.

"Even ogres have their moments." He broke eye contact and went back to work.

"You're not an ogre," Casey said, amazed that she actually meant it.

His dry chuckle let her know he doubted her. "You didn't think so earlier today. In fact, I bet you definitely considered me top ogre."

A smile tugged at her lips. "Maybe not top ogre...." He raised an eyebrow and she laughed. "But possibly vice ogre."

The humor on his face faded, and his expression turned thoughtful. "Sorry. I didn't mean to offend you about your chances of raising that money in time."

Casey twisted the sponge in her hand over the dented metal bucket and watched dirty water run through her fingers. "You didn't offend me, exactly—"

"Just really ticked you off."

She saw no point in denying the truth. "I don't like people telling me there's something I can't do."

"No one likes that."

"Exactly." She shifted so she faced him. "If only you understood—"

"Yeah, well, maybe I do. You know, there are things that are important to me, too."

Casey froze. Could the shark actually be human? "Like what?"

Michael hesitated, and Casey found herself holding her breath, willing him to tell her his thoughts. But he didn't. Instead, after long, agonizing moments, he shrugged.

"Did you get any ideas for your fund-raiser?" he asked.

Well, drat. She sensed he'd been about to tell her something important about himself. Something she wanted to hear. But as much as Casey didn't want to let him change the subject, she understood people well enough to know when not to push.

"The seniors are thinking about it. I'm not sure any of the ideas I've gotten so far will work."

"Tell me about them."

Casey debated whether he was truly interested or just humoring her. He seemed sincere, but still.... "Why? You don't think I can pull this off."

For a heartbeat of time, he just looked at her, and Casey felt the impact of his intent gaze. Then, he shrugged. "I had no right to say that."

Warmth spread through Casey at his words. He was so different tonight, not at all like a boardroom bigwig. For starters, he'd admitted he'd made a mistake. Plus now he was showing interest in her plans.

How odd.

"Thank you for saying so," she said. "I'll admit it's a long shot, but—"

"You have to try." He nodded slowly, the light gleaming off his dark hair. "Yeah, I know."

"You'd try, too," Casey pointed out.

"Dam—" At her warning glance, he grinned and started over. "Sure. I love a challenge. So what were the ideas?"

"A walk-a-thon, a bazaar, and an auction—but rather than auctioning off items, the gentleman who suggested it thought we should auction off dates."

"You mean like those bachelor auctions?"

Casey smiled, enjoying this conversation with Michael. "Yes. He thought the ladies in the center might be willing to part with serious cash to have a romantic night on the town."

"You can't blame a guy for trying." He added a wink for emphasis, making Casey laugh. How could she ever have thought him stiff and unfriendly?

"Yeah, well, it might be the solution to his dating problem, but I don't think it's the solution the center needs. But whatever we come up with, it has to be soon. I need to run the plans by the city council."

"You're a smart lady. You'll come up with something." His confidence in her caused an erratic fluttering in her stomach.

"Thanks."

"Once you decide, just tell the council this is what you're doing. Don't ask them," he said. "It's always easier to ask for forgiveness than for permission."

Michael's lopsided grin did funny things to Casey's metabolism. That grin invited her to share the joke, and she found she was smiling despite herself. She still couldn't believe he'd canceled a meeting to help. Michael was so approachable tonight he was impossible to resist. He genuinely seemed interested in what she had to say.

Which was a potent aphrodisiac.

As she continued to watch him, his eyes darkened and his smile faded. Casey sucked in her breath on a hiss and felt a wave of desire hit her. Who would have thought a man like Michael Parker would affect her this way? But here, now, in this quiet building on this lonely night, she couldn't remember ever finding a man as attractive as she found him.

Michael slowly set down his sponge, his heated gaze never leaving her face. With controlled, deliberate moves, he rose and extended his hand to her. Casey didn't have to ask what he was doing. She knew. Just like he knew. The air vibrated with the tension between them.

She took his hand, rose to her feet, and stood anxiously before him.

"This is a really bad idea," she said. But she made no move to resist when he placed his hands on her hips and pulled her forward until she pressed against him. This close, she could smell his tangy aftershave. He smelled like heaven, like temptation.

She was in big trouble.

"Yeah. I know." He kissed her neck, and she shivered. "Do you want me to stop?"

Casey pulled back just far enough to look at him.

She could see his desire, and she knew it mirrored her own. Desire born not of loneliness. Or fatigue. But of something stronger. Deeper. Certain now of her decision, she placed her hand on the side of his face and urged him forward.

"Hell, no," she murmured, a second before her lips met his.

She expected Michael's kiss to be forceful, taking more than it gave. But rather, with tenderness, he brushed his lips against hers. He moved with agonizing slowness from side to side. Reaching the corner of her lip, he nibbled softly, lingering just long enough to drive her wild. Then, he moved on, seeking, searching. When he continued to coax her with teasing brushes, she realized he wanted her to show him just how far he could go.

His thoughtfulness touched her. Most men she'd dated in recent memory kissed as if they were playing football. They turned a caress into a competition. But not Michael. Even though he no doubt possessed a keen killer instinct in business, he obviously understood that kissing was about pleasure, not conquest.

Tipping her head, she met his kiss more fully, wanting to savor the sensation. He made her feel not just desired, but cherished. Michael slid his arms around her, cradling her body tightly against his own. On a sigh, she parted her lips, and Michael slipped his tongue inside her mouth to meet her own. The rhythm of the kiss made her pulse race with excitement. A delicious ache settled on her, reminding her of how alone she'd been for so very long. This kiss was full of fire. And promise.

And magic.

Groaning, Michael cupped her face. Although his arms no longer held her, Casey felt her breasts pressing against his chest, her legs brushing his thighs. In the back of her mind, she knew she stood in several inches of water in the battered kitchen of the center, kissing a man who was completely wrong for her. But she couldn't help it. This embrace felt right. This kiss felt right.

Eventually, reluctantly, she pulled her head back, separating their lips. For a moment, she expected him to protest. She could read the banked frustration on his face. Then, he stepped back and moved away from her. Within the harsh light of the kitchen, she stared at him. His hands were knotted into fists at his sides. His face was taut, the muscles pulled tight.

And his eyes burned with the same fire she felt flickering through her veins.

"I didn't really intend that to happen," he finally said.

Casey nodded wordlessly, the reality of the situation overwhelming her. Michael Parker had kissed her. Holy cow. Worse yet, she'd kissed him back. Really kissed him. And she'd enjoyed it. Immensely. Immeasurably.

And she wanted to kiss him again.

"Aren't you going to say anything?" He had one dark eyebrow raised in question.

Great. Just what she wanted. A postmortem.

"What's there to say? We only kissed because it's late, and we're both tired." She moved past him and retrieved her sponge, ignoring the slight trembling in her hand. Talk about a dumb move. Kissing Michael ranked right up there with inviting a cannibal to brunch.

What had Elmira said? Men were like hats? Well, as far as Casey was concerned, she didn't need a hat, thank you very much. Even a hat that kissed as well as Michael did.

Kneeling, she resumed sopping up water, wanting to do anything but look at the man standing behind her. With uneven strokes, she rubbed the floor and squeezed the sponge into the bucket. The tingling on the back of her neck reminded her that Michael stood watching her.

What did he expect her to say? *Gee whiz, Mike, heck of a kiss you've got there?* What was the big deal? Okay, they'd kissed, whether they should have or not. The downside was she could no longer look at him and see just the suit and the job. Not now, when she knew she desired Michael Parker and hated herself for that weakness.

"You owe the center a dollar," Michael said.

Casey stopped in mid-mop and glanced at him over her shoulder.

"I what?"

Michael crouched next to her, a teasing gleam in his eyes. "You cursed."

Casey blinked. What in the world was he talking about? She rarely cursed, only when.... She gulped in a quick breath. He was right. She'd cursed. She turned back to her task, glad she no longer had to look at him.

"I did, so I'll pay," she said.

Michael moved to her side, picked up his sponge, and started wiping up water again. His movements were purposeful, his pace much faster than her own. Casey found herself watching his hands. The sure strokes. The wide swipes.

A bead of sweat trickled down her back. Suddenly, every move he made seemed seductive. His fingers flexed on the sponge, wringing the water into the pail. She couldn't help wondering how it would feel to have those same fingers caress her naked skin, rubbing against—

"I'll pay the dollar for you," he said, interrupting her thoughts.

Casey moved her gaze back to the sponge in her hand. Good grief. She'd just worked herself into a lather watching him wring out a sponge. Talk about being a basket case.

She forced herself to look at him. "I can pay for myself."

"No, really, I'd like to pay." Michael placed one hand on her arm, but when she jumped, he released her immediately. "What's wrong?"

Casey sighed. Why didn't he just let it go? She was going insane. That was the only logical explanation. "Drop it, Michael."

"But I really enjoyed that kiss, and it was worth a lot more than a dollar."

She half groaned, half laughed. What was with

this man? Wasn't the male sex the one who hated to talk about things like kisses?

"Let it go," she repeated. "Let's finish with the floor."

Her gaze met his, and she felt the same fluttering sensation she'd felt when he'd kissed her. Of all the men in the world, why did it have to be Michael who pushed her On button?

"Casey, I'm as confused as you are. It's a bit like Sitting Bull finding out he's got a crush on General Custer."

Absently, Casey smiled, but she had a sinking feeling Custer had fared better at Little Bighorn than she would fare with Michael. Suddenly, the mess of the floor seemed the least of her worries.

MICHAEL SAT in the meeting staring at the data projected on the screen. He hadn't a clue what he'd spent the last ten minutes looking at. All he'd been able to do was think about Casey. And last night. After the kiss, they'd finished wiping up the floor, annoyingly awkward with each other.

Talk about a stupid move. He hadn't even meant to kiss her, but once he had, he hadn't wanted to stop. She'd been soft and sweet and entirely too enticing in his arms. All sorts of great ideas had popped into his head.

But hey, he wasn't that stupid. He couldn't afford to get involved with Casey. Hell, last night had shown him how easily he'd change work plans to be with her. If he didn't watch himself, he'd end up like Jeff and the other managers—constantly having to choose between their personal life and work. No matter what decision those poor saps made, something ended up suffering.

But not him. Michael had figured out this rat maze as a kid. If you busted your butt and worked long and hard, you could make something out of yourself. Anything else was merely spitting in the wind. He'd spent his childhood living hand to mouth. Never again. Now he was only one tiny step away from being president of Noress. This was not the time to start thinking with his hormones rather than his head.

Gritting his teeth, he forced himself to concentrate on the meeting. The project was off-schedule, and the key personnel were presenting alternatives. Normally, he thrived on this kind of pressure. Nothing gave him a bigger rush than pulling off the impossible. But today it wasn't giving him the usual thrill.

Damn, why had he gone and kissed Casey? That kiss could cause complications. Sure, last night she'd said the kiss didn't mean anything to her, but what if she'd changed her mind? Well, he'd just have to tell her when he saw her this afternoon that they could never kiss again. Last night had been an aberration. A simple matter of satisfying curiosity. But now they both knew what they needed to know, so that was that.

Michael sighed, wondering if he had any chance of getting Casey to buy that load of crap. He sure wasn't. The bottom line was he'd kissed Casey because he'd wanted to. But he wasn't about to let

that kiss mess up his plans. There would be no re-
peats of last night. None. Ever.

"SO WHAT KIND of responses did you get?" Elmira
asked, entering Casey's office and sitting in the
chair.

Casey thumbed through the papers she'd gotten
this morning from the seniors and added them to
the pile she'd gotten the previous day. "The new
ideas are for a carnival, a casino night, a chili cook-
off...." She lifted the last paper and laughed. "And
a really big bake sale."

"Which one are we going to do?"

Casey placed the sheets of paper on her desk and
smoothed the creases. "That's up to the group. I
don't care, as long as it has the potential to make a
lot of money. I'll wait one more day to see what
other ideas come in."

Elmira regarded Casey with open curiosity. "Did
you ask Michael what he thinks? He seems like a
pretty smart guy."

The older woman's comment made the hair on
the back of Casey's neck stand up. Her internal ra-
dar said Elmira was in here to do a little lobbying
for Michael. Which was laughable. Michael was the
last person to need help with anything. She'd
learned last night how capable he was...at a lot of
things.

"I've mentioned that the center plans on having
a fund-raiser." Casey studied the older woman and
waited patiently for what she knew was coming. It

didn't take long. Elmira patted her hair, flashed Casey a tentative smile, then leaned forward.

"Dear, the real reason I'm here is because Dottie and I have been talking, and we think...." She gave Casey a sweet smile. "We think you should ask Michael out."

Astonished, Casey stared at her. "Ask him out?"

"Yes. Women do it all the time, and we think you should ask him rather than waiting for him to ask you. You need to be assertive in today's marriage market."

Casey bit back a smile. "Marriage market?"

Elmira wagged one finger at Casey. "Don't make fun of me. I read the paper. I know how hard it is to get a man these days. You have to remember, men are like fish."

"Fish? I thought they were like hats."

With a little *tsking* sound, Elmira said, "They're like fish. You can't let them know you're after them until you've caught them."

"But if I ask him out, he'll know I'm after him," Casey pointed out, more amused than annoyed by this latest matchmaking attempt.

"Casey, you ask him out, then once he's interested, you pretend you aren't."

Elmira delivered this advice slowly, as if she feared Casey wouldn't understand it. Which, come to think of it, she didn't. "Seems kind of manipulative to me," Casey said.

"No offense, but it isn't exactly as if your way is working. And you can't seriously want to spend your life alone. You need to get married and have

your children before it's too late." Elmira leaned
down and rooted through her large purse, which was
sitting on the floor. When she straightened, she had
a paperback book in her hand. "I borrowed this
from one of my granddaughters. It has all sorts of
suggestions you can use to get a husband."

She laid the book on the desk and pushed it toward Casey. The bright orange cover claimed the
book contained surefire methods for seducing a
man. Casey regarded it like a venomous snake. Gingerly, she nudged it back toward Elmira.

"Thanks, really. But I'm not interested in Michael that way," Casey said. She hated to lie, especially to Elmira, but in actuality, it wasn't a lie.
Well, not completely. She wasn't interested in Michael, despite the kiss they'd shared. He was all
wrong for her. Oh, he might have canceled one
meeting, but he was still a man rooted to the fast
track.

Now in the light of day, she knew she must have
been feeling weak last night. Yeah. That was it.
She'd been so worried about the money that a fog
had settled over her mind. And the kiss was just the
result of too little sleep and an unexpectedly kind
gesture from a handsome man.

Elmira rose, a serene smile gracing her face. She
made no move to retrieve the paperback. "Keep the
book just in case. You never know when you might
change your mind. In my own case, it took me
months before I'd even look at my husband. I never
considered him the right sort for me." She tipped
her head and regarded Casey over the top of her

glasses. "Then one day, he pulled up in a shiny new Mercury, and something magical happened. I saw him for what he really was."

"A good-looking man with a killer car?"

Elmira gave her one of those smug little looks she specialized in. "Amongst other things."

With that, she left Casey's office with her final words hanging in the air. Casey blew out a deep breath. Fine. Okay, so Elmira had been wrong, but she wasn't. Michael Parker really wasn't the right type for her. And last night had been one big, old fluke—a fluke that wouldn't happen again. She had way too much at stake to risk it all on a case of lust, regardless of how strong that lust was. She needed to keep her mind sharp and her senses focused on raising the money for the center. If she didn't get a grip on herself soon, she'd end up pulling petals off flowers saying, "He loves me, he loves me not."

"You are such a sap," she muttered. She picked up Elmira's book, intending on stuffing it in her desk, when temptation got the better of her. Slowly, she flipped through the pages, stopping when she reached the chapter on how to make sex interesting. The warmth of a blush crept up her cheeks. When she reached a particularly erotic illustration, she slammed the book closed and shoved it in her desk drawer.

Still agitated, she glanced out her open office door into the main room. She could see Michael talking to Al and Tommy. Today he had on his usual shark uniform—expensive suit, expensive shirt, expensive tie. Darn his hide, he looked incredibly...tempting. Especially when images from that book were still lodged in her mind.

As he moved through the room, he surprised her by stopping and talking to a few more seniors on his way to her office. Apparently he'd made a couple of friends yesterday afternoon. Drat. Lust she could fight. But he'd better not turn out to be a nice guy after all.

That would be way too much for her to take.

"Hi," Michael said, entering Casey's office cautiously. She looked flustered, which only made him curse himself more. Damn. What if she expected him to ask her out? He didn't want to hurt her feelings, but he also didn't want to mislead her. He sat in the chair across from her and debated how to approach this talk. He'd been less nervous firing errant employees than he was telling this woman he couldn't date her.

"Hi." Casey twiddled with a paper clip, her gaze skimming over him but not stopping. "Thanks for your help last night."

"No problem." He watched her mutilate the paper clip for a few seconds, then cleared his throat. "Casey, about last night—"

"Oh, yeah." She tossed the clip in the trash and flashed a too-bright smile at him. "We should just forget what happened."

"You mean the kiss?"

That too-bright smile seemed to stretch even wider. "Exactly."

Even though she was saying precisely what he'd planned on saying, she was strung like a tightrope. "I think that sounds like a good idea," he said slowly, trying to get her to meet his gaze.

She picked up another paper clip, and he pitied the tiny thing. "I mean, it was only a kiss. Certainly not the end of the world."

Soon, the twisted silver clip joined its mate in the trash. Michael shifted nervously in his chair. Was she upset they'd agreed to forget the kiss or was she worried he might not be willing to let go of one of the best memories he'd had in years?

"Okay," he said. "But you seem kind of upset."

"I'm not." Now even her voice sounded too bright. "I'm just not as good at this sort of thing as you are."

"What sort of thing?"

"Flirting. You've probably kissed hundreds of women."

What in the world? When she reached for another paper clip, he leaned forward and placed his hand over hers.

"Just for the record, I haven't kissed hundreds of women." He knew he might be digging his own grave, but he had to take a stand. "And I kissed you because I wanted to."

Casey finally met his gaze, and he felt his equilibrium rock. Of all the lame things to do. Why'd he have to admit something like that? He tried to backpedal, struggling to think what to say. He could hardly admit that she'd been kneeling there, looking sexy as hell, and then the next thing he'd known, he had her in his arms and was kissing her. He had no choice. He had to finish this discussion. There was too much at stake. His job. His sanity.

"Casey, I think we both agree the kiss was more intense than we expected," he said slowly, trying to gage her reaction. "But I think we also agree we shouldn't get involved."

"We're not involved. It was just one kiss."

Michael knew he should feel relief at her agreement, but it had been one *hell* of a kiss. Wait a second. Which side was he on? Annoyed at himself, he pushed on. "I think we need to agree to avoid kissing each other in the future. I personally think it's too dangerous, and we both have other things to concentrate on. So we need to be in complete agreement."

Casey frowned. "That sounds official. Do you want me to sign a contract promising not to kiss you?"

So she wasn't as cool as she pretended. He ran an unsteady hand through his hair. This was turning out to be incredibly difficult.

"Very funny. No. I just don't want us to get distracted from what's important. We need to work on the fund-raiser."

She had to know he was right. Deep down, she absolutely had to know he was right. They both had plans. Goals. They couldn't give up now.

His idea made perfect sense.

Finally, she nodded. "Fine. No more kissing."

"Great. No more kissing." The words sounded hollow, and he realized he felt just as empty. What was wrong with him? He was getting what he wanted. He should be dancing on her desk.

"Do we need to shake hands on this deal?" Casey asked.

Michael stood, knowing his best bet was to accept the agreement and leave. "I don't think it's a good idea for us to touch right now."

"Yes. You're probably right."

She picked up another clip, and Michael bit back a groan. Working here was going to be a nightmare.

"I guess we can try to be friends," she said, then she yanked on the clip, distorting it. Destroying it.

Michael made a strangled sound. "I guess that's the option we have."

"Yes. I guess so."

Friends.

Okay, so maybe it wasn't perfect, but it was a hell of a lot better than getting involved. And even though he knew Casey would make an amazing lover, he was also certain she'd make a great friend.

And hey, couldn't a guy always use another friend?

5

"SO HOW'S IT GOING at the center?" Cal asked as
he entered Michael's office the next morning.

*Not bad for a bona fide, full-fledged, all-out di-
saster.*

Michael pushed the thought away. "Fine."
Which was a huge lie. Yesterday he'd told Casey
they should just be friends. And the day had turned
out to be one of the longest of his life. Friends were
guys you played football with. They weren't gorgeous, auburn-haired women with sexy eyes who
watched your every move. They weren't daydreams
that turned around and haunted your nights as well.
And they certainly didn't drive you to distraction.

"Really?" Cal asked.

"Yeah. It's great." He wasn't about to tell Cal
the truth—that he had the hots for the center's director.

Cal chuckled and dropped into one of the chairs
in front of Michael's desk. "I think you're full of
it. Now tell me the truth."

Michael avoided making eye contact with his
boss. "The operation's a lot bigger than I expected,
but the director does an excellent job."

"And what have you been doing?"

You mean, besides coming on to the director? Michael shifted in his chair and met Cal's inquisitive gaze dead-on. "Helping."

Cal laughed again. "Could you be a little more specific?"

"Why don't you drop by the center and see for yourself?"

A twinkle settled in Cal's eyes. "Great idea. I think I'll do just that." He considered Michael, then he said, "You still think the time there is hurting your job?"

"Yes. You know as well as I do what happens to Noress if the merger falls through," Michael said. Yeah, Cal knew Noress could run into some serious financial problems.

Cal leaned forward in his chair. "So what do you suggest we do? Back out of our commitment to the community?"

Now that was a good question. Thoughts of Casey and the seniors filtered through Michael's mind. He was torn. Yes, he wanted out of the assignment. Boy did he ever, especially since he'd kissed Casey. He'd like nothing better than to spend twelve uncomplicated hours a day at the office.

Aw, but he couldn't just walk away. Maybe it was his past, his father. Or maybe it was the seniors themselves...or Casey. Hell, maybe it was all of that rolled up into one big muddled mess.

"They do need money," Michael said slowly. "So they're making plans to hold a fund-raiser at the end of the month."

"What for?"

"Modifications on a new facility."

Cal nodded. "So help them raise the money."

"I'm going to, but there isn't much time."

With a chuckle, Cal said, "They need a major miracle—just up your alley. Tell you what, you help with the fund-raiser, pull it off, and you're off the hook."

Cal's pronouncement caught Michael like a swift uppercut to the jaw. "Off the hook?"

"Yep. No more volunteering. You can spend the rest of your days glued to your desk without interruption, if that's what you want." Cal stood and headed toward the door. "There you go, Michael. You'll be a free man in a matter of weeks."

With that verbal wave of his magic wand, the older man walked out of Michael's office.

A free man. Great. Terrific. Just what he wanted. He ought to be one happy guy.

So why wasn't he?

"Dammit," Michael muttered, slamming shut the middle drawer on his desk. He was going to be happy about this if it killed him. He'd help with the fund-raiser, and when it was over, he'd wish the seniors and Casey well. He might drop by from time to time on his way to a meeting just to say hi. But that would be the extent of it.

After the fund-raiser ended, he was out of there quicker than a sinner leaving Sunday service.

CASEY ALWAYS KNEW the moment Michael entered the center, and this afternoon was no exception. The seniors seemed to liven, the volume in the main

room increased, and Casey was filled with...
expectation. She glanced out the door of her office
and saw him walk across the room, joking and smiling at several of the people. Her heart had developed a funny, flippy rhythm that she'd come to associate with Michael.

She wanted to think of him as simply a friend. A
volunteer who would provide invaluable help with
the fund-raiser, which was good since he'd proven
to be a disaster at helping with repairs around the
place.

Now if she could only forget the kiss they'd
shared. But it lingered in her mind, taunting her
senses. And darn it, she wanted to kiss him again.
She longed for the same feeling of oneness she'd
experienced briefly in his arms.

Michael appealed to her on a lot of levels, not
the least of which was the way he'd fit into the
center. She glanced out the door again and saw him
sitting at his now usual spot at the men's table with
a few of the guys. Casey had observed the same
scene several times over the past few days. She had
no idea what the group talked about, but yesterday,
Al Terford brought her a handful of money. He
muttered an apology, gave her a shy smile, then left.

She'd give the group a few minutes before she
gathered them to discuss the fund-raiser. Time was
running out. Just yesterday, she'd gotten two phone
calls from city council members who wanted to
know if she could raise the money. Crossing her
fingers, she'd assured them the fund-raiser would
be a success. Thankfully, neither had pressed her

for details, which was either a sign of their supreme confidence in her success or their absolute belief she was going to fall flat on her face. Either way, she owed it to the seniors to find a solution to this problem.

Unfortunately, her mind had turned to a big puddle of mush. Every time she sat down, determined to map out a plan, she'd ended up thinking about Michael. Repeatedly she reminded herself how friendship offered them a perfect solution. As friends, they could work beside each other day after day without worrying about emotions getting in the way.

But she knew the plan was worth zip. She couldn't be friends with this man. He made her stomach swarm with butterflies, her palms sweat and her breathing get shallow and rapid. She either was developing some really serious illness or an equally bad case of lust. More and more, she got the feeling that friendship just wasn't going to work.

Which left her with...what?

One heck of a problem. She needed to get her priorities straight. Okay, so he was handsome. And he could kiss. But she had to get over this infatuation she felt for him. She had to, so the only solution was to keep busy with the fund-raiser. Then she'd have no time to think about Michael Parker. That should do the trick.

At least, she sure hoped so.

"SO IF WE JUST got a band that could play the right sort of music, then I'm sure we could make lots of money," Al said.

"Let it go. You brought that up yesterday, and I told you, we can't get a band if we don't have any money to hire one." Tommy leaned forward and added a swirl of red paint to the ceramic bowl he was painting.

"Yeah, well, it's a good idea anyway." Al turned to Michael. "Don't you think so?"

Michael looked from Al to Tommy and then back again. These two men might be the best of friends, but they fought like old enemies. And Michael liked them both. A lot. His dad could have learned a thing or two from these guys.

Michael shrugged. "I don't know. Outline your plan."

Al slapped the table, causing Tommy to jump. "Michael, I knew you were a smart man."

"Dang it, Al, you made me ruin my art," Tommy muttered. Frowning, he turned his bowl around, studying the damage. Since his painting was—put nicely—abstract, Michael wasn't sure how Tommy could tell any harm had been done. But he decided to snuff out the brewing confrontation. Before Tommy launched into a verbal attack, Michael repeated, "Tell me the plan."

Al leaned back in his chair, and Michael braced himself for pontification. He wasn't disappointed. Before reaching the main point, Al waxed on about life in general for almost ten minutes. Michael was about to say something when Tommy burst out with

"Al, we're old men. Get to the point before Michael has to bury one of us."

With a snort, Al shifted in his chair to face Michael. "Anyway, as I was trying to say before I was interrupted, we should have a Big Band Night. You know, get a snazzy group in, serve a fancy dinner like they used to at the great New York clubs in the late forties, and have dancing. All the town muck-a-mucks will want to come." With a grin, he added, "Great idea, right?"

Michael had to admit, the idea had possibilities. "What did Casey say when you told her?"

"I haven't told her yet. Tommy thought it was a crazy idea since we'd need some money to secure the band and someone to guarantee expenses if we don't raise enough money. I think the city could back us."

"You know they won't," Tommy said, setting his bowl gingerly on the table.

"Like you know anything. You're just jealous 'cause I thought of it."

"Noress could underwrite it," Michael said, startling himself as much as he did both men. They stopped arguing and stared at him.

"You think so?" Al asked.

The more Michael thought about it, the more he liked the idea. "Where would you hold this fundraiser?" he asked.

"I don't know. We can't hold it here. The place is falling apart," Al said.

"I think we could use the cafeteria at Noress. It's

huge." Michael shrugged. "I'm sure my boss would go along with it."

"You really think he'd agree?"

At the question, the three men turned. Casey stood behind them. She smiled, somewhat self-consciously, her gaze skittering off Michael and landing on the two men. "Let me gather the group, and you can tell us your plan."

When everyone was assembled, Al recapped his plan, ignoring the occasional critiquing from Tommy. When he finished, Elmira said, "It sounds wonderful."

Al beamed. "I knew you'd like it, Elmira."

"I always said it was an idea with merit," Tommy piped in.

Michael bit back a smile. The two men reminded him of high-school rivals. To her credit, Elmira rewarded both of them with an equally bright smile.

"So do we all agree with Al's idea?" Casey asked.

The group made it clear they more than agreed. "It's going to be a lot of work," Casey pointed out. "And Michael will need to make sure we can hold it at Noress."

"We can do it," Tommy said. "We've got almost three weeks."

Casey laughed, the sweet sound pulling at Michael. He glanced at her and found her watching him. Their gazes met for a long moment, then she looked away. The look she had given him shot his pulse through the roof. He blinked and returned his attention to the group. What had they been talking about?

Oh, yeah. The fund-raiser. Now they were in his element. He knew how to put an idea into action, how to give a plan life. For the first time since Casey had told him about the fund-raiser, he started to think it might actually happen.

And after that, he'd be gone. He ignored the unexpected sadness that thought brought. All that mattered right now was that the seniors got their money.

CASEY GLANCED briefly at Michael. At some point, he'd taken off his jacket. As he listened to the conversation, he rolled up the sleeves on his white shirt. He picked up a pen off the table and grabbed a couple of sheets of paper.

"So, Casey, where do you want to start?"

Now she had expected him to hand her the paper and pen like she was his secretary. Instead, he clearly intended on letting her lead the conversation. It drove her nuts when Michael was considerate. How was she supposed to resist him then?

Casey tried to focus on the conversation swirling around them. When Al and Tommy burst into another vocal discussion, she used the distraction to lean slightly toward Michael.

"Thank you for taking notes," she said softly.

Michael shrugged. "Just trying to be a helpful volunteer. But I'll warn you, I'm sure I'll be an opinionated pain-in-the-butt before this is over."

She should be so lucky. If he annoyed her, then

maybe she'd stop thinking about how appealing he was. "I'm sure I'll have my fair share of opinions."

"Hey, you two, what do you think about Elmira's idea?"

With effort, Casey pulled her gaze away from Michael and forced herself to focus on the group. "I'm sorry, I missed the suggestion."

Elmira moved forward. "I offered a little something extra to the evening. My late husband had a car, a 1949 Mercury, which he just adored. Since his passing, I haven't had the heart to sell it, but I don't want to keep it in storage forever. No one in my family wants it. Do you think...." She waved one manicured hand. "Do you think people might bid for a car?"

"Elmira, we can't let you do that," Casey said, determined not to let the older woman part with something so valuable. "I'm sure your husband's car is worth a lot of money."

"But I want to donate it," Elmira said. "It's just sitting in the storage shed, costing me money. I've always thought of that car as, well, as almost magical. It's what finally made me fall in love with my husband. A car that special shouldn't be hidden away."

To her amazement, Casey realized from the approving gazes she was receiving that the group was siding with Elmira. "What? We can't let her make a sacrifice like that," Casey repeated.

"But I want to." Elmira turned toward Michael. "Do you like my idea?"

"I think it's a great idea," Michael said. "But I

have to agree with Casey. We can't let you make that sacrifice."

A sudden warmth crept through Casey, and she struggled to suppress it. But when Michael leaned forward and took Elmira's hands in his, her breath caught in her throat. He looked at the elderly woman with respect and kindness, and Casey couldn't believe she'd ever thought Michael was cold. Well, yippee and let the cows come home. Working with the seniors was obviously having a positive effect on him.

"Your husband would want you to use that car to help provide for your needs," Michael said to Elmira. "He would—"

"No offense, dear, but he would want me to do what I wanted to do," Elmira said firmly. "And I want to donate it."

Michael turned to Casey. "Looks like the lady has her mind made up."

Casey had to try one more time. "Are you certain about this?"

"Yes. Absolutely." Elmira added with a small smile, "Unless one of you two wants the car. Who knows? That Mercury could put a little magic in your love lives."

Casey refused to look at Michael. "Um, no thanks."

"I have an idea," Michael said. "We could find out what this car is worth. Then, after the auction, we'll pay that amount to Elmira and use any extra cash for the center. Add that money to what the dance brings in, and we…you should be set."

The seniors enthusiastically agreed with his plan.

"That's a great idea," Dottie said. "I knew you were a smart boy." She patted Michael's cheek, then looked at Casey. "And cute, too."

With amazement, Casey watched a tinge of color highlight Michael's face. He was embarrassed. When the seniors continued to fuss over him, she decided to take pity on him.

"Okay, so now that we've settled the car, let's get to work." Casey shot a smile at Michael.

After a second, he smiled back—a sweet, sexy smile that sent Casey's nerves into hyperdrive. Focus. All she needed to do was focus. Then she'd be all set. Yes-siree. All set.

MICHAEL GLANCED at Casey as they tugged the cover off Elmira's car. It had been four days since the seniors had come up with the idea for Big Band Night, and Casey was just now able to break free long enough to come see the car. But coming to the small storage shed together was probably a bad idea. Over the last couple of days, he'd found it increasingly difficult to treat this woman simply as a friend. Now, in the warm, close confines of the storage area, his libido was straying in dangerous directions.

Forcing himself to keep his mind on the task at hand, he helped Casey finish removing the cover. He'd found that the more days he spent at the center, the more he shared Casey's goal. Now, he too wanted Big Band Night to succeed. But not for him. Not even for Casey. He wanted it for the seniors who deserved a center that wasn't falling down around them.

"Wow" was all he could think to say once he saw the big, black Mercury. He'd never been a car nut, but this one might just change his mind. What had Elmira said? The car had made her fall for her husband. He shot a glance at the wide back seat and bit back a chuckle. He could only hope that wasn't what she'd meant.

"This is such a cool car," Casey said. "I can see why Elmira and her husband loved it."

Michael glanced at her and despite his good intentions, he felt his pulse rate kick up. Tonight she wore her usual outfit—jeans and a T-shirt. Her clothes were perfectly respectable, but somehow they did a little voodoo dance on his brain. The jeans were just a little snug, the T-shirt molded her curves with loving care. He wouldn't mind getting her into the back seat of that Mercury and seeing what sort of magic they could conjure up.

He blinked. Damn. He needed a cold shower— make that a dip in an ice bucket—and right now.

Casey grinned at him over the hood. "Do you think Elmira's right? Do you think this car could be magic?"

Michael pulled his thoughts away from his own little bag of tricks and focused on her question. "Didn't Steven King write a story about a possessed car? Seems to me that didn't work out so well."

Her soft laughter ran across his skin like a warm breeze, further fanning the flames he'd been trying to douse. "Oh, come on, you have to have a little fantasy in your life."

Oh, he was doing a bang-up job in the fantasy department at the moment. He could see himself tugging her T-shirt free from those tempting jeans. He'd run his hands up her torso, then slowly, with agonizing care, he'd run just the tip of his finger across her—

"Michael? Are you okay? You look kind of funny."

Before he could stop it, a groaning sort of sound escaped his lips. With effort, he switched his hormones off and jump-started his brain. What had she said? He looked funny. Yeah. Funny. Hell, he'd probably looked like a cartoon character with his tongue dragging on the ground and his eyes bugging out of his head. He scrubbed his hand across his face, shaking off the fantasy he'd woven around this woman.

"I'm fine," he managed in a strained voice. "Just fine." Except he wasn't. He was losing his mind in slow degrees to a sexy little siren of a director. Even his dreams were no longer sacred. She'd finagled her way into them in such enticing detail that he often woke up aching for her.

Up until now, he'd never believed a man could die from lust, but he seemed to be giving it one hell of a shot. Worse yet, she wasn't even his type, and although pretty, Casey certainly didn't possess the flawless looks of a model. Rather, her beauty grew from her personality, fueled by her kindness and humor. Her warmth drew him to her, enticed him into her circle of caring. Just looking at her made desire burn within him, licking at his soul.

He needed to do something about his feelings. The question was—what? A smart man would stop this disaster before it reached titanic proportions. A smart man would back away from this woman— and fast. Well, he might have been a smart man once, but he sure didn't seem to be one anymore.

He took a step forward, toward Casey. That wasn't so difficult. Then, he took another. And another. Until he stood directly in front of her.

A tiny frown crossed her brow as she gazed up at him. She must have seen the hunger in his face. "Michael," she said slowly, "I thought we agreed to just be friends."

He trailed his fingers down the side of her face. Her skin was so soft. "I've changed my mind."

"Maybe I haven't."

The teasing tone of her voice belittled her words. "Really? Sure we can't negotiate this? I'm one hell of a negotiator."

"I'll bet. And you owe me a dollar." Tipping her head, she gave him a flirty smile that made the blood pool beneath his belt. "I think the magic of this car is getting to you, hotshot."

Michael backed her up against the Mercury, pressing his body full against hers. "Lady, you have no idea."

When his lips met hers, he didn't even pretend to be a gentleman. He was hungry for her, and he let her know it. It was quickly obvious she shared his hunger. She wrapped around him like a vine, meeting his passion with her own.

It was crazy. It was wild. They were acting like two teenagers in heavy-duty lust. Hands wandered. Lips lingered. The only sound in the tiny storage areas was the two of them breathing deeply and murmuring words of pleasure and encouragement.

By tiny degrees, sanity started to seep into the corners of his mind. What in the great blue beyond was he doing? Okay, well, he knew *what* he was doing, but why? This woman was seriously dangerous to every single plan and goal he'd worked toward for years.

Yeow. But when her tongue slipped into his mouth, he figured reason and logic could just wait a couple more minutes. If he was going to do something so beyond stupid that it fell straight into the asinine pit—well, what could an extra few moments hurt?

Especially when she pressed to him harder, and he could feel her breasts against his chest. At this particular moment, he couldn't seem to get enough blood to his brain to form a sentence. All he knew was he wanted Casey. Wanted her with a driving need he couldn't seem to contain.

He slid his hands down to her hips and pulled her closer, letting her feel for herself just how much he did want her. Rather than being offended, Casey shifted even closer, her body pressed tightly to his. All Michael could think was how he wanted her in his bed. He wanted to watch her while he made love to her. He wanted to see her face in passion. He longed to hear her cry out his name in ecstasy.

Oh, yeah. Looked like reason and logic were doomed. Flat-out doomed.

WHEN BREATHING became almost impossible, Casey tore her lips free from Michael's. For one really long second, she just stared at him. Then reality flooded over her like a bucket of cold water.

She'd gone and done it again. She'd kissed Michael without making the slightest protest. Unless, of course, you considered kissing him back a protest.

Sheesh. Where was her mind? Better yet, where were her self-preservation instincts?

"That was a surprise." Casey slipped away from his arms and put as much distance as possible between them.

"It's getting to be more of a habit than a surprise," Michael said.

His rueful tone brought a reluctant smile to Casey's lips. It was a really dangerous habit.

Glancing at her watch, Casey realized she had absolutely no place to be for a couple of hours, so she said, "I'm late for a meeting. Mind driving me back to the center?"

At first, Michael looked like he might object. Finally, with a shrug, he said, "Sure. No problem. We can come back later and start cleaning up the car."

"The car. Right. We'll come back later." Not if she could help it. She'd come back later on her own and clean the car. No way was she coming back here with Michael.

Silently, they left the storage shed and climbed into Michael's Mercedes. Thankfully, once they were driving, Michael turned on the radio and it covered up the complete lack of conversation between them. It also gave Casey a chance to gather what little of her wits seemed to be left. She simply couldn't keep kissing Michael. The man lived and breathed his job, so kissing him was playing Russian roulette. Sooner or later it would blow up in her face.

By the time they reached the center, the tension level in the car was sky-high. After parking, Michael turned to face her. When his gaze dropped to her lips, Casey flashed him a warning look.

"Things between us keep getting out of control. We need a strict hands-off policy," she said, refusing to dwell on how cute he looked at the moment, with his hair slightly mussed. Okay, so he was cute. Oh, all right, he was sexy as sin. But he was a workaholic, and at times, well, a real pain in the butt. That was what she needed to focus on, not how cute he was.

Even if he was.

"I guess you're right. No more kissing," he said. When she moved to open her door, he placed a restraining hand on her arm. At her questioning look, he said, "But just so you know—I didn't want to stop back there in the storage shed. I couldn't help wishing things would get even more out of control."

Great. That helped a lot. "Think of something else to wish for," she advised him. Then she slipped out of his car and out of his reach.

6

FOR THE NEXT two days, Michael avoided Casey and refused to feel guilty about it. He was only doing what a sane man would do. After all, a sane man didn't drop an electrical appliance in his bathtub. And a sane man didn't hang around Casey Richards.

Not unless he wanted to find himself in deep trouble. Because Casey was soft, sweet and sexy, three deadly traits in a woman. She made him think things best not thought, and feel things best not...felt. Emotions made him uncomfortable. They made him antsy. The feelings Casey made dance around inside him were completely new to him. He hadn't grown up with kindness, and frankly didn't know how to handle it.

So he'd done the smart thing—he'd avoided her. Not that Casey had exactly sought him out, either. Even when he'd hired a handyman to come in and fix the hole in the wall, she'd just said thanks to him as she walked by on her way to her office this morning. Things would probably work out okay if he just kept his distance from her.

Yeah. Distance. That should solve the problem.

"You think Casey needs some help with the decorations?" Al asked.

Michael glanced up from his cards. They were playing a game called Wild Spud. As far as Michael could tell, there were no rules except those that Al or Tommy made up as they went along. At the moment, he had a six, two tens and two jacks. All he knew about Wild Spud was that whatever was in his hand was bad and whatever cards Al and Tommy held were good.

"I thought Elmira and Dottie were helping with the decorations." Michael threw down the two jacks, figuring if he was going to lose, he wanted to feel like he deserved to lose.

"They are. But there's not much money in the budget." Tommy picked up the discarded jacks and put them in his hand. Michael wanted to point out that Tommy now had seven cards, but decided what the hell. Tommy would simply make up a new rule that allowed the dealer to have more cards than anyone else.

"Noress can help with the decorations." Michael watched in bemusement as Al reached over and took two cards from Tommy's hand, gave him one, then placed the other card in his own hand. Amazingly, Tommy made no comment. What kind of card game was this? Even Go Fish made more sense.

With a grin at Al, Tommy said, "Lookee here, I've got a Wild Spud." He spread his cards out on the table. He had a four, a five, an eight, one jack and a queen. As far as Michael could tell, the man had zilch.

"Darn your hide." Al tossed his cards on the table. "You're the luckiest Wild Spud player I've ever met." Glancing at Michael, he added, "You should go tell Casey about the decorations."

"Maybe he's scared to talk to Casey." Tommy grinned at Michael. "We couldn't help noticing how you've avoided her ever since the two of you went over to look at Elmira's car. That Mercury didn't work a little magic on you, did it, son?"

Tommy and Al laughed as Michael shook his head. "No, I'm not afraid of her, and no, it didn't work any magic," Michael said, knowing he'd now painted himself into a corner and had to go talk to Casey whether he wanted to or not. "I've been busy the last couple of days. That's the only reason I haven't spoken to her."

Al nudged Tommy. "He's been busy learning to play Wild Spud."

Tommy chuckled. "Yeah. Except he stinks at it."

"How can you tell?" Al asked with a grin.

When both men laughed again, suspicion crept up Michael's back like a big bug. "There is no game called Wild Spud, is there? You two were yanking my chain."

"Just having a little fun, Mike. Nothing personal," Al said. "We thought it might do you good to relax a little. We're your friends. Both Tommy and I know men who died way too young by working too hard and being too serious. You're a good man, but you need to pop a few buttons.''

Michael laid his cards on the table and looked at the two men. He'd never had anyone care about him before. Not really. Certainly not his father, who'd been off in his own world. It felt nice knowing Al and Tommy considered themselves his friends. He smiled at them and rose to his feet. ''Okay, you got me with Wild Spud. And I'll think about the button-popping thing.''

He shot a quick glance at Casey's office. ''But I'm not afraid of Casey.''

Tommy grinned. ''Sure you're not, Mike. 'Course not.''

Michael groaned as he headed across the room to Casey's office. Behind him, he could hear soft chuckling coming from Tommy and Al. But they were wrong. He wasn't afraid of Casey. No, the lady stirred up all sorts on emotions inside him, but fear wasn't one of them.

In a strange sort of way, he wished it were.

WITH A FLOURISH, Casey crossed out the final item on her to-do list. She'd finished putting together the proposal for the city council meeting this afternoon and had even remembered to double-check on the cake for Elmira's birthday celebration.

Was she good or what?

Glancing out her open door, she looked over to where Michael was playing cards with Al and Tommy. When she saw him stand and head her way, the now familiar flitter-flutter started in her stomach.

"You're like a sixteen-year-old schoolgirl," she muttered, more than a little annoyed at herself.

"Got a minute?" Michael asked from the doorway to her office. He had an uncertain smile on his face.

Casey wiped her suddenly damp hands on her skirt. *Sheesh.* What a nutcase she was turning into. She picked up her notes for the presentation, needing something to keep her hands busy. "Sure."

Michael glanced over his shoulder, then entered her office and shut the door behind him. Suddenly they were surrounded by privacy. Being alone with Michael made her as jumpy as a canary at a cat convention.

"First, I want you to know I think you've done a terrific job with this fund-raiser. Really amazing," Michael said, walking over to her desk.

"Everyone's done it together." Casey fiddled with the pencils on her desk, avoiding eye contact with him. "I'm just part of the team."

"Most of the work has been yours."

At his gentle words, she made the mistake of looking at him. Aw, drat. His blue eyes held hers with an intense, sexy gaze. She needed to get him out of here. Proximity to Michael was hazardous to her health. Around him, her good sense evaporated.

"Um, thanks." She pulled her gaze away from his handsome face and restacked the papers for her presentation to the city council.

"You know, Noress has a lot of decorations we

can use for the party. That should save us some money," Michael said.

"Great. Thanks for the offer." She half held her breath, hoping he'd now leave.

"No problem."

He gave her that lopsided grin she'd come to know so well, and her heartbeat took off at a run. Desperately wanting a distraction, she tugged on the side drawer of her desk, finally giving it a swift yank to force it open.

"Well, thanks again. Now if you'll excuse me, I need to find a folder for this presentation. I want it to look nice." Knowing she was prattling, she ducked her head and rummaged through the drawer contents. When no folder floated to the top, she finally started unpacking the drawer. At the very bottom, she found a blue folder.

"Was that all you needed to tell me?" she asked, but when she glanced up at Michael, he wasn't paying attention to her. Instead, he stood looking at the top of her desk.

"What's this?" His hand snaked out, and he grabbed something from under a stack of papers. The second Casey saw the bright orange cover, she prayed for the floor to split open and swallow her up. Of all the dumb moves.

Ignoring the heat she felt rising on her face, Casey reached for the book. But with a smooth motion, Michael moved it out of her grasp. He scanned the back cover, then flipped through the pages, a smile tugging at his lips.

He glanced at her. His eyes sparkled with humor

and more. The humor she could take. The *more* left her scared breathless.

A double-dare expression settled on his face, and Casey knew she was in trouble. Why hadn't she insisted Elmira take the book back? Better yet, why hadn't she burned that stupid book? Elmira's granddaughter didn't need it any more than she did.

"Is this your book, Casey?" His deep voice rippled over her like warm fudge topping.

Good Lord.

"No. It's Elmira's."

He cocked one dark brow. "Really? Elmira's interested in seducing men?"

"No. She loaned it to me because..."

She snatched toward the book again, and again Michael held it out of her range. "This is so childish. Just give me the book. It isn't mine, and I intend on giving it back to Elmira."

Michael scanned the book again. "I don't think you should. Seems to me this book contains some interesting ideas." He chuckled. "For instance, Number 72 looks like fun."

He turned the book toward her, keeping it far enough away that she couldn't grab it. Casey frowned at him, but he just laughed again. Then despite herself, she glanced at the book. Number 72 deepened the blush on her face.

"Is that possible?" she asked, without meaning to.

Michael turned the book and studied the picture again. For a second, he said nothing, then he gave her a heated look. "I don't know. We could find out."

The thought of being in such an intimate position with Michael made her blood rush like floodwaters. Memories of their kiss a few nights ago flashed through her brain. Funny how she could be so determined to avoid involvement with Michael when he wasn't around, but the second he came near her, all her good intentions disappeared. Still, she made a feeble attempt. "I'm pretty sure we've agreed to just be friends."

The softly spoken words didn't seem to convince him. Rather, Michael moved forward, placing the book on her desk. "Are we? Are you sure?" he muttered, dipping his head.

"Friends don't keep kissing each other," she pointed out, stopping him with a restraining hand on his chest. He felt warm and oh so tempting. Reflectively, she contracted her fingers. He sucked in an audible breath.

Michael's gaze never wavered from her own. "I've given this a lot of thought, and I no longer want to be your friend."

HE HAD THE WILLPOWER of a sinner. He'd come into this office determined to tell Casey about the decorations, wish her well this afternoon at the city council meeting, and then make a hasty retreat. But he'd forgotten everything except his name the second he'd seen that book. Maybe even before he'd seen the book. Around Casey, he had a hard time thinking clearly.

Was that pathetic or what?

At this particular moment, he wasn't thinking at all. He brushed his lips against hers lightly, waiting for her to pull back. Waiting for one of them to have enough sense to stop this nonsense. But she didn't move away. Instead, she came closer, close enough to fit snugly against him. Her hands ran over his shoulders and around his neck.

Danger signals flashed in his brain. He needed to exercise some basic self-control. Simple as that. The only problem was he seemed sorely lacking in the precious commodity of control.

So when she moaned, he tipped his head and slipped his tongue inside her inviting mouth. She met him with an eagerness that filled him with desire. Need curled through him, wrapping around his heart, his lungs. But even as he explored her mouth, he felt something different in the embrace. Beneath his desire lay a tenderness he'd never experienced before. Pretty scary stuff. It unnerved him to admit it, even to himself, but he cared for Casey. Cared about what she felt.

Thankfully, at the moment, she felt like pressing against him. He shifted so her belly rubbed against his arousal. She felt so damn good, the lady should be illegal. When she moved against him with a seductive intent that matched his own, he figured at this rate, they might be able to accomplish Number 72 without even taking their clothes off.

He moved one hand from her waist and slid it slowly up her torso. When he reached the underside of her breast, he hesitated, the tips of his fingers tingling in anticipation. Casey murmured something and turned within his embrace. The motion moved his hand higher, and with relief and gratitude, he cupped her full breast.

She continued to make hungry noises as he discovered her firm curve. When she pressed against his hand, he ran his thumb across her taut nipple. She shivered slightly. The sensation made him crazy. Wild. Knowing he affected her deepened the sensations. It felt right holding this woman, which was both frightening and exhilarating. He nudged her toward the desk. He wanted to make love to Casey. Here. The hell with their surroundings. With convention. Need had turned him crazy.

With unsteady hands, he grabbed the bottom of her sweater, intent on pulling it over her head. But noises from the main room drifted through the fog in his brain. Casey wrenched her mouth free from his and pressed her hands against his chest.

"No, Michael. Not here."

He froze as if he'd been tossed into a snowdrift. With effort, he struggled to get his body under control and drew in several deep breaths, willing his rushing blood to cool.

"Yeah. You're right." His arms still held her tightly. "Just give me a minute here."

Actually, he probably needed closer to an hour. What was it about Casey that turned him into a man who couldn't control his own actions? This time he didn't have a supposedly magical car to blame. This time, the fault was one-hundred-percent his. He'd always prided himself on his ability to remain emotionally separate from the women in his life. But now, holding Casey, he knew he was fighting a battle he could easily lose.

Damn. There was a scary thought. He dropped his arms from around her and moved back. Getting involved with Casey could really screw things up. She would further distract him from his job, which would probably cost him the promotion.

"Um, Michael, I—" Casey got no further. A brisk tap barely preceded the opening of the door.

"Hi, there." Calvin Desmond walked in, flashing his usual self-confident smile.

Michael groaned. He'd forgotten Cal had said this morning he might drop by today. Naturally Cal would pick right now to show up. And knowing Cal, he wouldn't miss a thing. Hell, the man could have his eyes shut and still know what had just happened in this room. The atmosphere was ripe with tension. Casey looked flushed and mussed and thoroughly kissed. His own appearance probably mirrored hers.

Well, hell.

No sense avoiding the inevitable. Michael met Cal's quizzical gaze full on. "Hey, Cal. Glad you could make it."

Cal strolled into the office, looking straight at Michael. Then, he turned his gaze toward Casey. A smile as big as a canyon split his face.

"Thanks, Michael. I wanted to see for myself all the great things you're doing here."

A soft noise escaped Casey that sounded something like a smothered giggle. Moving farther away from him, she circled her desk, then she extended her hand to Cal.

"Hi. I'm Casey Richards, the director of the center."

Cal pumped her hand like a thirsty man working a well. "I'm absolutely delighted to meet you, Casey. When I looked into a charity for Michael, I knew he'd be perfect for this place. Guess I was right. I understand you're planning a fund-raiser."

Michael had to hand it to Casey. She looked calm and collected. Still, he couldn't help thinking Cal's interruption had saved him from making a big mistake. He'd been this close to losing control with Casey.

"We hope Big Band Night will be a success." Casey's voice sounded just a tiny bit husky, reminding Michael all too well what they'd been doing just moments ago. "I hope you'll be able to attend."

Cal laughed and winked at Michael. "She's a lot like you. She never misses a chance to make a sell." Turning his attention back to Casey, he said, "I'll be happy to help in any way I can."

An awkward silence settled on the room, and when Casey picked up a stray paper clip, Michael decided to hustle Cal out of the office before the innocent clip was tortured.

"Cal, let me give you a tour." Michael stepped forward, ushering the older man toward the main room. After saying goodbye to Casey, they headed out. Right before leaving her office, Michael glanced back and met Casey's gaze. When she winked at him, he knew he was standing knee-deep in a big pile of trouble.

CASEY SAT facing the members of the city council and the mayor and wished she'd brought reinforcements. What was intended to be a nice, simple meeting had turned into a fiasco.

"Look, all I'm trying to do is preview the fundraiser for you. You've already committed the money needed to buy the house," she said, studying their faces. Two of the members, the ones who had assured her repeatedly that everything was fine, refused to look at her. Something was up.

"We've been rethinking the money allocation for the house," one of the council members said. "There's only a few days left, and we doubt you can raise the rest of the needed money."

Annoyance bubbled up in Casey. Oh, no. They were going to play the chase-their-tails game again. It seemed like every time a new council member was elected, everything had to be completely reexamined. Well, she was downright tired of being examined by these people.

"Of course I can raise the money," Casey said firmly. "I've just shown you our plans. Besides, we have to move. The current building is falling apart. And unsafe. And much too small."

"Well, maybe we should talk it over again," another council member said. "It is a lot of money."

Sheesh. Lord save her from politicians. "What's really going on here?" she demanded, pinning each council member with a hard stare. "Why are you backpedaling?"

Finally, Drew Charlin said, "We're not. It's just this fund-raiser you have planned seems risky. What if it doesn't work?"

She glanced at the council members then back at Drew. "Then I'll find another property and we'll try again. One way or the other, I am going to find a new location for the center."

"Casey, some of the members are new to the council and don't know that much about the center's condition," Drew said. "Why don't you start back at the beginning?"

Oh, for crying out loud! Talk about returning to square one. With a sigh, she settled in her chair, knowing she was in for an annoyingly long meeting.

"Fine, I'll recap why we need the new center, and what changes we envision to our program," Casey said. "Then I'll walk you through the plans for our fund-raiser, Big Band Night."

"MICHAEL, I knew this would be the perfect place for you," Cal said, once their brief tour returned them to the main room. "I can see how much influence you're having."

Michael frowned, unhappy with Cal's assessment. "I haven't done anything." Well, if you didn't count the hole in the wall. "Casey and the seniors have done all the work for the fund-raiser."

Cal dismissed Michael's words with a wave of

his hand. "Nonsense. You got me to agree to holding it at Noress."

Before Michael could comment, Cal nodded his head toward the far corner of the main room. "There is something I'm curious about. Tell me about that lovely lady."

Huh? Confused, Michael looked across the room. A group of women sat talking. If memory served him, they were in charge of publicity for the fundraiser.

"Who?"

"The beautiful one in the blue dress."

Elmira. Michael should have known. Both Tommy and Al had already treated him to long dissertations on the charms of Elmira Ross. Dottie claimed all men were besotted with Elmira, even without benefit of her magical Mercury.

But for Cal to be interested was truly amazing. Cal's wife had died five years ago, and since then, the man had lived like a monk. Michael would have known if there had been a lady in Cal's life. But Cal lived at the office, just as Michael did.

"Her name is Elmira Ross," Michael said, not sure he liked being a matchmaker for his boss. "She's a very nice lady."

"Married?"

Michael shifted, really uncomfortable with this conversation. He liked Cal. He liked Elmira. He felt like a high-school freshman. "Widowed."

"Introduce me."

Even expecting the request, it caught Michael off guard. No doubt about it. The center had a strange effect on Noress execs. They arrived as perfectly sane professionals, but quickly turned into slobbering piles of mush.

Knowing protest would do him no good, Michael led the way across the room. Cal had guts, he'd give him that. He was about to flirt with Elmira under the very watchful eyes of Dottie and the rest of the ladies.

The man had solid-gold guts.

After introducing Cal to the ladies, Michael stepped back and watched his boss in action. Even though Cal had been out of the game for many years, he still hadn't lost the knack. Although polite to all of the women, Cal managed to convey to Elmira that she held a special interest for him. He asked her questions and listened to her answers with just the right degree of attentiveness. And when he asked his final, go-for-broke question, even Michael held his breath.

"A date?" Elmira's voice rose a tiny bit. "You want to take me out to dinner?"

"Say yes," Dottie hissed. "Or I'll never speak to you again."

Intrigued, Michael watched the scene before him. How in the world did Cal imagine he'd have time to date Elmira? Okay, so he'd slowed down since his heart attack, but he continued to work long hours. When did Cal expect to have a social life?

An attractive pink tinge settled on Elmira's cheeks. Michael glanced at Cal. Beguiled. Definitely beguiled. Elmira was still a heartbreaker.

"I'd like to, but I'm afraid I'm too old for you," Elmira finally said.

Cal moved closer. "No, you're not. Please reconsider."

Good manners told Michael to move away, to give these people privacy. But he just couldn't. Natural curiosity forced him to hold his ground until he knew what happened.

"Oh, dear." Elmira looked at Dottie. Then at Michael. And finally at Cal. When she smiled, Michael knew Cal had won.

"I'd love to go."

Michael felt like giving Cal a high five. He'd never seen this side of his boss, hadn't even given any thought to Cal as a man. But the center had a way of getting to people. Heaven knew, these people got to him.

And Casey got to him, too.

Two hours later, Michael knew something was wrong. Casey should have been back by now. Glancing at his watch, he realized she'd never have time to pick up Elmira's birthday cake. He still had some time before his meeting at four, so he grabbed his coat and headed off to the bakery.

When he got back and Casey still wasn't there, he realized the council meeting must be going badly. Casey never missed a birthday party, and she wouldn't start now with Elmira's. He looked at his watch again. Damn, if he didn't hurry, he'd miss his meeting. Maybe he could just leave the cake and the seniors could hold the party themselves. Casey should be here soon.

"Do you think we should start bringing out the plates?" Dottie asked him.

"Actually, I have a meeting—"

Tommy patted him on the back. "That's okay. We can handle this. You head off to your meeting."

Michael glanced around, uncertain what to do. "It is an important meeting," he said lamely.

"You know, we don't need a baby-sitter," Dottie said. "We can be left alone."

Stunned, Michael turned to stare at her. "I don't think of myself as a baby-sitter. I know you don't need me to stay."

Tommy nodded. "That's right. So what's the problem?"

The problem? Michael looked from Tommy, to Dottie, then to Elmira. Something tugged at him, pulled on emotions he didn't even know he had. He wanted to sing *Happy Birthday* to Elmira, listen to Dottie tease her about her age, and then also listen to Tommy and Al come to her defense. He wanted to stay and be part of the fun and the warmth. Looking at Elmira, he knew he wanted her to know she was special to him.

"The problem is, I want to stay," he admitted, tossing his jacket on the back of a chair. "Let me make a quick phone call, then I'll rustle up some balloons." He grinned at Elmira. "Can't forget the balloons, now can we?"

SHE'D DONE IT. Was she hot stuff or what? Casey grinned as she locked her car and headed across the parking lot to the center. There had been several times this afternoon when she'd thought the council would turn her down, but somehow, she'd managed to slam-dunk the presentation.

And now she felt terrific. She could hardly wait to tell the seniors. And Michael.

Shoving open the door to the center, she was all set to share the great news when she noticed the scene before her and stumbled to a stop. Cake. Party plates. Balloons.

Oh, no. She'd forgotten Elmira's birthday party.

"Oh my God," she whispered. From the look of things, the party was over. Most of the seniors were gone. Only a few remained, and they were picking up. How could she forget something so important? Elmira was like a member of her own family. Casey loved her. Images of her own birthday parties as a child hit her. Her father, always so wrapped up in his job, would arrive just as the party ended. If he arrived at all.

She was a horse's patootie. Glancing around, she saw Michael walk out of her office talking to Elmira. When he noticed her, he smiled and waved her over.

"Elmira, I'm so very sorry," she said when she reached the older woman's side. "The meeting ran late, and I didn't dare leave until they agreed to Big Band Night. Please forgive me."

Elmira patted her arm. "That's okay, dear. No harm done. But if you'll excuse me, I'm in a bit of a hurry."

With a final wave, Elmira walked out. From her distracted attitude, Casey didn't believe for a second that the older woman forgave her. With a mental kick to herself, she turned to Michael. "Thanks for staying."

"No problem. I stayed because I wanted to. So how did everything go this afternoon?"

Casey picked up one of the balloons. "They agreed to our plans. Finally."

"Great." He frowned. "You okay?"

No. "Sure. Well, I know you need to get back to your office," she said, her voice overly bright even to her own ears. "And I need to work out some last-minute details."

Casey thought he would argue with her, but eventually he said, "I'll see you tomorrow."

"Tomorrow, yes." Then she walked into her office, quietly shutting the door. How in the world had she forgotten? She hadn't just been late. She'd gotten so caught up in the meeting that she'd completely forgotten about Elmira's birthday party.

Right now, she felt like pond scum. No, it was worse than that—she was so low, she was whatever pond scum despised.

MICHAEL FELT LIKE A FOOL as he climbed the stairs to Casey's apartment. Only a fool would rush through an important meeting so he could go check on a...a what? What was Casey to him? A friend? Naw. She was right. Friends didn't kiss the way they did. No, Casey was a woman who made him feel like he was riding a roller coaster. Dealing with her was both exhilarating and terrifying.

But today, something strange had happened. He'd worried about her. She seemed so unhappy when he'd left her at the center. Worrying about someone was a brand-spanking-new experience for him. An uncomfortable experience that made it difficult for him to concentrate on his meeting. Was this what men like Jeff felt all the time? That they should be somewhere else? It was like being dragged in two different directions by wild horses—not exactly a sensation he wanted to duplicate on a regular basis.

But, fool or not, he had to make certain Casey was all right. So he'd come to see for himself that she was fine. He tapped lightly on her door and waited, uncertain of what to expect.

When she opened the door and he saw her face, he knew he'd been right. She was upset. Her eyes were red-rimmed. His heart twisted when he realized she'd been crying.

"Mind if I come in?" Michael asked.

Casey stood staring at him as if he'd dropped from the sky. Finally, she moved aside so he could enter.

"What are you doing here?" she asked, shutting and locking the door behind him.

Michael didn't answer right away, wanting to first gauge her mood. So instead, he moved into the living room, noticing how it reflected Casey's personality. Two brightly flowered, overstuffed couches filled the small room. Flowers tumbled out of an eclectic assortment of vases, giving the room a cozy feel, and books lined several long shelves. Casey had created a warm room, an inviting room. A room just like her.

Michael turned to face Casey. "I came to make sure you're okay. You seemed upset this afternoon."

Casey nibbled on her bottom lip, and Michael sensed she wanted to talk about it. Deciding to make it easier, he said, "You feel badly about missing the party, right?"

Wordlessly, Casey nodded, the gleam in her eyes telling him she wasn't far from tears again. "I can't believe I missed it."

He gently took her hand in his. Warmth tingled through his fingers. He led her over to one of the couches and sat, pulling her down next to him. When she settled deep into the cushions, he turned to face her.

"You had to go to the council meeting. Elmira understands that," he said emphatically. The unhappiness he saw on her face tugged at him. His need to console her was making him damn nervous. He didn't need a metal detector to know he was smack-dab in the middle of an emotional minefield when it came to this woman. She stirred up all sorts of foreign feelings, and to a man like him, a man who made a point of never getting seriously involved, feelings were the bogeyman. Something scary enough to make him turn tail and run.

But right now, he didn't feel like running. He also didn't want to put a name to these new feelings. Hey, just because he cared about Casey didn't mean he'd totally lost his mind. Just maybe misplaced it temporarily.

Casey sighed. "Being at the party was important to me."

Michael shifted closer to her on the sofa. He didn't even try to be coy. He boldly slipped his arm behind her and gathered her to his side. Dipping his head, he said softly, "And why is that?"

He half expected Casey to refuse to explain, or to at least move out of the circle of his arms. But she did neither. If anything, she snuggled deeper against him.

"Birthdays are special to me."

Brushing a stray strand of hair off her forehead, he asked, "Now why is that?"

She looked faintly self-conscious. "It's silly, really."

"Tell me," he prompted, wanting to understand.

"I wanted Elmira to know I care," Casey said.

"She does. She understood. You had to secure the funding for the center." He frowned, sensing there was something more here. "What's really bothering you?"

With a shake of her head, Casey said, "Never mind. I told you it was silly."

"I won't think it's silly," he said, his gaze never leaving her face. "Well, not unless you tell me you've always secretly wanted to be a clown because you admire their wardrobes."

Casey gave him a faint smile, and he felt some of the tightness around his heart ease.

She shot him a brief glance, then blurted, "See, my father missed almost every birthday party I ever had."

Silently, Michael willed her to go on.

"I know it sounds crazy," she finally added. "But the more parties he missed, the more I wanted him there."

Michael was half-afraid he knew the answer to the question hovering on his lips. Since there was no sense avoiding the inevitable, he bit the bullet and asked, "Why wasn't your dad there?"

She gave him a rueful smile. "He was always working. Always too busy to spend any time with his family. So he missed birthday parties, Thanksgiving dinners and more than one Christmas. My father was a true-blue corporate shark."

Ouch. Michael pushed away memories of how he'd spent Christmas last year at his desk eating vending-machine cuisine. Hey, he could spend

Christmas by himself if he wanted to. He didn't have a family waiting on him. But in his way, Casey's dad was as selfish as Michael's old man had been. Neither one made a place in his life for his children.

This little history lesson sure explained Casey's attitude toward him. She thought that as soon as something important came up at the office, he'd bail on her quicker than a gigolo after the check cleared.

Which of course was exactly what he planned on doing after the fund-raiser.

He pushed aside that anvil-sized block of guilt and focused instead on Casey. Hoping to put a positive spin on this, he asked, "So your father was into his job?"

"That's all he cared about. All he ever thought about."

"And that still bothers you," he said.

"Not really." At his dubious look, she added, "Only in as much as I don't want that kind of obsession in my life. I don't ever want to be that kind of person. To me, life's about more than the next deadline, the next promotion." She shot him an apologetic look. "No offense."

At any other time, Michael would have complimented her on the swift blow to his chin, but he let it slip by. Sure, in his book, working hard was important. But he wasn't so callous that he couldn't understand how long days at the office would strike a child as not caring. "Your father probably worked hard so he could make a good life for his family."

"It was more than that. He felt his job was always his first priority. His job was his whole world, and it didn't seem to matter if he disappointed his family.''

This conversation was hitting a little too close to home for Michael, so he decided to fandango it in a new direction. ''Well, I wouldn't worry about Elmira. She's an adult and knows you wanted to be at the party.''

He sensed Casey wanted to believe him but didn't. ''It doesn't matter what your age is,'' she said. ''You can still have your feelings hurt.''

There were those scary feelings, raising their evil little heads again. Up until a week or so ago, he'd pretty much been able to steer around those bugaboos. But feelings for Casey had brought him here tonight. And feelings for Casey prompted him to say, ''Why don't you call Elmira and talk to her?''

Casey studied him. ''Do you really think I should?''

Like he was an expert on the polite thing to do. Still, he said, ''Yes.'' He shifted away and picked up the portable phone from the end table. ''Do you know her number?''

Casey nodded. ''Elmira and I sometimes talk in the evenings.''

Michael stood and moved across the room while Casey made her call. In a couple of minutes, he knew from the happy tone in Casey's voice that Elmira wasn't upset. With a smile on his face, Michael wandered into the kitchen.

And found ducks. Lots of ducks. Flocks of ducks. Ducks on the wallpaper. Ducks on the dish towels.

Ducks on the oval throw rug on the floor in front of the stove. On one white counter, a large ceramic duck held an assortment of cooking utensils. Then, perched on the side of the sink was another duck with a large blue sponge in its mouth.

Holy…duck.

"You were right," Casey announced from the doorway. "She wasn't upset. She said she knew the meeting was important."

Michael turned toward her, thrilled to see a genuine smile on her face. "Great."

"Actually, she was giddy when I talked to her." Casey leaned against the oak table in the corner of the kitchen. "Apparently, she's getting ready for a date with your boss."

"Oh, yeah, they hit it off while you were at your meeting." He moved toward the door, suddenly uncertain what to say. "I'm glad everything worked out."

"Thanks." She shifted a duck spoon holder around on the table. "Any chance I could convince you to stay for dinner? I'd like to thank you for…tonight." She smiled. "I can't promise anything fancy, so you'd have to settle for potluck."

Of course, a smart man would leave before he got himself in trouble. But then again, a smart man wouldn't have come here in the first place. Hadn't he already decided he was a fool? No sense being a fool with an empty stomach. "Potluck? Exactly what does that mean?"

Casey tossed a duck-covered dish towel at him,

which he caught with one hand. "It means you're lucky you're getting fed at all."

With a grin, Michael placed the towel on the counter. He liked the sparkle in Casey's eyes, the happiness in her smile. There was no sense kidding himself—he wasn't going to be leaving for a while.

"Then I guess I'd better help, just so I can make certain this potluck of yours is safe to eat," he said.

"Trust me, you'll be safe."

Yeah, Michael amended in his mind, *but maybe not smart*.

"I WAS WONDERING if you could help me finish waxing Elmira's car tomorrow," Casey said, stacking the rest of the dishes in the dishwasher. She glanced over at Michael. Dinner had been fun. They'd kept the conversation light and impersonal. "I've moved the car over to the center so we can finish getting it ready."

"Sure. I'll help." Michael said as he wiped the table. "Tommy and Al told me you've been working on it. So what do you think? Is it magic?"

Casey shrugged, suddenly wanting to talk about anything but magical cars that made you fall in love. Truthfully, she didn't believe a word of that nonsense, mostly because she and Michael didn't need to be anywhere near the classic car for their hormones to fly out of control.

"I think Elmira would have fallen for her husband without the car," Casey said, suddenly realizing how cozy she and Michael were in her tiny kitchen.

Michael crossed the room and stopped directly in front of her. He had a teasing gleam in his eyes that was incredibly appealing.

"Aw, come on," he said. "Don't blow an age-old belief right out of the water. Men have been buying fancy cars to impress women for years. Don't tell me that trick doesn't work when I've just bought a brand-new Mercedes."

No fair. Michael was attractive at the worse of times, but when he was teasing with her, he was downright irresistible. Needing to put some distance between them, Casey led the way out of the kitchen and to the living room. "Okay, I won't totally discount the theory. But I still don't believe the car is magical. If it were, we could auction it off for a lot more money."

Michael laughed, the deep rumble coursing through Casey. "Your bottom line is showing."

She smiled and sat down on the sofa, tucking her feet under her. "I guess there's a little of my dad in me, after all. Anyway, let's talk about something else. I told you about my family. What was your childhood like?"

Oops. Wrong question. She watched Michael tense.

"You don't have to talk about it if you don't want to," she said quickly. "We can talk about the fund-raiser instead."

Michael sat near her on the sofa. "No. It's okay. Let's just say I just didn't have a Norman Rockwell-style upbringing."

Indecision filled Casey. She wanted to respect his

privacy, but she also wanted to know more about him.

"Were you an only child?" she asked.

His blue gaze sought and held hers. Reaching out, he took her hand, winding his fingers through hers. Michael looked at their joined hands. "You really want to hear this?" At her nod, he sighed. "You may regret asking, but okay. Yes, I'm an only child."

"Where did you grow up?"

"Oh, all sorts of places. Mostly dumps."

"I'm sure your parents—"

"Casey, before this turns into a daytime talk show, let me sum it up for you. My mother left when I was a toddler. My father stuck around, but he had a heartfelt aversion to work. Of any kind. So he rarely participated." He glanced at her. "He wasn't really mean to me. Just unaware that I was around."

"Oh. I'm sorry."

He shrugged. "Don't be. My childhood taught me to appreciate hard work and the benefits gained from it."

"Like the car that impresses women?" she teased.

Michael smiled. "Maybe. But it's also about having food and a place to live that isn't about to be condemned. It's about feeling your life means something." His blue gaze caught and held her attention. "It's about making a difference."

Boy, did she ever know what he meant. She felt exactly the same way, except she didn't want to make a difference by pulling in a big paycheck. She wanted to bring joy to the people in her life. She struggled to keep her voice steady as she asked, "Where's your father now?"

"Dead. He died the second year I was scrapping my way through college." Michael turned toward her, his large hand cupping her cheek. "Bet you're sorry you asked about my family now."

Blinking, Casey covered his hand with her own and leaned against his palm. He felt warm and secure. And exciting. Very exciting. "To tell you the truth, I'm proud of you."

He stilled. "Proud?"

"Yes." Tenderness for Michael overwhelmed her. How could she have ever thought he was a heartless shark? He'd come here tonight just to make certain she was okay. Not exactly the actions of a man with no heart.

"I'm proud of the man you've become, of the things you overcame," she said. "Look at what you've accomplished."

He started to lean toward her when abruptly he stopped. A groan escaped him seconds before he pulled away from her. "I'd better go."

Drat. She must have said the wrong thing. Casey halted him before he stood. "I didn't mean—"

"You know, I'm sorry, but I can't do this." He leaned back out of her reach. "I shouldn't have told you about my past. I don't want your sympathy."

Sympathy? He thought what she felt for him was sympathy? Casey bit back a laugh and watched as he stood and took two steps away. Then she said, "I don't feel sympathy for you."

He turned and looked at her, his blue eyes darkening dangerously. "You don't?"

She stared at him, her heart in her throat, her palms sweating. Didn't he feel it? The sexual pull between them was so strong she felt it like an undertow. Dragging her toward him. Making rational thought impossible. Even now, looking into his mesmerizing blue eyes, she felt herself falling like Alice down the rabbit hole. She wanted to kiss him, to touch him, to drink her fill of him.

"Oh, Michael, what I feel is desire," she said, her voice a mere whisper in the quiet room.

"DESIRE," Michael repeated, his gaze never leaving her face. He hadn't expected her to say that. Slowly, he moved back to the couch, and when he stood in front of her, brushed the back of his fingers across her cheek. She shivered, and he knew he was lost.

"Casey, are you sure?"

She nodded once, and that was all he needed. He gathered her into his arms, finding her mouth with an overwhelming urgency. When she slid her arms around his neck and parted her lips, he slipped his tongue inside, meeting her own in a seductive dance. He wanted as much as he could get, needing this woman so much it defied logic.

He'd never experienced such intense emotions. Hell, he'd never really experienced any emotions when it came to sex. It had always been about physical needs. But with Casey, it was so much more than just lust. He wanted her body, but he also wanted something more. Something he couldn't name, but felt with equal urgency.

With effort, he pulled his lips away from hers. "Are you *really* sure?" he rasped, not wanting to think about the possibility of her saying no. His heart skipped a beat when she smiled at him.

"Yes, I'm really, *really* sure." Tipping her head, she asked, "What about you? Are you really, *really* sure? I don't want you waking up in the morning and claiming I seduced you."

Michael chuckled. "Don't worry about that. I want to be seduced."

She climbed off the couch and took his hand. "In that case, my bedroom is this way."

Anticipation clawed at him. His body tensed. Silently, he twined his fingers with hers and followed her down the darkened hallway to the last room on the left. She reached inside and flicked on the switch, causing the lamp on the night table to illuminate the room.

Michael's gaze dropped to the double bed, then returned to her face. She was flushed. Worried that she might be feeling shy about what they intended on doing, he freed his hand from hers and raised her chin. When he saw the glow in her green eyes, he was pleased that the flush was due to excitement, not embarrassment.

She tucked a lock of hair behind her ear and gave him a flirty smile. "I want everything to be perfect," she murmured.

"It's already perfect." Michael tugged her close, his lips finding hers again. He sipped at her sweetness as he walked her backward toward the bed. Desire thickened his blood. How could this not be perfect? She made it perfect.

When he felt her bump the bed, his hands slipped down to the hem of her T-shirt. He pulled it free from her jeans, desperate to feel her. A sigh escaped him as he touched the delicate skin on her back, then skirted around to her stomach. He flexed his fingers, slipping them farther under the smooth material. When he grazed the bottom of her bra, she muttered something he didn't quite catch.

Unable to resist, he teased, "Just so we're clear on a few things...." He ran his fingers lightly across the lace of her bra. "I want no cursing here tonight. Groaning is fine. Moaning is great. And it's perfectly acceptable for you to say 'Oh, Michael, you're magnificent.'"

Casey laughed. "Really? Magnificent?"

"Yes. I think *magnificent* will probably sum things up nicely." He moved back far enough to tug her T-shirt over her head. She reached to turn off the light next to the bed, but he stopped her.

"Don't," he whispered. "I want to see you."

Casey studied him. He wondered what she saw in his face. Did she see how special she was to him? Did she see how much he wanted her? She must have, because eventually she nodded and pulled her hand away from the light.

When he met her gaze again, he gently reached around and freed the hooks on her bra. Then, he slipped the straps over her shoulders and down her arms.

At her questioning glance, he said, "Looks like you're pretty magnificent, too."

Before she could cover the beauty he'd exposed, he dipped his head and drew one taut nipple into his mouth. He heard her sighs of pleasure as he tugged on the delicate flesh. His own body was aroused to the point of pain, but he didn't want to rush her. He didn't want to rush himself, either. He wanted to experience this moment with Casey, to be one with her. When she stumbled, he followed her down onto the bed. And when she pulled at his shirt, he sat and quickly shed it, needing to feel her soft breasts against him.

Finding her parted lips again, he lowered his torso over hers until he felt the tight points of her nipples brush against his chest. With a groan, he slid his hand between them and tenderly fondled her. She gasped, and he used the opportunity to deepen his kiss. Unfamiliar emotions coursed through him and mingled with his desire.

He knew Casey would only let him take the lead for so long. When her small hand brushed the front of his pants, he knew she'd decided it was her turn. Through the thickness of his slacks, she explored him, cupped him. She squeezed ever so slightly, and he yanked his mouth free.

"Dangerous move, sweetheart." Gently, he moved her hand. Rolling to his back, he sucked in several deep breaths, trying to slow things down before he lost any chance at being *magnificent*.

Casey sat up and smiled at him, her hair a glorious cascade over her shoulders, her full breasts peaking from between the auburn strands.

He couldn't help himself. He said, "Damn."

She laughed, then reached over and unbuckled his belt. As she slid down the zipper on his pants, she said, "Looks like I'm going to make some money tonight."

"You may not need to hold the fund-raiser after tonight."

Still wearing a teasing smile, she helped him strip off his pants and briefs. Before he tossed them on the floor, he removed his wallet and took out two foil packets.

Then, working together, they removed her jeans and panties. When finally—finally—they were free of their clothes, he leaned her back into the soft mattress, kissing her face, her breasts, her belly. Casey was so beautiful.

When her sighs became urgent, he opened a foil package, rolled the condom in place and parted her thighs. With care, he entered her slowly, squeezing his eyes shut with the intensity of the pleasure. He'd been right. She was perfect.

Although he intended to go slowly, she didn't share his sentiment. She thrust toward him, drawing him deeply into her body. When he filled her completely, she rocked against him, urging him into a rapid tempo.

He didn't need much persuasion. Withdrawing almost completely, he drove into her again. And again. And again, murmuring endearments he didn't even realize he knew into the satiny curve of her neck. Her arms held him tightly, her legs wrapped around his hips. Michael had never felt this way before—the blinding intensity of his own pleasure, the overwhelming wonder of hers. He never slowed his pace, but kept moving, kept pushing them both toward the brink.

Finally, Casey's quiet gasps grew in volume until she clutched him to her, squeezing him tightly with her arms and her body. She tossed her head back and cried out his name. The sound of her climax was more than enough to push Michael over the edge to join her.

"Well, damn," she muttered a few moments later into his damp neck.

Despite knowing that what had just happened between them was a lot more than just killer sex and that he should be terrified clear down to his bones, Michael laughed. At this moment, he couldn't remember ever feeling so happy.

MICHAEL HADN'T LEFT HER, Casey realized with a start when she awoke in the middle of the night. Instead, he lay sprawled next to her, his arm tossed across her stomach. Turning her head, she watched him in the moonlight seeping through her thin drapes. Michael asleep was a marvel. Awake, he always seemed busy, doing something, rushing somewhere. Asleep, he looked so peaceful it reminded her just how sweet and tender he could be.

She sighed. Now why'd she have to go and fall in love with a corporate shark? But she was in love with him. No doubt about it. The feeling washed over her, and she realized she was hopelessly, completely, probably stupidly in love with Michael. Her heart had made its own decision, and there was nothing she could do about it. She could either go looking for trouble or just accept what had happened. Granted, this affair of theirs couldn't go anywhere. After the fund-raiser, Michael no doubt would be back to working nonstop. And she would be busy with the modifications on the new center.

Still, there was now, this night, and the other nights between now and the fund-raiser in a few days. Was there any reason why she couldn't grab the happiness she had within her grasp without worrying about tomorrow? Sooner or later, she knew this thing between them would end, but why did it have to be sooner?

The arm across her tightened. "You're thinking so hard, I can hear you," Michael drawled, his voice sleepy. "Are you making plans for the new center?"

Casey smiled. "No. I was thinking about you."

With a chuckle, he rolled over to face her. Propping his head on one hand, he said, "I hope you're thinking good things."

"Yes."

"No regrets?" She could hear the tension in his voice.

"No." Glancing behind him, Casey noticed a faint glimmer in the moonlight. She realized it was the other condom, as yet unused. Smiling, she decided she wanted whatever time she could have with him. She needed this. These precious days would keep her going long after she and Michael had gone their separate ways.

Her decision made, she leaned across him to pick up the condom. As she started to move back, Michael grabbed her around the waist. She squealed, but didn't try to get away.

"I was thinking, since we have this, maybe we should use it." She held up the condom for him to see.

Michael chuckled. "Waste not, want not."

8

MICHAEL SAT in his office Thursday afternoon staring out the large window behind his desk. Big Band Night was on Saturday, and he still hadn't told Casey he wouldn't be coming back after that.

You might as well paint a yellow stripe down his back and call him a coward. Because that's what he was. A coward. He'd meant to tell her. He really had. But things between them were so great he didn't want to rock the boat. Telling Casey he wasn't going to help at the center anymore would more than rock the boat. It would sink it straight to the ocean floor. More than likely, Casey would take his leaving as further proof that he really was an unrelenting workaholic who only cared about his job.

But that wasn't true. He cared about Casey, too, and didn't want their affair to end. Not now. Not when things between them were so spectacular that his life felt perfect for the very first time. It was selfish of him, but he didn't want to stop being with Casey.

Still, he had to be honest with her. After the fundraiser, he couldn't afford to spend any more time away from work. Turning back to his computer, he studied the piles of paper on his desk. He had to be crazy to be thinking about Casey now. His work needed his full attention for the next few weeks, if not months, and yet here he sat, mooning over Casey. He had to face facts: he didn't have time for an affair, especially a hot, wild, all-consuming... amazing affair. Being with Casey was a distraction. A major, serious distraction that could easily cost him the promotion to president of Noress if he didn't watch himself. He needed one hundred percent of his concentration focused on work. Then he had a real shot at the job.

A job that was going to be available soon. Cal had mentioned a couple of days ago that he planned on retiring after the merger went through. So Michael knew he couldn't lose his focus now. Not now when everything he'd ever wanted was almost within his grasp. If he continued to see Casey, she'd need to understand about his job.

Which meant there was a pretty good chance Casey would tell him to buzz off. But still, maybe they could reach a compromise. They were both intelligent, reasonable people. Maybe, despite the way her father had treated his family, maybe she'd understand if he couldn't be with her very often over the next couple of months. And just as soon as the merger crisis ended, they could be together more.

Michael sighed. It would be easier to convince Casey that he was the Easter Bunny than convince her the merger would be the last crisis dropped in his lap. There was always a crisis at work, and the employees depended on him to keep the company

running. They would depend on him even more if
he got promoted and became the president.

"Drat," he muttered, then smiled. Casey sure
had him trained. He couldn't even curse in the privacy of his own office anymore without wanting to
pay someone a dollar.

There had to be a solution to this problem. He
didn't want to stop seeing Casey, but he knew she
deserved better than a man who was hardly ever
with her, a part-time lover who came to see her only
when his schedule allowed it.

Which, unfortunately, was all he had to offer.
Well, the only fair thing was to let Casey decide.
She needed to make up her own mind, and he'd just
have to live with the consequences.

He'd also pray she didn't ask him to put his feelings for her into words because he flat-out couldn't.
Was what they had love? How would he know? He
didn't know what love looked like, how it felt. And
it wasn't as if there was a standardized test you
could take to find out for sure. No, figuring out his
feelings was going to be a lot more difficult than
choosing: A—She has a great laugh. B—She makes
me smile. Or C—She really, *really* turns me on.

Of course, he'd have to choose D—All of the
above.

But was that love or just really great lust? He
didn't know. All he knew was he wanted to keep
seeing her as much as their schedules allowed. So
tonight, he'd take her out to a romantic dinner, explain how important she was to him, and then see
if there was a compromise they could reach. After

that, he'd pray she didn't tell him to take a flying leap.

Because if she did, he didn't know what he'd do.

"I'M NEVER GOING TO FIND something to wear." Casey paced around her bedroom, tossing dress after dress on her bed. *Sheesh.* There was no reason for her to be nervous. They'd spent the last three nights making love in her bed. Still, she'd been jumpy since Michael had asked her out today when he'd been at the center. He'd seemed so serious that she got the feeling he wanted to talk.

For them, talking could only lead to trouble. Really big trouble. Maybe he'd decided he didn't want to see her anymore. Maybe he'd realized their being together was a huge mistake. Which, of course, it was. They both had things to accomplish in life, and they certainly didn't have time for a relationship.

But she wanted to be with him. Love flowed through her for Michael. How could he not feel the same magic? He had to. If she were a brave woman, she'd ask him how he felt, demand he admit he loved her back. She knew she wouldn't do it, though. In some ways, she was brave. But not brave enough to ask Michael if he loved her.

She finally decided to wear a short black dress. Placing it on her bed, she reached for her perfume and dabbed a drop between her breasts. Before she could slip into the dress, she heard a definite knock on her door. She looked at the clock. It was seven. It was Michael.

Feeling mischievous, she vetoed the dress and put

on her robe instead. When she opened the front
door, the sight of Michael looking tall and handsome and sexy did nothing to settle her already fraz-
zled nerves. Yep, she wasn't brave at all. But she
knew he felt the magic between them, too. She
could see it in his heated gaze.

"Hi," he said in that deep voice that made shiv-
ers run up her spine. "You look great."

She laughed. "No, you look terrific. I'm in my
bathrobe."

He raised one dark brow. "Need some help getting dressed?" he asked as he moved farther into
her apartment, closing the door behind him.

Looking up at him, Casey felt her love for this
man lodge in her throat. She couldn't ask him how
he felt, but she could show him her feelings.

"Let's stay here," she blurted out.

"Here?" He studied her for a moment, then
grinned.

"Yes." Her voice sounded husky, laden with desire.

"And talk?"

Casey sucked in a deep breath. "No." With one
pull, the knot came undone on her robe. The sides
parted. Now seemed like a good time to go for
broke, so she shrugged the robe off her shoulders.
It dropped to the floor, leaving her standing in only
her strapless black bra and panties.

Silence settled on the room, broken only by the
ticking of the grandfather's clock in the corner of
the living room. Casey would have felt incredibly
self-conscious if it hadn't been for the way Mi-

chael's gaze wandered over her, lingering occasionally on things he apparently found interesting. The look he gave her when his gaze returned to her face was nothing short of incendiary. Wearing a tiny smile, she took a step forward. Then another. And finally, she took the last step that brought her directly in front of him.

In that moment, standing before Michael and looking up into his handsome face, Casey felt as if she was drowning and going down for the third time. Her love for Michael overwhelmed her. Even if he was the wrong man, she loved him. And the thought of that love filled her with joy.

Michael slid one strong arm around her waist, pulling her flush against his body. She felt how aroused he was, how much he desired her. He bent his head and found her lips. This time, his kiss didn't start out gentle. Instead, the kiss was about hunger and need. About temptation and fulfillment. Casey wrapped her arms around his neck, meeting his urgency with her own. She opened her mouth, granting him access, and moaned when he accepted her offer. Then he startled her by lifting her off the ground. At his prompting, Casey wrapped her legs around his waist and squeezed him.

"I'm too heavy," she said, looking deep into his darkened blue eyes. "I don't want you to strain anything."

Michael chuckled as he carried her the few feet to her bedroom without showing the slightest sign of difficulty. "I get the feeling there's a purely selfish motive behind your concern."

As he walked, he never took his gaze off her face. Love spilled through Casey like a waterfall. They hadn't settled anything about their future. She knew that. But she had tonight with him. And maybe tomorrow.

And that would have to be enough.

"I was hoping to seduce you—unless, of course, you'd rather still go out to dinner," she teased, holding him tightly.

"Honey, you couldn't blast me out of here with dynamite," he said seconds before his lips found hers.

WHEN SHE WOKE the next morning, he was walking out of the adjoining bathroom, drying his hair with a blue towel. Unconcerned with his nakedness, he walked over to the bed and kissed her lightly. "Want to join me for breakfast?"

What she wanted to do was convince him to come back to bed, but then they'd end up late for work. "Just give me a minute."

"Sure," he said.

She sat up and stretched her arms above her head, enjoying the hot look he gave her as he stared at her naked breasts.

With a groan, he pulled on his pants. "I can't stand here and be tortured. I'll see you out in the kitchen."

Casey immediately missed the warmth of his body but had to admit that food sounded wonderful. After he left, she took a quick shower, pulled on her robe and padded down the hall.

When she reached the kitchen, he gave her such a sexy look she decided to play it safe and stay on the opposite side of the table while he poured some coffee and put bread in the toaster.

"Why don't you come over here?" he asked, when she evaded his grasp.

Casey shook her head. "You said you wanted breakfast. I'm hungry, and when I get near you, we both seem to have trouble keeping track of our hands."

"I don't mind."

She shook her head again. "Because you're a good sport."

He started to say something but the toast was done. Grabbing a piece, he buttered it and handed it to her. "Here's food. As promised."

Taking the other piece of toast for himself, he ate it slowly.

"Aren't you going to butter that?" she asked, unable to stop staring at him.

"No. I'm in a hurry to finish breakfast."

Casey smiled. "Now why is that?"

"Have you had enough to eat?" he asked rather than answering her question. Slowly, deliberately, he circled the table, a heart-stopping grin forming on his face. When he reached her side, he picked her up and set her down on the edge of the table. She grabbed his shoulders and started to protest. But before she could say anything, he nudged her legs apart and stepped between them. Desire flared through her like a brushfire. She draped her arms around his shoulders and then wrapped her legs around his hips.

"We never did try Number 72," he muttered before his mouth claimed her lips in a deep kiss, his tongue seeking hers out. His hands pushed her robe out of their way and found her breasts. He tugged softly on her nipples. Moaning, she kneaded the muscles in his back, then moved her hands down his torso to his pants. Her fingers fiddled unsuccessfully with the fastening until she said against his lips, "How do you get this open?"

He lifted his lips for a second. "What are you looking for?" he teased, one of his hands dropping between her thighs and nuzzling against her soft hair. He slid one finger inside her and recaptured her mouth in time to swallow her moan. Slowly, he stimulated her, stroking her until she rode the waves of pleasure he created. When she climaxed, he released her mouth and watched her face.

When the delicious tremors ended, she blushed as the realization of what had just happened flooded through her.

"Michael," she murmured with embarrassment, burying her face in his shoulder. When she lifted her head, he smiled.

"You think you're so smart," she said yanking on the top of his pants.

"Brains had nothing to do with it."

Casey feathered kisses on his face, then leaned back and cupped his cheek. "That was fun. But that wasn't Number 72."

His eyes twinkled. "Why don't you show me what is?"

She pulled his head down and rested her lips against his. "Okay," she whispered, her tongue outlining his lips and then dipping inside. Michael always made her feel so empowered while they made love.

As she kissed him, he dug his hand into her hair and met her hunger. She could feel his smile when she finally released the clasp on his pants. She lowered the zipper, freeing him. Her robe still hung from her shoulders, and she fumbled in the pocket for a condom. When she had him covered, he pulled her forward on the table and entered her with one powerful thrust.

Then his movements gentled. His kiss turned so tender she almost cried. He made her feel wanted and treasured at the same time. Behind the gentle brushing and lifting of his lips, the passion they ignited in each other smoldered, held in place by Michael's strong will.

When he caressed her, his hands were equally gentle. They touched and savored her curves, cupping her breast lightly until she arched into his palm. Tentatively, his thumb rubbed her nipple, bringing it to a peak. Then, he tugged until her breath came in tight gasps. She raked her fingers through his hair, drifting down to his shoulders and kneading his taut muscles. She chanted his name softly until his lips returned to hers.

Suddenly, his thrusts turned urgent, almost frantic. He drove into her deeply as if trying to possess her completely. Matching his rhythm, she threaded her fingers through his hair, holding his mouth on hers. As the intensity of his thrusts increased, she pulled her mouth free and clung to him. The tension grew within her, strengthening, tightening, until with a moan, she clutched his shoulders and savored her release. His own climax quickly followed hers.

For a moment, they held each other, their breathing ragged and deep. She rubbed his back, feeling the tightness in his muscles slowly seep away. When he lifted his head, he kissed her. Then he moved away, closing her robe and helping her down.

"Wow," she said, not sure her legs would hold her. "Double wow."

Michael gave her a wry smile, his gaze direct and intense. A knot formed in her throat. Something was up. She could tell.

"Casey…you mean a lot to me," he finally said softly.

Oh, no. That didn't sound good. "Um, me… too."

"I feel whole when I'm with you," he finished, his voice thick and husky.

Okay. That didn't sound as bad. Right now would be a good time to tell him she loved him. But as overwhelming and wonderful as the thought of Michael caring for her was, she sensed there was more to come.

"But?" she prompted.

He looked away, his jaw tight. She held her breath, willing him to say he loved her, that he'd be with her, that he'd put her before his job. But that was asking for the moon.

After an eternity, he glanced back at her. "As soon as the fund-raiser is over, I need to go back to work full-time."

Casey turned his words over in her mind. He wasn't going to volunteer anymore, but she really wasn't surprised. She'd expected this. Michael wanted to go back to working fourteen-hour days. To living and breathing his job.

Moving away from him, she carried her plate to the sink. "I understand." And she did. He wanted to spend all of his time at work, so this was the end of them.

"No. You don't," Michael said.

Bracing herself, she turned to face him, trying to force air into lungs that seemed to have forgotten how to breathe. "So what are you saying?"

"I think we should live together."

DAMN. He hadn't intended on saying that. He hadn't intended on saying anything *remotely* like that. But that was what Casey did to him. She made him do things completely out of character. But when the words jumped out of his mouth, he realized he meant them. He wanted to live with Casey so he could at least see her every night.

Casey, though, stood staring at him as if he'd been possessed by a demon. "You're kidding."

He realized she wasn't asking a question, but making a statement. "No." He moved forward and took her hands in his. "I guess you know that once

I go back to work, I'll have to put in long hours." Before she could say anything, he added, "But you'll have to put in some long days at the new center."

Casey slowly sank into one of the high-backed kitchen chairs. "Michael, I don't—"

He moved to stand directly in front of her. "What bothers you about the idea?"

Casey shrugged. "Everything."

"Such as?" He sat in the chair next to her, forcing himself to stay calm. But it was hard. He wanted her to say yes.

"Have you thought this through?" she asked.

He hadn't, but he wasn't about to admit that. Because now that he'd suggested the idea, he was convinced it would work. "I'm certain."

She leaned forward, her scent surrounding him. "I think it's just the sex—"

"This isn't about sex, Casey. This is about..."

Her intense gaze focused on him. "About what?"

What was it about? Love? He didn't know. "It's about caring for each other. I enjoy being with you." His words were tame compared to the emotions surging through him. Casey's expression made it clear she wasn't swayed by what he'd said.

"I don't think it will work," she said quietly.

"What do you feel for me?" he asked.

Wide-eyed, Casey blinked at him. "I'm in love with you," she said, her voice brushing over his skin.

He hadn't expected that. A surge of happiness

shot through him. He pulled her into his arms. "Then don't say no. We can make it work."

"Michael, we're so different," she protested. "Your job is everything to you. And I need a man who will be there for me."

He bent to kiss her sweet, sexy lips. "My job's not everything. Sure, I love my job, but I'll make this work, too. I promise you. I'll make this work."

Knowing it wasn't fair, he kissed her before she could argue. As always, she melted against him, and he knew he would keep his promise. He would find a way to make this work.

Resting his forehead against hers, he said, "Just think about it, okay? Please, think about it."

He held his breath until she nodded. Then he knew, everything would be all right. Everything would be fine.

CASEY FINISHED polishing the hood of the old Mercury and stood back to admire her handiwork. Boy, if she could afford it, she'd buy this gorgeous car in a heartbeat.

"Hello, Casey," Elmira said, coming to stand next to her. "You look very happy today."

Casey wasn't sure she'd call herself *happy*. Sure, the plans for Big Band Night were coming along nicely. And sure, everyone's spirits were high, and Casey was thrilled for the seniors. And sure, it was definitely starting to look like the fund-raiser would work.

But was she happy? Tough question. She still didn't know what to do about Michael.

"I'm doing okay," she finally said.

Elmira nodded. "I understand." With a quick pat on Casey's arm, she added, "Hon, men are like shoes. It takes a while to break them in."

Casey laughed. "Shoes?"

Elmira glanced over Casey's shoulder, then gave her a conspiratorial wink. "I think Michael's coming over to help you. I'll go...um, check on my surfboard. Have fun."

As Elmira hurried away Casey heard Michael walk up behind her. Gathering her courage, she turned to face him. Ever since they'd become lovers, they'd pretty much left their personal relationship outside the center. Although judging from Elmira's words, the seniors knew all about them.

"Hi," he said.

"Hi." She wiped her hands on her jeans. "I think the car's about ready for tomorrow night."

He stood back and studied the Mercury. "So I see. Anything I can do to help you?"

Sure. Fall in love with me. Deliberately, she moved away from him. She needed time to think. She'd never really considered living with a man before, for a lot of reasons. The main one being she'd never been in love before.

But she was now, and like Michael, she wanted to spend whatever time they could find together. But was that building a future or just postponing the inevitable? When push came to shove, would he choose business over her? Would she end up like her mother, bitter about the days and nights she spent alone? Casey couldn't let that happen to her.

"Can I help?" Michael repeated.

She blinked and turned to face him. "Al and Tommy are finishing the final preparations for the auction. Maybe you can help them."

When she started to walk past him, he blocked her way. He placed one hand on her shoulder, the warmth of his touch having its usual effect on her hormones. "Casey, have you thought about what I suggested this morning?"

"Yes."

"And?"

She looked up into his face, love filling her. How could she say no? But how could she say yes? Reluctantly, she said, "I don't think it's a good idea."

"Why not? You said you love me."

She didn't want to make this choice. Not now. "I do love you, but like I said, I think we're too different."

"We can work out any problems," he rasped, moving closer to her. "If we want to."

She looked beyond him. Several of the seniors were milling about, and Al was heading their way.

"Do you love me?" she whispered.

Now it was Michael's turn to stare at her. "I care about you—"

She waved one hand. "That's not the same. Do you love me?"

His silence pretty much answered her question. Finally he said, "I don't think I know how to love."

Not the answer she wanted. The world seemed to lurch beneath her feet, but she couldn't waver.

"Then you have to learn before we can have a future."

"Casey, don't do this. I just need some time to sort through what I'm feeling. All I know is you're too precious to me to lose."

"Can we talk about this later?" she asked, feeling self-conscious having this conversation at the center.

Michael seemed oblivious to the seniors. "Fine. Later. Just tell me one thing, why won't you live with me if you love me?"

Sheesh. He was making this difficult. She would prefer to stand in the middle of a room of supermodels with a serious case of bed head rather than tell Michael the truth, but she couldn't lie to him.

"I won't live with you because I don't trust you to be there when I need you," she said.

ON THE DRIVE to his office, Michael admitted to himself that he was angry. Not at Casey, but at himself. He should be able to tell her he loved her, to promise he'd always be there. But he didn't know if he could. It wasn't as if he didn't care about Casey, but he didn't know if what he felt was love.

Didn't she know that asking her to live with him was a huge step for him to take? He'd never even considered the possibility of a long-term relationship before. But he was more than willing to consider it now.

Still upset, Michael found Cal pacing in his office when he got to work. One look at Cal's face was more than enough to convince Michael something was wrong.

"The merger's going down the toilet," Cal said without any preamble.

Michael set his briefcase on his desk, dread filling him. He knew he shouldn't have spent so much time away from the office. If he'd been spending his days at his desk, he could have prevented this.

"What happened?" he asked Cal.

"They withdrew the offer. You realize what this means, don't you? If this merger falls through, we have to close the Michigan plant. That's almost four hundred jobs lost."

Michael leaned against his desk, alternatives running through his mind. Unfortunately, he couldn't come up with any other solutions. Noress needed this merger like a dying man needed a transfusion. "We have to save the deal."

Cal stopped directly in front of him. "How? They've called off negotiations."

Michael was living his worst nightmare. He knew how to solve this problem, and it was killing him. Why did everything in life have to be so damn hard?

"They'll listen to me if I fly up there tonight and fix it," he said finally.

"Isn't your fund-raiser thing tomorrow? I thought you had to be there," Cal said.

Michael felt like alcohol had just been poured into a gaping wound in his heart. There was no way he could save the merger and be back in time for Big Band Night. Casey would never understand him missing the fund-raiser. Moreover, he had wanted to be there, not only for her, but also for the seniors. Over the last few weeks, those people had come to mean a lot to him.

He looked at Cal. He hated this, but he had no choice. Not really. Those employees needed him. If he didn't go up there and work this out, they would be out of work within a matter of weeks.

"It's more important I try to save the merger," Michael said. "I don't need to be at the dance."

"But Casey—"

"Will be fine," Michael said, knowing he was lying. She would never forgive him. He ran a weary hand through his hair. "I guess I can explain what's happening to her—"

"Not unless you want to get us in a real mess. You preannounce this merger, and we're in deep legal trouble," Cal said.

"Casey won't tell anyone."

"Doesn't matter. *You* aren't allowed to tell anyone."

Michael nodded, knowing his boss was right. He couldn't tell her what was happening. Could this get any worse? Casey was going to hate him.

Cal patted him on the arm, compassion evident on the older man's face. "Just tell her it's important business. I'm sure she'll understand."

Yeah, right. And pigs could learn to fly. "I doubt it," Michael said.

"Sure she will. She cares about you. And I know she means a lot to you, or you wouldn't be worried about what she'll think."

"Cal, this morning, I asked Casey to live with me."

Surprise crossed Cal's face. "Really? Good for you. Well, then, that's even more reason why she won't mind you missing the fund-raiser. If she's willing to live with you, she knows how important your job is."

"She'll be devastated," Michael said, knowing it was true. Tomorrow night meant everything to Casey. How could he miss one of the most important nights of her life?

Cal continued to watch him. "Maybe we could get Jeff to—"

Michael waved away the suggestion. "No. It's my deal, so I'll save it."

With a nod, Cal headed toward the door. Right before he left, he turned and looked at Michael. "I'm proud of you, Michael. You've made the right choice."

"I know," Michael said. It *was* the right choice. But as he watched Cal leave his office, he knew there was no way Casey would understand. She'd think he'd chosen business over her, and she wouldn't understand.

He knew it as well as he knew his own name.

9

CASEY HALF EXPECTED the knock on her door about an hour after she got home. Michael hadn't said he was going to stop by, but she wasn't surprised he had. They needed to talk, but boy, was she dreading this conversation.

Peering through the peephole, she saw him standing outside and the butterflies in her stomach turned into giant, flying bats. Taking a deep breath, she tried to calm her nerves and opened the door. Why did love have to be so complicated? As much as she wanted to tell him that she would live with him, she just wasn't certain it would work.

One look at Michael's expression, and her anxiety was immediately replaced with fear. Cold, alone-in-the-house-with-a-psycho fear. Something bad had happened.

"What's wrong?" She stepped aside so Michael could enter her apartment, but he remained standing in the doorway.

"I have to leave town for a couple of days," he said bluntly.

Casey sucked in a startled breath, feeling like he'd thrown a sucker punch. "What? Will you be back in time for Big Band Night?"

He shook his head. "I can't tell you how upset I am about this," he said. "I want to be there tomorrow, but a problem has come up at work, and I'm the only one who can solve it."

Casey's throat closed up. After everything they'd done, after all the plans, he was standing her up so he could go on a business trip. She'd heard this song played time and again while growing up. Got to go. Be back sometime. Love ya.

Yeah, right.

"I see," was all she said, all she could think to say. She leaned back against the wall, needing the support. How could he do this? More important, how could she have been so foolish as to fall for a workaholic? Sooner or later, corporate sharks always reverted to type.

"Casey, I don't *want* to go. I *have* to go. I want to be here with you," he said, his voice strained. "You think I'm like your father, but I've changed. Right now, I don't want to be anywhere other than with you. But I can't let the Noress employees down."

Casey registered the sincerity in his voice. She knew Michael felt he was doing the right thing by taking this trip. He truthfully believed he was doing it for the employees. Normally, Casey would have cut him some slack, but she'd seen her mother swallow that same line year after lonely year. She didn't want the same solitude for herself. She didn't want to spend countless nights alone while the company took precedence.

And she wouldn't do it. She might love Michael,

but she couldn't spend her life with him. If he would miss the fund-raiser, knowing what it meant to her, then he would miss other important moments in their life together.

So she'd stop things right here, right now, no matter how much it hurt. In her mind, this breakup was like yanking a bandage off a cut. If she did it fast, the pain wouldn't hurt as much. Well, at least not in the long run.

"I don't think we should see each other anymore," she said softly, ignoring his loud protest at her words. "You have different priorities than I do, so I think—"

"Dammit, Casey, don't do this. I can't tell you why I won't be at the fund-raiser. This trip is confidential. But you need to believe that I don't want to go. It's important."

"Big Band Night is important, too. Now if you'll excuse me, I don't think we have anything else to say to each other."

"Casey, no," he begged.

She wiped a couple of stray tears off her cheeks. Where had those come from? She never cried. Ever. And she wasn't going to start now, even if the anguish in his voice made her heart constrict. "It's over, Michael."

"Don't do this," Michael said again. "I know now I love you."

A sob caught in her throat at his words. "I love you, too. Except love isn't enough. I refuse to be in love with someone who isn't there for me. So it has to end now. I'm sorry."

Not daring to risk the possibility that Michael might say something to weaken her resolve, she moved to shut the door. "I have to go."

He slapped his palm against the door, keeping it open. "I can't send someone else. This is my responsibility."

"Then go. Do what you have to do."

They stood, for timeless moments, facing each other across the threshold. Casey knew how much it had cost Michael to admit that he loved her, and his admission made her heart break even more. He was a good man who wouldn't mean to hurt her. But he would always choose business.

Silently, she pushed on the door. This time, Michael didn't stop her. He let go, and the door swung shut. And once it was closed, Casey realized it was over. It had only been a matter of time before this happened. She should have known better than to fall for a corporate shark like Michael. Whenever you needed them most, they were always somewhere else.

More tears threatened to fall, but she held them back. She would not cry. Not about this. But the dampness on her cheeks was making a liar out of her. Finally, a couple of tears broke free and ran down her cheeks. Drat. She was tough. She was strong. She didn't want to cry over a man. But when more tears escaped, she decided she would hate Michael Parker for the rest of her life. She would also love him for the rest of her life.

Dragging in a deep breath, she headed to the living room, snagging a handful of tissues before she curled up on the sofa. She'd done the right thing. Someday, she'd find someone else. She'd fall in love again. Maybe he wouldn't be quite as handsome as Michael. And maybe his hair wouldn't droop across his forehead in that cute way Michael's did. And maybe he wouldn't make her laugh like Michael could. But he'd still be a great guy. And he'd be there for her. And for their children.

He just wouldn't be Michael.

That thought twisted her heart, but she reined in her grief. She could be strong about this. She *would* be strong about this.

After all, no one had ever died of a broken heart.

"WOULD YOU LIKE something to drink?"

Michael looked up at the flight attendant and shook his head. "No thanks." After she wheeled her cart away, he turned his attention back to the window next to him. Normally, he loved to fly. He enjoyed the thought of being so far above the ground. But today, he couldn't relax. All he could think about was Casey and what had happened between them.

He'd finally told a woman he loved her, and she'd literally shut the door in his face. Not that he could blame her. She'd made it clear to him several times how important it was that he be there for her. And he'd wanted, more than anything, to be there tomorrow.

But the merger was just too important. Damn. Wasn't this just like life? Here he'd finally found a woman to love, and he'd had to toss her love away in order to save Noress. This was what he'd tried to avoid all along with Casey—this feeling of guilt, of remorse. He'd never resented his job until today. He loved working for Noress, cutting the deals, seeing the profits grow. But right now, he'd give anything to be back home. With her.

Except four hundred jobs depended on him. He couldn't throw them away. Those jobs represented the hopes and dreams of other people. And those people trusted him. So he had to do what he could to save their jobs.

As much as he liked to think he could convince Casey to reconsider when he got back home, he knew he had a better chance of sprouting wings and flying to Michigan himself. Her father had laid the groundwork for her prejudice against corporate execs, and he'd finished the job. Part of what he loved about Casey was her determination. But now that determination would cost him everything. She wouldn't change her mind, wouldn't give him an inch. Nope, Casey Richards was one tough lady.

But what had he expected? He'd known all along he wasn't cut out for love. He couldn't finally discover love at thirty-four and be any damn good at it. Besides, Casey was right. This trip wouldn't be the last emergency he'd face during his career. There would be plenty more. Another crisis, or emergency, or opportunity. He'd have to be there. He'd have to be free to hop on a plane and go where he was needed without worrying about hurting someone. He couldn't spend his life constantly making those kinds of choices.

He also knew it wasn't fair to expect someone to always let him leave. No woman deserved to be left alone all the time. That wasn't love, and it sure as hell wasn't a life. Casey deserved so much more than he could offer her.

No, they'd both be better off if things ended here. Sure, he'd hurt for a while. She'd hurt, too, and that thought made him almost frantic. But in the end, in a couple of years, they'd both be better off. He'd have the promotion and everything he'd ever worked for, and Casey would have the new center and probably find another man who would be there for her.

That thought made Michael's stomach drop. Another man with Casey. Holding her. Loving her. Having children with her.

Damn, he hated his job right now. Almost as much as he hated himself.

"Wow, THIS PLACE looks like a fairyland," Dottie said, tugging Casey farther into the cafeteria. "Noress sure knows how to throw a party."

Casey glanced around and had to agree. With silver and white decorations everywhere and small twinkling lights cascading down the walls, the room did resemble something out of a story. Every table was draped in a cream linen tablecloth and had an impressive flower centerpiece with a large flicking candle in the center.

The decorations were so much more than she had hoped for. When she'd showed up this morning, she'd found a professional crew already at work.

The foreman of the group explained that Noress often held large functions in this room and had the necessary supplies. When she saw Cal tonight, she would thank him for his generosity.

"It does look pretty terrific," Casey agreed. "Plus it's a good thing we've got a room this big. Michael and Cal have invited everyone they know."

"Hey, what about me?" Dottie put her hands on her hips. "I rustled up more than a few people for you by using some heavy guilt on all my relatives. After this, I'll be getting fruitcake from everyone at Christmas."

Casey chuckled. "I appreciate your sacrifice."

"No problem." Dottie squeezed her arm. "I'm really sorry about Michael. Are you okay?"

Casey nodded. "Sure. I'm going to have a great time. Why don't you go mingle?"

Dottie studied her face. "Are you sure? Because I can stay with you if—"

Shaking her head, Casey nudged her friend toward the crowd. "No. Go. I'm fine."

After Dottie walked away, Casey rubbed a nervous hand against the side of her calf-length black dress. Getting ready for the party had been a nightmare. She'd run two pairs of hose, smeared her eyeliner and been unable to get her hair into a bun. Finally, she'd dug up a spare pair of hose, taken off the eyeliner and decided to leave her hair loose. She was in no mood to fight with anything tonight.

Glancing around the room, she realized couples were starting to drift in, so she went over to greet them. Everyone looked so terrific, all dressed up for the party. The seniors, especially, had dressed to the hilt. She spotted both Tommy and Al wearing tuxedos, while several of the women had on glittering long dresses.

Casey was too jumpy to sit while dinner was served. She circled the room, making certain everything was perfect. Finally, after the plates were removed, the band arrived and launched into a loud, upbeat song. Smiles covered each face, and Casey knew she had to smile back, so she did, but found it difficult pretending to be happy. As much as she hated to admit it, she was downright miserable. She missed Michael and desperately wanted him next to her tonight.

For the millionth time, she berated herself for being silly enough to fall in love with a shark. She, of all people, should have known better. Of course he'd chosen his job over her.

"Looks like the party should bring in some serious cash," Cal said next to her.

Casey turned and shook his hand. Elmira stood by his side, her hand resting on his arm. Apparently their romance was progressing far better than her own had with Michael.

"I'm keeping my fingers crossed. You and Michael sure convinced a lot of people to come. The advance ticket sales alone had almost brought in enough money. And thankfully, we're getting quite a few last-minute attendees, so we should be all right." She smiled at Elmira. "You're looking beautiful tonight."

Beautiful was an understatement. The older woman practically beamed with happiness. Dressed in a floor-length blue velvet gown, Elmira looked elegant.

"Thank you, Casey. I'm having a wonderful time." Elmira looked around. "Where's Michael?"

Apparently she hadn't heard the news yet. Before Casey could answer, Cal said, "He had to go away on business."

Mouth open, Elmira looked up at Cal. "You sent him away the night of the party?"

To give him credit, Cal seemed unruffled by her question. "I didn't send him. He made his own choice. But it was vital he go." Then he led Elmira off toward the dance floor.

Casey resisted the impulse to follow Cal and ask him to explain just what was so vital it couldn't wait twenty-four hours. Michael could have caught a plane after the party if he'd wanted to. It was the weekend. Who worked on the weekend? Well, other than a shark.

Glancing over at the dance floor, she watched Cal and Elmira. The couple danced together as if they'd been doing it for years. Standing alone, Casey couldn't help feeling happy for them and sad for herself. Cal had managed to be here tonight. He hadn't been called away on some last-minute business.

She would have loved to have Michael hold her like that and spin her around the dance floor. She felt her eyes misting, and struggled to remain in control. But she wouldn't cry anymore. Her pity party was officially over.

Deciding to dry her eyes before any tears fell, she hurried toward the bathroom, hoping no one saw her. She wouldn't ruin tonight, no matter what had happened with Michael.

Tonight was too important to spoil.

HE WAS GOING to be late, Michael decided with a curse. He increased his speed, running through the airport for all he was worth. Until now, he'd thought he was in pretty good shape, but sprinting for a plane was the way to find out.

Reaching the gate just as they were shutting the door, he hollered for them to wait and handed his ticket to the startled gate agent.

"You're cutting it close, aren't you?" she said, pulling off his ticket and handing him the boarding pass.

"You have no idea," Michael said. He grabbed the stub from her and hurried down the jetway toward the plane.

"Glad we didn't leave without you," the flight attendant said when he stepped inside the plane. "Let's get you in your seat."

Glancing at Michael's boarding pass, the attendant directed him to the remaining empty seat in first class. Michael shoved his small suitcase in the overhead compartment and dropped into his seat. He'd actually made it. He hadn't thought he had a chance when he'd grabbed a cab to the airport a half hour ago. But luck had been with him. There'd been a seat left in first class, so Michael had taken it, regardless of the cost.

Unable to stop himself, he smiled. If the winds were with him, he should make it back in time to catch some of the party. Maybe he even could convince Casey to share a dance with him.

That was, if she didn't mind dancing with a man who'd just thrown away his chance of a promotion. Oh, he'd done his job, all right. He'd started the meeting at six this morning and kept things moving until they'd pounded out an agreement a little over an hour ago. Once he knew the deal would go through and the jobs were secure, he'd turned it over to Jeff. Now Jeff would put the final shine on the package and get all the glory. Cal would probably pick him as his replacement.

But Michael no longer cared. He'd sat in the meeting and realized he didn't want to be president of Noress if he couldn't have Casey. He'd pump gas before he gave her up.

The sentiment had seized him with such urgency that he knew better than to ignore it. For years, he'd worked his butt off. He was successful, but he had nothing to show for all those years except a big bank account and an empty life.

Until he'd met Casey. Now he knew he had a new focus in life. A life that he hoped would include Casey, and someday, children. She'd told him the night they'd first made love that she was proud of him. Today, when he'd decided to come home to Casey and left the meeting early, he'd been proud of himself, too. All he had to do was convince Casey to give him another chance. But this time, he wasn't going halfway. He wasn't just going to ask her to live with him.

He was going to ask her to marry him.

"CAL WOULD LIKE to dance with you," Elmira said, coming into the ladies' room.

Casey dabbed at her cheeks with a tissue, wiping away the rest of her tears. Checking her reflection, she realized her eyes were still slightly red, but there was nothing she could do about it. With luck, it was dark enough at the party that no one would see. Elmira noticed, though, and she frowned at Casey's reflection in the mirror.

"Don't cry. Things will work out."

"I'm not—"

"Yes, you are," Elmira said, moving forward and taking Casey's hand. "You're crying about Michael, aren't you? Casey, men are like flypaper. Once you're stuck on them, it's hard to break free."

Casey smiled ruefully. "Guess I'm a fool, aren't I?"

With a shake of her head, Elmira nudged Casey toward the door. "No. Just a woman in love. Now get out of here and go dance with Cal. He wants to talk to you."

Casey followed the older woman from the bathroom. They walked over to where Cal stood at the edge of the dance floor.

"Come on, let's dance," Cal said to Casey.

Uncertain, Casey looked at Elmira. "I don't want to interrupt."

Elmira waved them off. "Don't worry about me. I'd like to sit for a while and visit with Dottie. We'll do our own fashion assessment of all the dresses." Glancing at Cal, she added, "Be certain and get me before they auction the car."

Cal nodded. "I won't forget."

A look passed between them that made Casey wonder if these two might end up together. They had already developed a shorthand that only those in love seemed to have.

When Cal took her hand, Casey followed him out to the crowded dance floor. A lot more people had arrived in the past few minutes.

"The party is going to make more than enough money for the modifications," Cal said, smiling. "Businessman that I am, I went and checked on the total while you ladies were talking. Your fund-raiser is a hit."

"That's wonderful." Casey smiled, genuinely pleased. Now the new center could have all the facilities she'd always dreamed of. Of course, it would take a lot of work to make the changes to the house, but she didn't mind. They'd find a good contractor and some talented workers, and she would work with them to make certain everything was perfect.

"And you haven't even auctioned off the car yet," Cal pointed out. "That should bring in even more money."

"I hope so," Casey said. Michael had already had the car appraised, and all the seniors had agreed to pay Elmira top dollar for her husband's pride and joy.

"So, your party's a huge success, but you look really sad, as if your best friend ran away with your dog. What's the problem?" Cal asked.

"I'm not sad," she protested.

Cal snorted. "The hell you're not. Elmira noticed it right away, but even an old goat like me can see it a mile off. You can smile fit to beat the band, but those smiles aren't real. I should know—as a boss, I get lots of fake smiles flashed at me all day long. So what's wrong? Elmira thinks you're upset about Michael. Is that true?"

Casey's gaze flew to meet his. She could lie, but there didn't seem much point. "Yes. After all he's done for this fund-raiser, I'd hoped he'd be here."

Through narrowed eyes, Cal appraised her. "Didn't Michael explain he had to go? You know he wanted to be here."

"I can't help thinking if he'd really wanted to be here, he would be," she said, hoping Cal would drop it. Despite everything that had happened, she didn't want to criticize Michael in front of his boss.

"Lot you know about business," Cal said, leading her through a series of intricate steps. When they settled back into a normal rhythm, she frowned at him.

"I may not know about business, but I know people. Michael made a choice. He wanted to impress you, to get another promotion," she said quietly, the truth of her words causing a new wave of pain to go through her. "That promotion's worth more to him than I am."

Cal stopped dancing. He ignored all the other couples swirling around them and just stood, staring at Casey. "Excuse me, Casey. I like you, so take this the way it's intended, but you don't know diddly-squat."

Casey blinked. She should have known another corporate shark wouldn't understand. "I think I do. Michael wanted to go on the business trip more than he wanted to be here."

"So he didn't tell you why he had to go?"

She shrugged, feeling self-conscious. "He said it was important…to him."

"Not to him. But it's sure important to more than four hundred other people who will lose their jobs if Michael doesn't pull this off."

Stunned, Casey looked up at Cal. "What?"

"Casey, Michael went because it was the right thing to do. The boy was in a tough spot, between a rock and…" He grinned. "And you. But in the end, he went because he had to. Sure, you would have liked him here with you, but those employees needed him at these meetings." He cocked one white eyebrow. "Why? Did you give him a hard time about going?"

A hard time? That was an understatement. "I broke things off with him."

"Hell." Cal took her hand and started dancing again. "I thought you were in love with Michael."

"I am." She swallowed and amended her answer. "I mean, I was."

"Was? Past tense?"

At his dubious expression, she relented. "Okay, I am. I'm still in love with him."

"Then you should feel damn proud of our boy. He made a tough decision, but the right one. Those employees have families. A lot of people depend on him." He smiled at her. "Michael's changed in the last few weeks, Casey."

She saw that now. Michael wasn't a thing like her father. Her father had worked so hard because he wanted to get a promotion—for himself. Michael had left her because he'd needed to do this. Or had he?

"But if he pulls this off, won't he end up getting promoted?" she asked.

Cal chuckled. "You're one tough lady. Maybe. It's up to me. If I think Michael has the stuff to run Noress, then I can give him my job when I decide it's time. But there's more to running a company than just putting in the hours. You have to have a heart."

Casey nibbled her bottom lip, suddenly uncertain. Had Michael really gone on the trip to save those jobs or because he thought he'd get Cal's job? She wouldn't know if she didn't ask Michael.

"Do you have a phone number where I can reach him?" she asked, needing to know.

"No. Michael's in nonstop meetings this week-end. You'll have to wait until he gets back." With that, Cal finished the dance and then led her over to the table where Elmira sat. After kissing the older woman lightly on the cheek, Cal asked, "You ladies ready to do this auction?"

Elmira smiled and stood. Casey went to the band, borrowed the microphone and gathered the group. Then Tommy, who used to be an auctioneer, climbed on stage, cracked a few jokes about the supposedly magical car, and began the auction. Bidding started out slow, and for a while, Casey worried that they wouldn't earn back the money the center had promised Elmira.

Then, as if a dam had burst, the bidding took off. Three men were in heavy competition, each upping the amount by several hundred with each bid. Finally, the competition dropped to only two bidders and eventually, it became clear one man would win. The man's final bid wasn't as much as Casey had hoped for, but it would do nicely.

Tommy raised his gavel to accept the final bid when from the back of the room, a man said, "Fifty thousand dollars."

A gasp went through the room. Casey recognized that voice. Or at least, thought she did. She searched the crowd looking for the benefactor. Finally, the crowd parted enough so she could see Michael walking toward the stage.

She borrowed the microphone from Tommy. "Are you certain?" she asked Michael, love filling her. He'd come back. To her.

"I'm positive," he said loudly enough for Casey to hear.

Tommy laughed and slammed the gavel on the

podium. "That's good enough for me. I'm calling this before that man changes his mind."

Bemused, Casey stepped down from the platform and crossed the room. When she stood directly in front of Michael, she said, "I didn't know you liked antique cars."

"I didn't," he smiled down at her, a teasing twinkle in his sexy blue eyes. "Until recently. But I've become a believer in the magic of that car."

Dancing started again, so the crowd wandered off as Casey continued to stare at Michael.

"Looks like the evening was a huge success," Michael said.

Casey nodded, still unable to believe he'd come back. Still a little uncertain why he had. "Yes. We made more than enough money."

Michael took a step toward her, his gaze holding hers. "Casey, I want—"

She couldn't stand it anymore. She rose up on her toes and pressed her lips to his. When he didn't kiss her back at first, she decided he was surprised, so she brushed his lips again. This time, Michael pulled her close, his head bending to her, his lips seeking hers in a deep kiss.

He'd come back. He'd left his meeting and come back to her. Abruptly, she realized what that meant and leaned back from the temptation of his kiss.

"The meeting. The jobs," she whispered, floundering.

"I hurried things along, but I got it settled enough to leave." He cupped her face, his eyes glittering as they studied her face. "I had to go, Casey. I didn't want to—"

She laid a finger across his mouth. "I know. I realize that now. You made the right choice."

Before she moved her finger away, he nipped playfully at it, making Casey laugh. Then he took her hand in his, tugging her close again.

"I love you, Casey Richards. I'll do anything for you."

Lovingly, she gazed into his eyes. "I love you, too."

He kissed her again, tenderly, then said, "But you have to know before we go any further that I've decided I don't want to live together."

Her stomach dropped. "If you're not ready—"

Shaking his head, he said, "I want to get married. I want to spend the rest of my life with you. Say you'll marry me. I promise I won't let my career come before what's really important in life—you."

"Now how can I resist a promise like that? Yes, I'll marry you," she murmured against his lips. He rewarded her with a thorough and enthusiastic kiss.

"One more thing," he said when he ended the kiss. "I hope you didn't have your heart set on me getting promoted to president. By leaving the meeting early, I'll probably get chewed out big-time. In fact, I'll be lucky if I'm not demoted because of this."

"I don't care," Casey assured him. "But I know how much it means to you." She caressed the side of his face. He didn't look unhappy. He looked ecstatic.

"Not me. Not anymore. Sure, I want to do a good job, but it's more important to have a life—a life that you're part of. No more workaholic days for me."

A new thought occurred to her. "Michael, with the new center, I may have to put in some long days."

He grinned. "Okay, I'll work late when you work late. Then we can meet back home and see if we can get into trouble."

"We can only get into trouble on the nights we work late?" she teased.

Michael leaned forward and started to murmur something naughty in her ear, but before he could, Cal said, "Hi, Michael. Hi, Casey."

They moved slightly apart and turned to face him.

"I guess you've heard from Jeff that I decided to leave after we worked through the major details," Michael told his boss. "And I stand by my decision, Cal, even though I know it will reflect on my career." Michael glanced at Casey. "It was important for me to be here tonight. Jeff will do a great job finalizing the deal."

Cal shrugged. "Doesn't bother me. I'm all for delegating. I'm a firm believer in sharing the workload so no one ends up having to do everything."

He wrapped his arm around Elmira's waist, then turned his attention back to Michael. Casey could see the love radiating off the older couple.

"Truthfully," Cal said, "I've wanted to retire for a long time, but I wasn't certain who could replace me. You had the brains and the talent, but frankly, you lacked heart.'' He smiled. ''I see now, you've got that, too. The president's job is yours.''

Next to her, Casey felt Michael stiffen. ''Cal, I can't put in those kind of hours.''

''So don't. Spread the work around. Hire an assistant or two. You don't have to personally do all the work. Live your life at the same time, son. You only get one.''

With that, Cal patted Michael's arm and headed back to the dance floor with Elmira. Stunned, Casey looked up at Michael and laughed when she saw the bemused expression on his handsome face.

''I have to agree with him. You certainly have a heart,'' she said.

He pulled her close, hugging her. ''I do now. Thanks to you.''

''You are the most perfect man,'' she said quietly, cupping his face.

He chuckled and shook his head. ''Me? Perfect?''

''Darn near it,'' she whispered, standing on tiptoe to press her lips to his. ''Darn near perfect.''

If you enjoyed what you just read,
then we've got an offer you can't resist!

Take 2 bestselling love stories FREE!

Plus get a FREE surprise gift!

**Start celebrating Silhouette's 20th anniversary
with these 4 special titles by
New York Times bestselling authors**

*Fire and Rain**
by Elizabeth Lowell

King of the Castle
by Heather Graham Pozzessere

*State Secrets**
by Linda Lael Miller

*Paint Me Rainbows**
by Fern Michaels

On sale in December 1999

Available at your favorite retail outlet
**Also available on audio from Brilliance.*

Silhouette®
Where love comes alive™

HEART OF THE WEST

Every Man Has His Price!

Lost Springs Ranch was famous for turning young mavericks into good men. So word that the ranch was in financial trouble sent a herd of loyal bachelors stampeding back to Wyoming to put themselves on the auction block!

July 1999	*Husband for Hire* Susan Wiggs	January 2000	*The Rancher and the Rich Girl* Heather MacAllister
August	*Courting Callie* Lynn Erickson	February	*Shane's Last Stand* Ruth Jean Dale
September	*Bachelor Father* Vicki Lewis Thompson	March	*A Baby by Chance* Cathy Gillen Thacker
October	*His Bodyguard* Muriel Jensen	April	*The Perfect Solution* Day Leclaire
November	*It Takes a Cowboy* Gina Wilkins	May	*Rent-a-Dad* Judy Christenberry
December	*Hitched by Christmas* Jule McBride	June	*Best Man in Wyoming* Margot Dalton

HARLEQUIN®

Makes any time special™

Visit us at www.romance.net

PHHOWGEN

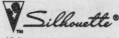